Chanel Sweethearts

CANCELLED

S0-AQK-598

By the same author

Gucci Mamas
Versace Sisters

Chanel Sweethearts

Cate Kendall

Macquarie
Regional Library

BANTAM
SYDNEY AUCKLAND TORONTO NEW YORK LONDON

A Bantam book
Published by Random House Australia Pty Ltd
Level 3, 100 Pacific Highway, North Sydney NSW 2060
www.randomhouse.com.au

First published by Bantam in 2010

Copyright © Lisa Blundell and Michelle Hamer 2010

The moral right of the author has been asserted.

All rights reserved. No part of this book may be reproduced or transmitted by any person or entity, including internet search engines or retailers, in any form or by any means, electronic or mechanical, including photocopying (except under the statutory exceptions provisions of the Australian *Copyright Act 1968*), recording, scanning or by any information storage and retrieval system without the prior written permission of Random House Australia.

Addresses for companies within the Random House Group can be found at
www.randomhouse.com.au/offices

National Library of Australia
Cataloguing-in-Publication Entry

Kendall, Cate.
Chanel sweethearts

ISBN 978 1 86325 694 0 (pbk).
A823.4

Cover illustration and design by www.saso.com.au
Internal design and typesetting by Midland Typesetters, Australia
Printed in Australia by Griffin Press, an accredited ISO AS/NZS 14001:2004
Environmental Management printer.

10 9 8 7 6 5 4 3 2 1

FSC
Mixed Sources
Product group from well-managed
forests and other controlled sources
Cert no. SGS-COC-005088
www.fsc.org
© 1996 Forest Stewardship Council

The paper this book is printed on is certified by the © 1996 Forest Stewardship Council A.C. (FSC). Griffin Press holds FSC chain of custody SGS-COC-005088. FSC promotes environmentally responsible, socially beneficial and economically viable management of the world's forests.

For Jacque Ford, 5 June 1963 – 20 October 2009,
Andy's Paper Nautilus. LB

To Mum and Dad. Thank-you. For everything. MH

Prologue

It was the smell that really knocked her sideways. She was expecting the heat, the smoke and the noise, but not the sickening stench of burning oil and blistering paint mixed with sizzling eucalyptus from nearby trees.

Jess stood numb as the miasma of smoke and the acrid smell wove thick, black plumes around her. It was surreal, it couldn't be happening. It couldn't end like this; all her dreams and hopes burnt to nothing.

She pressed the sting of tears from her eyelids. She put her head up and stared at the purple–red flames leaping into a night sky that was bruised with black smoke.

'Stand back, love,' one of the CFA volunteers shouted. 'She's coming down.'

The wrenching squeal of corrugated iron announced the roof's collapse.

The crowd gasped and hurriedly shuffled to the other side of the road. Des and Merle from the supermarket up the road stood distraught in each other's arms. Fat tears on Merle's cheeks glowed orange against the blaze.

The cafe's frontage was the last to go. In her mind Jess saw the ghosts of that afternoon's customers dancing in the haze. Rainbow and Songbird had been there; and Steve the milk-bar guy, laughing and chatting together. Here they all were again, just a few hours later, but now everything had changed.

There was a loud pop as the fryer exploded, sending the stink of burnt chip fat into the night air.

'Where's Nick?' someone called from the crowd.

Nick!

Jessica turned wildly to the speaker, then back to the store, terror prickling her skin. Nick had been with her just two hours earlier. He'd left, saying he had work to do. Had he come here to fix that loose floorboard for her? She wasn't sure whether she was going to faint or vomit. Bile rose in her throat.

'Gas!' someone shouted and soot-faced men spilled from the shop.

'Please, there's someone in there, there's someone in the kitchen!' Jess shrieked, her words distorted, breaking in anguish. She rushed towards the inferno, wild with fear. Not Nick; not him too, not after so many losses that year. Not her Nick.

'Get out of there.' A fireman grabbed Jessica and dragged her roughly across the road. 'We checked out the whole place when we got here, there's no one in there.' He held her arms to her side to stop her battering his chest with her fists.

'Are you sure? Are you absolutely definite?' she screamed at him.

'Yes we're sure, now stay over here,' the firefighter shouted.

Rainbow ran over to her in the lurid orange light. 'We saw Nick pass our place about an hour ago,' she said, and Jess felt her legs collapse beneath her with relief.

Rainbow and Songbird sat with her in the gutter, holding her, as the chaos continued around them. A series of deafening booms split the air as gas bottles exploded one after the other.

Jess watched it all from the safety of her friends' arms. Tears spilled down Rainbow's face, running under her chin and off the end of her nose, but she ignored them and continued to whisper, 'It's okay, it's okay, it will all be okay' in Jess's ear as she rocked gently beside her. Songbird said nothing, but her arm was firm and strong behind Jess's back.

Jess suddenly felt strangely detached from the scene, as if she were watching it all unfold from above. As the store's weatherboard facade finally gave in, ending its eighty-four-year history, she felt nothing. She was empty. She watched, mesmerised, as the '*GEN*' in General Store blackened first, then the scorched letters fell one by one to the verandah below. The fire was almost like an interactive artwork, she thought; so beautiful in its destructive force.

Then there was nothing but charred timbers and the insatiable flames.

It was all over.

~ 1 ~

TWELVE MONTHS EARLIER

Jessica Wainwright twisted her gingham seersucker skirt around her fingers. It was actually a vintage tablecloth held in place with a chunky leather belt. She hadn't got around to turning it into an actual garment yet. But the look was so eclectic, so funky, so . . . Jessica . . . that it was actually catching on and some of her younger staff were stealing their mums' tablecloths to emulate her style. But on Jessica it looked anything other than homemade craft, as she'd teamed the skirt with a TL Wood short-sleeved Montego cardi, from which long, white peasant-blouse sleeves billowed. She'd loved fashion ever since her dad had given her a biography of Coco Chanel when she was a teenager. The sophisticated designer had quickly become her creative idol.

But fashion was the furthest thing from her mind right now. She sat, stunned, at one of the tables in her cafe, struggling to take in what she had just heard.

'What do you think about coming to work with Mimsy and me at Still Life?' The words echoed in her head. Jimmy McConnell's Hugo Boss suit sat perfectly on his square shoulders; his hands swept appreciatively over her latest artwork — a sculpture in found recyclables. She could see he meant business; that he really wanted her to work at the prestigious inner-city design firm at which he was the headhunter and second-in-charge. It made her nervous. She wasn't the headhunted type. Of course her nervousness might just be about having Jimmy so close again. He certainly still smelled as good, looked as good, and – she put her fingers up to her face to hide a sudden rush of blood to her cheeks – probably felt as good as he used to.

She made a pretence of adding more sugar to her latte to hide her glowing face. For God's sake, her crush on him had been twenty years ago, this was embarrassing.

'I'll be back in a tick,' she said, jumping up from the table and knocking her latte over in the process. 'I'd, er, better check on the kitchen.'

Jimmy gave a low seductive laugh and casually threw some napkins on the mess, waving her away. 'Do what you gotta do, girl. I'll be here.'

Jess scurried into the storeroom off the kitchen to give herself a moment to gather her thoughts. She stared at the boxes of organic vegies and packets of wholemeal flour as she remembered the first time she'd seen Jimmy, at design school in Melbourne. He'd been in the year above her and they'd moved in different circles, but she'd noticed him straightaway in the halls. With his confident, charismatic air and striking looks, he was hard to miss.

They'd fooled around briefly at a party one night when they were both drunk. Jess blushed again thinking back on the inebriated fumble that had been enough to ignite her crush into a full-blown obsession. She'd spent the next few months checking her answering machine constantly, dying a little bit with each disappointment. She stopped going out, just in case he rang. Even when he took up with the leggy Stephanie Smyth she still remained convinced he'd be hers one day. And she'd relived that one passionate evening over and over until the memory got worn out.

Then socialist, idealist and egotist Danny Mulroney had walked into her life, Jimmy had graduated from design school and their paths hadn't crossed again. But now Jimmy McConnell was out there in her store, all these years later and as charming as ever. She peeked around the storeroom to check him out again. His dimples were a little deeper and although his hair had a sprinkling of salt and pepper, he still wore it tousled and long, thrust behind his ears with lank locks falling over his forehead.

Maturity had sharpened his looks, making him even more gorgeous than she remembered. She noticed with pleasure that his eyes were more penetrating, his flirting more polished and his laugh lines more plentiful. He obviously worked out: he was broad across the chest and finished at the waist in a very tidy V-frame. He certainly still had his x-factor and it was having the same effect on her as it had two decades ago.

She took a deep breath, straightened her skirt and smoothed her wayward curls before walking slowly back to the table.

His eyes stayed on her as she crossed the room, nodding appreciatively at her.

As she sat down, he rubbed his goatee and cocked his head to one side, staring at her enquiringly, his grin forcing her to smile back.

'So what do you think, Jess? I've been admiring all your publicity.' He inclined his head towards the magazine articles hung on the wall.

'Oh, well, a friend framed them for me, and insisted I hang them, so you know . . .' Her voice trailed off. It had been fun to have her artwork and cafe profiled in magazines and the weekend papers, but it didn't mean she was a serious artist or anything.

'The gallery space works well,' Jimmy said. 'How much of your own work do you sell here?'

'Not much, really. You know how it is, there's so much time involved in every piece, I just don't have enough hours in the day to do much – though, well, lately I've been freer.' She bit her lip and looked down at the table. 'Can we get some more coffee here please, girls?' she called out to her staff, breaking the moment. 'Another espresso for you, Jimmy?'

'Oh yeah,' he tapped his head. 'I need regular infusions to keep me sharp. But you are still selling your work?' He turned back to the topic at hand.

'I sell them here and there,' she said, nodding, 'but usually I just give them away to friends and family.' Colour crept into her cheeks again as she added, 'That way I get to visit my favourite pieces whenever I want.'

'Aww, you always were the sentimental type,' he grinned, stroking the back of her hand. 'So is Chanel still your favourite designer?' he asked.

'Oh, yes,' she said with an emphatic nod. 'I'll always be a Chanel girl.'

One of Jess's waitresses slid fresh cups of coffee in front of them and cleared away their used cups, giving Jess a minute to think. Nick didn't take his eyes off her face as she tried to make sense of his offer.

'So you're seriously offering me a job at Still Life, one of the biggest design firms in Melbourne; just like that?' Jess asked, stirring her latte slowly.

'Not just like that, Jess. I've been keeping up with your work. I loved those collages you did with those whimsical collections of found objects: the vintage buttons cascading from an antique tin button box and the lace doilies, ribbons and collars, folded into intricate shapes – they were stunning.'

Jess leaned forward in excitement. 'You saw those? How?' She was incredulous.

'A friend bought the button piece and showed me your exhibition flier, which had a photo of the doilies piece – it was inspired stuff.' He threw back his espresso in one quick swallow and returned the cup to its saucer. 'I showed it to Mimsy and we both agreed you are just what we need at Still Life.'

Jess's thoughts whirled at the idea of working with the stylish, creative entrepreneur Mimsy Baxter. She knew the woman's work and reputation from regular articles in her favourite design magazines, and she had studied her early work at design school. A recent profile about her in *Frankie* magazine had celebrated Mimsy's vision in creating the hugely successful Still Life chain, which created semi-permanent art pieces, usually from reclaimed materials, as an alternative to floristry.

With Still Life boutiques in Albert Park, South Yarra, South Melbourne and in the foyer of Space in Church Street, Richmond, there was no denying that right now Mimsy was the most powerful person in the Victorian design and decor industry, and just the thought of working with such a legend made Jessica feel dizzy.

'But I would have to leave my business here, my friends, the property,' Jess said, abruptly coming back to earth.

'Hey, it's up to you, but these sorts of opportunities don't just drop in your lap every day. There was a time I remember when you were serious about art and wanted to prove something to the world.' Jimmy leaned back in the chair, placing his right ankle on his left knee and clasping his hands behind his head. The 1920s-style wingtips he was wearing took the look of his double-breasted suit from conservative executive to sophisticated whimsy. He continued to stare at her as if she were a fascinating type of sea creature.

Jess blushed: he *had* noticed her all that time ago after all. He was right, though, she had wanted all that – once – but she'd been just a silly teen back then. Instead she'd gone straight from design school to work in a well-known Peninsula interiors-cum-homewares shop because she'd wanted to be close to her family. She relished the coastal life and had found it difficult living, for the four years of her study, in the concrete jungle of the big city.

Six years of advising wealthy weekenders which navy-and-white regency stripe would work with their lime-washed floorboards finally wore her down. 'If I have to do one more bowl of river pebbles or hang another freaking oar above a stone fireplace I'll go nuts!' Jessica had complained to her dad.

The two had become business partners in the General Store, which had been the centre of Jessica's life for fourteen years as she worked to build it up into the stylish eatery and summer tourist destination that it had become.

But then her life had taken another massive turn five years ago. Joy had floated into it in the form of Graham and his two beautiful boys – they were an instant family and instant happiness for Jess and nothing could have enticed her to leave her patch of paradise and move to the big smoke to pursue her once-promising career.

But that was all gone now. So why not take Jimmy up on his offer? The store was so successful now that a competent general manager could run it.

'Let me know what you decide,' Jimmy said as he stood up to leave. 'Ever since your store appeared in *Gourmet Traveller*, Mimsy's been desperate to get you, and she always gets what she wants so you may as well say yes now and save us all a lot of hassle.' He gave her a sexy wink that made Jess want to squirm in her seat.

He picked up his mobile phone and satchel. She looked up at him. He smiled gently. 'Don't look so nervous,' he said. 'You're fantastic. Look at this place.' They both turned to look around the store. Jessica saw it through Jimmy's eyes. She took in the vintage Chanel fashion ads she'd had enlarged and framed as posters. The Eames-style lounge furniture around the open fire. Her array of *Black & White* magazines and back issues of *Dumbo Feather* enticed customers to stay a while longer. Even the reclaimed timber chairs, every one different, created a unified look by virtue of their randomness.

The sun-filled art gallery attached to the cafe by a glass tunnel was her biggest triumph. Local artists took turns exhibiting in the compact space. It *was* beautiful. He was right.

Jimmy leaned down and brushed his lips over her cheek in farewell, filling her nostrils with the scent of CK One. 'You're as beautiful as ever, Jess,' he whispered, running his fingertip down her face and sweeping a stray curl from her forehead. Her heart thumped in her chest and desire swirled through her. She closed her eyes and tried to calm her breathing.

'Let me know your decision, soon.' Then he was gone and she sat trying to collect herself; her face still hot from his touch and her nerve endings tingling. She turned to watch as he walked through the cafe area and wound easily through the crowded grocery store section and out the door. He was lean and languid like a cat. As he opened his car door, he glanced up and saw her watching. His eyes held hers for a few seconds, then his lips turned slowly upwards and he gave her a small wave before climbing into his gleaming Jaguar XJS.

Perhaps there was more than one reason to take Mimsy Baxter up on her offer, Jess mused. She poured herself a glass of water and found a quiet seat at one of the old timber dining tables. She fiddled with the sugar packets as she turned the idea over in her mind. Leave her home, her General Store and try her hand at a design career in the city? It seemed too massive to even comprehend. She loved living the quiet country life. But then she thought of her empty house: the empty bedrooms, the quiet nights alone and the even quieter mornings . . . She needed a change, a challenge, something to shake things up, shake the past away.

She could do this, surely; she, Jessica Wainwright, could prove she was a skilled artist who could cut it in the commercial world with the best of them.

~ 2 ~

The next morning Jessica stepped over the rake lying across her back doormat. She banged her Blundstones against the step to scare out any uninvited guests and sat to pull the boots on.

She gazed across her property's broad expanse and beyond to the whitecaps darting across Westernport Bay. The waves roared and crashed, urged on by a strong southerly. This was the homestead's best view.

But although Jess saw it, it didn't move her as it normally would. She sighed and looked at the crazy cottage gardens that flanked the gravel path. She should be concerned that a yellow broom seed had sown its wicked work and was infiltrating her wildflower bed, but really she couldn't care less.

Usually the chaos and colour of her native wildflowers made her smile, but not today. They hadn't for some time. Maybe Nick could come and give her a hand, although his job description supposedly kept him in the paddocks, not in the domestic garden.

She forced herself to her feet, restrained her wild curls with an elastic, and wandered down the wide garden steps. She saw with a start the daisy grubber that sat rusting in the same spot where she'd jammed it over a month ago. It wasn't like her to neglect her beautiful garden for so long.

But it was hard work to maintain the property now that she was on her own.

It just seemed so much easier to cook, clean and garden when she knew that others would enjoy it too. She couldn't seem to dredge up any joy these days. Everything was mere duty: the gardening, the General Store, her friends, even her art.

All night she had mulled over Jimmy's job offer and the whole idea was just giving her a headache now. What he'd said was true, she had wanted an artistic career – once. But she'd changed. Nothing excited her or moved her anymore; nothing gave her that swell in the guts that she used to get when she spied a piece of nature balanced well against its backdrop, or an old chair that needed just a splash of paint in a vintage shop, or the perfect colour of ochre in a pebble . . . it was all gone. Graham had taken so much more than the boys when he'd left her.

A movement in the corner of the yard caught her eye and she turned to see the empty swing, hanging from the boughs of the she-oak, swaying in the wind.

She glared at it and turned away, redirecting her glare at the overgrown garden.

The native flowers, oblivious to their owner's despondency, gaily bobbed their heads in the brisk breeze from the south. The dietes lining the homestead's baseboards were beginning to pop out their mini iris-like heads. The scarlet running postman wandered lazily across the path, while pink fairy orchids and blue periwinkles jostled happily together, ignoring the threat of the greedy agapanthus lurking behind.

Jessica was proud of her drought-tolerant Australian garden, but even the most self-sufficient flora needed some TLC occasionally and, thanks to this rotten immobilising malaise, they had been neglected for too long.

She looked down to the orchard. The bulbs around the fruit trees were on their last legs. She should pick the remaining few dozen blooms and take them to the General Store. There were enough for each of the tables. Maybe she could create a tall centerpiece for the entrance table from the cherry blossom branches. Or maybe not. It was too hard. It never used to be too hard. It used to be fun. There was lots in her life that used to be fun.

What had she done wrong in the relationship? What could she have done better? Why didn't Graham love her? Why did he have to take the boys away from her? Her heart resumed its familiar frenetic increase in pace and her breathing shortened. She shook her head and tried to snap out of it. It had been eight months. Why was she punishing herself with the same questions; the same interminable thought patterns, over and over; again and again? It didn't help; it just made it worse. She breathed deeply, slowing down the panic.

Shielding her eyes, she looked up at the sun. She had to get to her afternoon shift in about an hour. She had a tremendous manager at the General Store, Linda Dundas, so Jessica's presence wasn't crucial, and she didn't have to be on time, but she liked spending time at the store, chatting with customers, maintaining the look of the place, and ensuring the gallery ran smoothly.

She took a deep breath and attacked the garden beds; she pulled out weeds, evicted snails and wrestled with aggies using the physical toil as therapy to channel all her sadness and frustration.

~ 3 ~

The sweat dripped off Nick Johnson's forehead and onto the parched earth. Catriona Bayard stood over him, hands on hips.

'No, I think it's a bit crooked. How about you twist it about thirty degrees?'

Nick stood up slowly, easing the crick out of his back and stared at the lady of the manor. He was a patient bloke. He was tolerant and empathetic. But some of these tourists who came down to his township on the weekend were complete shockers.

'I've . . . umm . . . already planted it,' he explained. The mature crepe myrtle loomed above them.

'Oh, I don't mind if you have to dig it back up,' Cat said with a flick of her hand. 'But it must match the other one,' she pointed to a second crepe myrtle on the other side of the driveway. 'Let me know when you shift it – I'll be down at the manège.'

Nick glared at the generous jodhpur-clad bottom as it swayed off towards the dressage arena.

Surely Cat wasn't seriously expecting him to dig for another two hours just to twist the thing around? He stared at the crepe myrtle's mate. It had long limbs reaching out eastwards while the new tree's limbs reached northwards. Simple. Nick grabbed his shears and snipped the overgrown boughs off each tree and gave the foliage a clean-up until the two silent sentries were twins, impossible to tell apart.

The bright late-morning sun filtered through the pencil-pines and dappled the mulch.

Now he had time for more satisfying design pursuits. He worked his way down the exposed aggregate driveway towards the manor, where he tidied up the overgrown English-style garden. He pulled a few errant weeds from the rose garden and noted with pride that the savage pruning months earlier had resulted in a bounty of blooms.

The daphne beneath the French windows was awash with buds and as he hacked it back from the path he grinned at the powerful fragrance that clouded the air. He cut some for Jess, hoping it would bring a smile to her face. She'd been so miserable since that bastard broke her bloody heart. God, what he wouldn't give to smack that guy in the mouth sometime. The idea of it made Nick grin happily as he chose blooms for his friend.

Once he'd amassed a sizable bunch he turned to survey the grounds. Nick was no trendy landscape designer, more a general hand, really, but he had long been popular with the holiday-makers who flooded into their rural properties over the warmer months. Apart from Cat Bayard's occasional eccentricity, he enjoyed this job – and it was the only other regular gig he did now that he worked full-time at the Wainwrights' Springforth Estate as Richard Wainwright's farm manager. He'd taken the job on a few months ago, thrilled to be able to help Jessica manage her dad's property. It gave him a chance to be there for her more and support her as much as he could as she dealt with the heartbreak of losing those boys. Nick smiled to himself again as he imagined their cheeky faces lit up with joy as they played hide-and-seek around the property with him and Jess.

He'd been managing the farm unofficially for years anyway: as Jessica's friend and advisor he'd been happy to help where he could. After all, they'd been friends since high school. They'd drifted apart for awhile in their twenties, which he knew was his fault, but things had been, well, difficult back then. Now they were as close as ever, and he loved it.

'Oh, good, you did it,' Cat said, waddling back an hour later draped in various pieces of riding tack. 'See, it's so much better facing the other direction, isn't it?'

'Absolutely, Cat, your suggestion was spot on,' Nick said, managing to keep a straight face.

'Sorry I couldn't be here to supervise, I had to see to Lady. She's fussing with her new snaffle, the minx. Can you believe the farrier suggested an Uxeter Kimberwicke?'

'Err, no, I, guess I can't.'

'Outrageous! Anyway, next time, Nick, I'd like to improve the ambience of the kitchen, so I'd like you to create a window in the rear hedge so we can enjoy a water view.'

'Riiiight,' Nick said. 'I'll see what I can do.'

'And do you think we could grow some aubergines and cour-gettes in the vegie patch? Apparently they're culinarily *de rigueur*. Not that I'd know,' – she snorted a rather equine laugh – 'I'm a hopeless cook! If it doesn't come in a packet I wouldn't have a clue! But in the country one really must do a kitchen garden à la Stephanie Alexander.'

'Let me work on that for you,' Nick said.

'Brill, you're a marvel,' Cat brayed with pleasure, flashing her impressive teeth. 'You mightn't guess, but I don't really have much of a green thumb, so you're my absolute saviour.'

'Really?' Nick said, a smile playing at the corner of his mouth.

'Yar, yar, absolutely. House plants take one look at me and run screaming to the compost heap in a suicide mission,' she said and snorted happily.

'Well, it's a magnificent garden.'

'As long as the horses are happy, that's all that matters. Leave your invoice in the mud-room: I'll have Freddy draw you a cheque. Which reminds me, must get those frozen Yorkshire puds in the oven,' she said, and she tottered off to the stables.

Nick threw his tools into the back of the truck. Cat was all right. They all were, really, these townies who used his hometown as a holiday village. Many of his local friends couldn't stand the city folk. 'Swanning in as if they owned the place,' Mrs Carmody from the bookshop complained every weekend. It didn't matter how many times Nick pointed out to Maude Carmody and her cronies that the city dwellers with their fancy holiday houses kept the village alive, they'd still grumble. 'Real show ponies, the lot of 'em!'

Nick slammed shut the rear door of the ute's tray and walked around to the driver's door. Sure, parking became nightmarish in the small main street on the weekends and nigh impossible during school holidays. And the visitors' voices did grate as they complained loudly to each other about the substandard cheese platter at the local winery, or the poor weather that had 'ruined' their mini-break.

Oh well, Nick thought as he started up the engine, tourist season would soon be here in full force, so they'd just have to make the best of it. The summer school holidays were only a few weeks away, bringing with them a stampede of Toorak Tractors and Balwyn Buses. The bottle shop owner would shortly order Stoli and Veuve to replace the Bundaberg Rum and ten-dollar plonk on his shelves, and the little town's economy would start to whir into life, to the sound of the grumbles and mumbles of the checkout chicks, waitresses and footy-club lads who could no longer get a table at the pub.

As Nick drove down the shady drive and out to the main road, he chuckled again as he thought of the dozens of eggplant and zucchini plants already growing in Cat's vegie patch.

Thank goodness they were gone. Caro Wainwright's luxuriously appointed and generously proportioned Malvern house was her own for six glorious hours.

Wednesdays were bliss. It was Angus's bonding morning with the children. He started work late so that he could drive them to their exclusive inner-city school and catch up with them during the ten-minute commute.

She leaned against the front door for a few moments, listening for a last-minute return for forgotten books or homework. No, they'd gone. She smoothed down her long brunette bob and scurried to the kitchen as fast as her Bally mules would allow.

Had she locked the front door? She nearly turned back. Yes, she had, no chance of being caught. She opened the gift cupboard and removed the box of wrapping paper.

Her teak stash box was at the back, under a scarf. She pulled it out and opened the lid. Her blue-and-gold pack of mother's-little-helpers lurked in all their carcinogenic glory. It was wicked, stupid and frightfully politically incorrect, and her husband would absolutely kill her if he found out, but God she loved her morning ciggie.

She didn't even have any smoking friends anymore. Or if she did, they'd never admit it. We're a dying breed, she thought, and laughed at her cynical joke. She wandered out into the morning sun that bathed the generous courtyard, clicked her gold lighter into life and drew in her first satisfying puff.

The patio and surrounding gardens appeared immaculate, but she knew she would find something out of place. Sure enough, an ugly little weed was threatening to upset the uniformity of the recently spread black mulch. Holding the cigarette aloft, she leaned down and tore the offender from her garden bed, tossing it into the weed bucket hidden behind the Japanese screen.

The topiaries rustled in a slight breeze and she glared at them, daring a leaf to drop onto the sandstone pavers. The leaves thought better of their intention and held fast.

An English box hedge neatly bordered the courtyard's edge and the espaliered fruit trees clinging to the back fence were her clever answer to Angus's desire for a country touch in their urban home. Angus adored his father's large country estate; he'd grown up there and still enjoyed taking the family down for weekends. Caro enjoyed going too, of course, but the country was ever so dusty and played havoc with her blow-wave.

Caro smiled at the lushness of the camellia plants: they were sure to flower well this season, she thought with satisfaction. Now that they'd been pruned back into square blocks they were quite architectural and would render a welcome fragrance. It had been worth the effort of having that mulch brought in and applied last month (she didn't enjoy touching soil, it reminded her too much of dirt). The entire look was going to be perfect for the patio party she was planning to farewell summer. Although summer hadn't yet arrived, Caro liked to be organised.

She pursed her lips as she stared at the large maple stretching tall from its pride of place front and centre. It had better jolly well turn bright red next autumn. Its recent installation had required a crane and several thousand dollars. Though of course it would be worth it, because her horticulturist had assured her it would complement her drapes perfectly.

She carefully butted out the cigarette and hid it inside a can at the bottom of the recycling bin. No one would find it there.

Eugene, the alpaca, stared down his nose at Rainbow. His eyes were half closed in a haughty glare and his nostrils flared. Rainbow put her hands on her hips and stared back. There was no way Eugene would let her pass. This was his turf. He'd staked it out. There was a nice water supply nearby and a pile of fruit. He was very happy where he was and he wasn't planning on letting some upstart hippie unsettle his little piece of paradise. A sprinkling of alpaca pellets pattered onto the floorboards behind him.

Experience told Rainbow there was no point trying to negotiate with Eugene in this mood, so she stretched over his warm, solid back to open the fridge and squeeze a bottle of iced dandelion tea from the door.

She now needed glasses, but the beast's firm buttocks were leaning on the door to the cupboard. 'Come on, Eugene, get out of the way.' She flung her long, dirty blonde dreadlocks to one side and nudged his bottom with her bare toes.

Eugene gave a long-lashed look of superiority, then, without shifting position, leaned over to the fruit bowl where he selected the choicest organic apple from the pile and munched it noisily.

Rainbow sighed and grabbed two disposable cups from above the fridge instead.

'What the hell are ya doin'?!' Songbird's rough baritone broke through the screen door a second before she did. She clutched her short, cropped auburn hair in disbelief. 'I don't believe it.'

'I know, I know,' Rainbow hurried to excuse herself, 'it's just that –'

'I can't believe my eyes. Rainbow, darlin' heart, what are you thinking? Disposable cups? As I live and breathe, disposable cups in my own house!' Songbird rubbed the dirt off her hands onto her folded-down dungarees. She lived in dungarees and workboots and would rather eat at McDonald's than be caught dead in any clothing that even hinted at femininity. Especially make-up, which to Songbird's reckoning was about as sensible as organised religion or day-spa treatments.

Rainbow rolled her eyes. 'Eugene is blocking the glassware cupboard and anyway, I'm going to plant herbs in them after our morning tea.' She pulled her long tie-dyed skirt out from under Eugene's foot. Rainbow's look was more feminine, a blend of hippie chic meets tooth fairy.

Songbird's hands dropped in relief.

'Oh, that's all right then. Are they the cups we got from the tip last week?'

'Yes, sweetie, don't panic.' As Rainbow patted the air to calm Songbird down, her mass of skinny silver bangles jingled, competing with the wind chimes blowing outside the kitchen window.

'That's my girl! For a terrible minute there I thought you'd bought new ones.'

'Yeah, and then I carried them home in a plastic shopping bag while spraying my dreads with hairspray.'

'Ya dag!' Songbird grinned and took the iced tea from her partner with a smile. 'Thanks, darl, you're grouse.' She downed the tea in one, carefully rinsed the plastic cup and put it on the draining board.

'Now, back to the terra preta,' Songbird said.

'Yeah, now tell me the plan again?' Rainbow asked, finally convincing Eugene to go outside.

The women stepped over the two preschoolers who were marking out a racetrack in the dirt by the back door, and surveyed the back paddock.

'We're enriching the soil and sucking carbon back,' Songbird explained with a sweeping arc of her arm.

'Oh, goody. How?' Rainbow asked.

'It's very simple. We're making an underground oven, if you like. I've borrowed an old plough and Eugene and Ralphie are going to pull it –'

'Eugene?' Rainbow looked at her partner skeptically.

'Okay, we'll get Digger. Digger and Ralphie are going to plough up the paddock. Then, essentially, we're going to plant compost, grass cuttings, garden rubbish and food scraps, then backfill the lot.'

'We're going to need a lot of rubbish,' Rainbow said, frowning as she looked at the acre of grassy field.

'Yep, we can ask around the area.'

'Yeah! We can get all the rubbish from the neighbours,' Rainbow said excitedly. 'We can become the town's compost dump! What a great saving for everyone, they won't have to use the tip.'

'Yeah, it's good already and we haven't even started.' Songbird put her hands on her hips and stood staring out at the potential landfill site.

'So that's stage one,' Rainbow said, eyeing off their own compost heap.

'Yep, then in a couple of months it'll be ready for the next bit; that's where we suck up the carbon and start making a difference.

The women ensured their children were all working together happily in the vegetable garden, then picked up their tools and started turning their compost mountain, discussing, in detail, their plans for saving the planet.

Tori lugged a washing basket full of new linen through the front door. She felt like she was wagging school, coming down to the holiday house on a weekday, but there was so much to do to prepare for the season.

The beds had to be made up, so she left the new Sheridan linens on the end of each bed for Joy the cleaner. The pantry had to be cleared and restocked. She wrote Joy a detailed note explaining her alphabetical storage system. The outdoor furniture had to be sanded back and oiled; she sent the handyman a text. What next, she wondered, rubbing her hands with satisfaction at how well she was powering through her duties.

Right, windows. Trickier chore, that. She didn't have the window cleaner on speed dial. She shuffled through the kitchen drawer until she found the business card holder. First one. She called and booked him in for the following weekend. Job done.

She popped out to the car to scoop up the box of summer tableware she'd picked up at Country Road and the fluffy new towels in aquamarine and teal, which were her colours this summer.

As she lugged the homewares inside, she bubbled with excitement at the summer ahead. She couldn't wait for the kids to break up from school so they could load up the four-wheel drive and spend two glorious months in the country. Besides, she needed a break from her husband, Owen. It was a real struggle living under the one roof at the moment so a summer break would do them all good.

She dropped her load at the front entrance and stood admiring her beautiful garden. White sand spilled from the drive through the meandering paths that had been painstakingly styled by the landscaper to look natural and beachy. Wide driftwood bench seats dotted along the pathways overlooked feature acacias, she-oaks and flowering gums.

Her favourite trees, her magnolias, flanked the front door. She'd argued with the landscape designer over those. He'd suggested they weren't native, would probably struggle to live without regular water and, more importantly, wouldn't suit the overall design, but she absolutely loved them and insisted. He was probably right in the end. They did look a bit dead.

She stepped over the knobby club-rush that was overgrowing onto her jetty-style front walkway. Her next priority was to get stuck into the garden. She pulled out her phone and booked the landscape gardener. Excellent.

Tori looked out at the exterior of the house. The place really could do with a good clean. Algae grew up the sides of the bollards she'd bought from the Flinders Pier renovation. Country dust coated the weatherboards. And the big artistic granite rocks lining the garden's entrance could use a thorough scrub – they were filthy. She phoned Nick to organise an external mini-facelift before next weekend.

He protested that he was too busy working full-time next door, but she sulked loudly until he gave in.

'Why can't your handyman do it for you, Tori? Dave's a good man,' Nick said.

'Oh no, I only use him for the basic jobs. We really need you for the more high-level work,' Tori insisted before bidding him farewell and tossing her phone on the kitchen bench.

She was exhausted. Time for a cuppa. Maybe Jessica was at home. She went out onto her back deck and looked over the post-and-wire fence to the neighbouring property. Although Jessica's land was several hundred acres, the homestead was just a few hundred metres from the boundary. No, Jess's old Patrol wasn't in the drive. She must be at the General Store. Well, that was as good a place as any for a break.

Tori unloaded the rest of her summertime essentials from the car: Saeco espresso machine, new beach towels, boogie boards, wetsuits, pantry items from The Essential Ingredient that couldn't be sourced at the local IGA, new cushions in teal and aqua and, finally, ramekins. She certainly couldn't do an entire summer without ramekins, now, could she?

At last it was time for a well-earned break. She hopped into the BMW, retracted the convertible's roof to enjoy spring's nervous sunshine and headed down to the General Store.

★

Richard would never tire of this view. There it was, his precious MCG right in his backyard. He may have been a country boy at heart, growing up on the Springforth Estate, then raising his two children, Jessica and Angus, down there with his now late wife Eva, but Richard Wainwright embraced every aspect of his city lifestyle.

Sporting events within a stroll; exhibitions, theatre and shows next door; bars, clubs and restaurants rendering his kitchen redundant. Even his daily espresso was taken care of by the barista in the five-star apartment building's lobby.

He plucked a cherry tomato from the ornamental tree perched on the stone patio table and popped it into his mouth. Definitely lacking the country composted flavour, but never mind. At least it gave the stone and stainless steel balcony a touch of green. He poured a cup of water into the plant.

He gave one more look at his beloved sporting arena. Cricket season was around the corner and so was The Long Room; come on summer! He sniffed the smoggy spring morning and went back into the apartment.

The phone on the kitchen bench caught his eye and he frowned. His beloved daughter, Jessica, hadn't called for two days. Perhaps he should ring and see how she was. But he already knew. She'd been miserable ever since that bastard–. No, he stopped himself. He wouldn't allow negative thoughts to block his energy. His tai chi instructor advocated eliminating such bitter emotions.

He took a calming breath and opened his MacBook. It hummed to life with an aerial shot of Springforth Estate. God he loved that place. He could see the old lavender fields where Eva had run the Lavender Lunches cafe in the early eighties. Good lord, was it really almost thirty years ago? The beef cattle were grazing in stasis and Jess's crazy garden looked like a lace doily resting under the house.

Richard checked his email. Board papers had been sent for his next directors' meeting. He had been one of Australia's largest beef cattle breeders but had long since sold off the business and was now semi-retired as a board member and shareholder of the company Beef Bargains of Queensland. He enjoyed the advisory role as it freed up his time for more pleasurable pursuits. His mind flickered over to the sultry Genevieve Walters and he smiled in memory of their last get-together.

Genevieve was a stunner; all voluptuous curves, flashing white teeth and big blue eyes that shone with life and fun.

They'd been seeing each other for a few months now and he loved her feisty nature and glamorous looks. He flicked through his emails quickly and was disappointed to see there was no news from Jess, just another message from his daughter-in-law complaining again about the long hours Angus worked and how annoying the children were being. Richard shook his head and wondered anew how his son coped with his high-maintenance wife.

He shut his laptop and put family out of his mind for a while; he'd ring Jess tonight, but right now he was late for Genevieve.

~ 4 ~

Nick was at the top of his ladder, his voice muffled as it drifted down from inside the ceiling cavity. 'So, how's Blondie MacBrilliant working out?' he asked.

'Look, she might struggle to tell her lattes from her laksa, but she's really sweet, and besides, she needs the work,' Jess said. She frowned crossly at the Excel spreadsheet on her computer.

'You're a real softy, Red.'

'Don't call me that,' she replied.

'What? Softy?' he teased.

'No, you know what I mean.'

'What, "Red"? Why not? It's your name; you earned it!'

'Just don't do it in front of people.'

'What people? Everyone in the village knows it's your nickname. Are you worried the posh city girls might hear?'

'No,' she said defensively, stabbing the keyboard of her laptop. 'It's just got a bit old, that's all.'

She'd acquired the nickname in her late teens. She, her boyfriend Mark and Nick had been building a chook house at Springforth and Jess had insisted on painting its exterior in lurid cherry to cheer up the chooks. As Nick brought the can of paint to her he had tripped on a rock and a sheet of bright red had sailed through the air and landed all over Jessica. It coated her hair and face, dripped from her chin, soaked her chest and ran down her legs.

Mark and Nick had stared aghast in silence for about two seconds, then laughed so hard neither could stand up. They'd rolled around on the gravel path almost in pain with mirth.

The oil-based paint took days to wash off completely, leaving Jess with a faint pink tinge to her skin and hair for several days. Every time Mark or Nick passed her in the school halls they'd burst out with fresh laughter and ask, 'How's it going, Red?' Somehow it just didn't seem as funny to her as it did to them.

'Hellooo, are you here, Jessica?' Tori popped her head through the servery window. 'Any chance of a coffee around here? I haven't seen a waitress since I arrived.'

'Tori!' Jess exclaimed, walking into the cafe to greet her friend.

'Hello, daaarling!' Tori smiled, and gave Jess a bear hug.

'You haven't been down in ages. I've missed you,' Jess replied.

'I know, bloody weekend sport. It's a real pain. I've half a mind to have the boys join the local footy team down here.'

'You should, then I'd get to see you more often,' Jess said as they sat down at a corner table.

'I was kidding, I like their limbs intact, thanks all the same. I've heard how rough the locals play.'

'Hmm, good point,' Jess answered, looking round to see her new waitress standing in the corner frowning at a box of napkins.

'Trixie, two lattes over here, please,' she called with a wave.

'Oh, sorry,' Trixie said, dimpling her cheek. 'I didn't see you there.'

'Is she new?' Tori asked, stowing her Fendi Zucchino bag safely under the table.

'Yes, still learning the ropes. Last Wednesday was a nightmare: she left meals going cold in the kitchen while she fiddled with her iPhone. Somehow she'd changed it to Mandarin and then couldn't read the phone menu to change it back to English.'

'Well, she seems nice. By the way, the place looks brilliant, Jess,' Tori said, looking around. 'And the gallery has so much great stuff to buy. I can't decide on that duck-egg blue vase or the canvas totes. I think I'll get both, they'll work well with my summer theme this year.'

'Yes, I've made it summer-ready,' Jess said and followed her friend's eye around the room appraisingly. 'The holiday hordes are about to hit.'

In the corner the overstuffed sofa piled high with cushions sat behind a sixties boomerang-shaped coffee table. Magazines from the seventies and eighties spilled from an old brass news-paper rack on the floor. The fireplace, cleaned of winter's cheery warmth, was decorated in Jess's signature styling with accessories from the nearby beach: driftwood sticks with shells and urchins dangling from their limbs.

'I love how you make the cafe look like just one more of your sculptures,' Tori commented.

'Thanks.' Jess squeezed her friend's hand. 'That's what it feels like for me too. Aaaand,' – she drew the word out for dramatic effect – 'you'll never guess what happened to me last week.'

'Ooh, gossip, you know how I love that, sweetie,' Tori said. 'It's almost as fun as shopping!' She smiled her thanks as the waitress put a frothy coffee before her.

'Thanks, Trixie.' Jess waited till the girl was out of earshot before she continued. 'I had a very interesting visitor, and an even more interesting offer.'

Tori squirmed with excitement. 'Don't hold back, darling, give me the details.'

'Well, I don't know if I've ever told you about Jimmy McConnell?'

'Hunky heart-throb from design school?'

'Oh, yes, I did, ridiculous really, can't believe I had such a crush. Although he's still rather gorgeous. And anyway, he's offered me a job.'

'What? Where?'

'In town!'

'No way!'

'Yes way.'

'Where in town? That'll be great, you'll have access to much better retail opportunities. What would you be doing?'

'I would be a designer, chief designer in fact, at Mimsy Baxter's Still Life.'

'Wow, Jess, that's brilliant. I love that store. I'd never send a bunch of flowers ever again – why would you when you could send a sculpture? I love their stuff. I'm in there all the time snapping up gorgeous bits and pieces.' Tori's eyes shone with excitement.

'I know. Mimsy's fab, isn't she?'

Tori gave a shrug. 'Well, you have to take the job of course,' she said.

'You think?' Jess twirled one long blonde curl around her finger. 'You really think I should?'

'Of course, darling, it's exactly what you need. It will be a breath of fresh air after the sadness of the past year and you'd be much closer to the boys up in the city.'

'I thought of that,' Jess nodded, dropping the tendril of hair. 'Imagine if Graham changed his mind and let me see them sometimes; how amazing would that be?' She clapped her hands with excitement at the idea. 'It really could work, couldn't it?'

Suddenly her face clouded over. 'But then again, this is my home. What about the store, the gallery, Springforth and . . .' An image of Nick's smiling face flitted through her mind. '. . . And, you know, my friends down here?'

'Darling, it's the city, not Europe,' Tori scolded, lightly tapping Jessica on the wrist. 'You have everything running smoothly here with Linda in control, and Melbourne's only an hour-and-a-half away. You could come home on weekends and have the best of both worlds.'

'Yes, that's true. There's nothing really stopping me,' Jess said, and chewed her thumbnail thoughtfully.

Tori waggled a finger at her. 'What about Nick? What will he say?'

Jessica frowned. 'What are you talking about? What's Nick got to do with it?'

'Found your problem, Jess,' came Nick's voice from the kitchen. 'I found what's making the god-awful smell.'

'Oh, Jeezuz! Keep it down!' Jess leapt up from the table. 'Excuse me, Tori, kitchen issue. I'll get Trixie to bring you some lunch.'

As she entered the kitchen, she fumed. 'Could you not announce to the entire restaurant that we have a stinky kitchen?' she demanded.

Nick's cheeky grin emerged from the manhole. 'Keep your hair on, Red. Look.' A dead mouse dangled by its tail from his fingers.

Jess flew over and slammed the lid on a stockpot that was bubbling away precariously close to the carcass.

'Shit!' she whispered in horror. 'We haven't got mice, have we?'

'No, this little guy's a one-off. The traps are all empty and the bait hasn't been touched. Have you noticed any mouse droppings?'

'None at all. You're a star. How about a steak sandwich for your efforts?'

'With fries, cos I'm about to nail that loose verandah board down.'

'Your prices have gone up,' she told him, smiling.

'I'm a skilled worker, you know. You can't expect me to charge mere bread and water.'

She laughed as she wrote down his order and took it over to the chef.

It was funny that Tori had mentioned Nick. It wasn't as if they were an item – never had been – though they'd been the closest of friends at high school. Back then he'd constantly had a troupe of admirers happy to be his girl but he'd never settled on any one favourite. Then, during their HSC year, Imogen had come along with her sleek big-city attitude and had finally tamed the most popular boy in school. They'd got married after she fell pregnant but tragically the baby had died just after birth and the relationship ended soon after. Nick had simply seemed to disappear for a few years after that, and when he did resurface it was without his trademark confidence and easy smile. Both had taken longer to restore, but now he seemed to be in a good place again. Four years ago, just before she met Graham, Nick and Jess had picked up their friendship where it had left off. Nick had been an absolute star since Graham walked out, supporting her through the darkest times, but they were still just best friends and nothing more.

'I'm off, darling,' Tori said, peeping around the swinging kitchen door.

'We haven't finished our chat,' Jessica protested. 'I haven't even asked about your life.'

'Never mind, I can see you're busy. Hi, Nick.'

'G'day, Tori,' Nick said, leaning against the bench. 'I'll get to your place tomorrow first thing.'

'Thanks, that'd be fabulous. I might catch you at home later, Jess. But right now, I'm going shopping: there's a new home-wares shop in Red Hill.'

Then she looked back at Nick as a thought struck. 'Hey, you don't know a cobweb guy, do you? I have cobwebs in the corners of my windows and I need an HLM to get them off.'

'An HLM?' Nick asked.

'Yes, a Helpful Little Man,' Tori said. 'I've never done cobwebs before and I don't know how.'

'Er, yeah, I'll think about it,' Nick said, wondering quietly if the city folks' requests could get any more bizarre.

'*Grazie, ciao,*' Tori said and waggled her fingers on her way out the door.

Nick dug through his toolbox for a hammer. As he stood, Jess suddenly had a throat-closing thought. 'Oh my God, your birthday's coming up, isn't it?'

'Well, you could say that, in fifty-one weeks.'

Jess looked up and cringed. 'What? You mean I missed it? It was your birthday last week? Oh Nick, I'm so sorry I forgot. I'm such a ditz.'

'Don't be silly, we had a nice day together anyway.'

'When was the twentieth? What day was that? Tuesday? Oh shit, Nick, that's the day we cleaned out my filthy gutters. What kind of birthday is that?'

'The best kind,' Nick replied. 'Sludgy leaves, rusty gutters, possum poo and you. Doesn't get any better than that!'

'I am so sorry,' she said. 'I had it in my mind the week before; I even knew what I wanted to give you.' Bugger, she thought. She'd planned to buy him an iPod shuffle so he could listen to his favourite music while he worked, but somehow she'd just lost her train of thought yet again and forgotten one of her closest friends.

She sighed and shook her head. 'Sorry,' she said again.

Nick smiled at her as Trixie brought him over his steak sandwich. 'You could just give me a kiss,' he grinned and made a grab for her.

'Oh stop it, you flirt,' she said and whipped him with the tea towel.

Trixie stuck her head back in the door. 'Have we got any milk?' she asked.

'Did you look in the other fridge, the one in the storeroom?' Jess replied.

'Oh, yeah,' the waitress said and went back into the cafe.

Nick rolled his eyes. 'How do you stand it?'

'She's nice,' Jess replied. 'There's more to a waitress than just remembering orders and serving food, you know.'

'This place would grind to a halt without you,' Nick said as he poured tomato sauce all over his chips.

'Hmm,' Jess replied, dropping her gaze. 'We'll see.'

'What does that mean?' Nick asked.

'Well,' – Jess grabbed some bread and ham to make herself a sandwich – 'I was thinking of maybe trying something new for a while – in the city.'

'What?' Nick put down his knife and fork. 'You can't leave here, Jess, it wouldn't suit you. Look at you, with your whacky clothes.'

Jessica assessed her Bettina Liano skirt and distressed Collette Dinnigan tee and shook her head at Nick. She thought the look was pretty fashion-forward really. But she wondered how the chic professional women of Melbourne might see her. Maybe Nick was right. 'Oh settle down,' she said. 'So what if I do stretch my wings? This will always be home.'

Nick fixed her with a steady gaze. 'Is this something to do with that bloke who was in the store the other day? The one in the tosser suit and the wanker car?'

'Nick, can you not be such an alpha male for one second? That was Jimmy McConnell, you don't know him. He's the second-in-command at Still Life in Melbourne.' Jess slathered mayo on the rye bread and added some of chef's new chutney.

'Still Life? Never heard of it. What did he want?' Nick asked through a mouthful of chips.

'I knew him at design school and he just wanted to toss some ideas around, that's all.' Jessica definitely wasn't about to reveal details of the job offer while Nick was in such a filthy mood.

He grunted.

She arranged some roasted capsicum and fetta on her sandwich and sliced it into triangles.

'Well, I'm off,' Nick announced, wiping the edge of his mouth on his sleeve.

'Bye,' Jess answered, as he sauntered out the door. It was a relief to be rid of his grumpy face for a while.

That evening Jess pulled into her driveway and killed the engine. She stared at the weatherboard homestead that sat amid the dry paddocks. The last rays of sun stroked its west wall and the orange glow settled on her arum lilies, staining them peach.

How much longer could she face walking into that empty house? She couldn't believe she used to grumble about the noise and nag for the kids to pick up their Lego.

She sat in the car, dry-eyed and empty. She was so tired of faking brightness and cheer all day.

Jessica clearly remembered the day Graham and the boys had come into her life. She'd been walking from the kitchen to cross through the cafe when she'd noticed a little shoe wiggling from the top section of the shelving unit. She'd sped up her journey, fearing the worst. Sure enough, a baby, about a year old, had managed to use the shelves as a ladder and was now balancing precariously between the linguine and the one-and-a-half-metre drop to the timber floor.

'What are you doing?' Jess had grabbed the chunky, squirming babe around his tubby little belly. 'Are you a monkey? This isn't a palm tree, you know!'

The boy squealed and kicked his little legs in glee at having been caught. Jessica laughed. She loved children, she always had, and this one was gorgeous with his wispy soft blond toddler bob, red denim overalls, and eyes the colour and clarity of a Whitsundays' sky. Jessica felt a tightness in her chest, one she hadn't known was even there, snap and release. It was like ice-cream melting on the inside.

'Who are you?' she whispered as she stood there, holding this magic little person around the waist.

'Callum?' A deep rumble called out and the owner of the voice quickly followed. A tall, thin man emerged from the glass hallway that led to the gallery.

'Oh, there you are! I've been looking for you.' He sounded very terse but Jessica could only presume he'd been worried.

'I am sorry, has he been bothering you?' the man asked. At his first glimpse of Jessica, a smile came to his tanned face.

'Not at all, I just rescued him from the top shelf, that's all. I was worried he might fall. But no harm done, he's delightful,' she said as she reluctantly handed her new charge back to his dad.

'No, he isn't!' The man looked at his son disbelievingly. 'Oh, you're a monkey!' he said. The scolding was met with peals of giggles. The child clambered up to his dad's shoulders and grasped handfuls of the thick, overgrown ginger hair.

Jessica giggled right along with him. 'That's exactly what I called him!' she said. 'He certainly likes climbing.'

'Yes, too much, I'm afraid. He's a real worry.' He leaned down, unattached Callum and placed him on the ground. Doing so allowed his eyes to wander over Jessica's open, friendly face, surreptitiously taking in her attractive figure and her wild blonde locks.

'His name is Callum, and I am Graham,' he said putting out his right hand to shake Jessica's. Their eyes met and Jessica smiled shyly at Graham's frank and open gaze. The freckles smattered across his whole face made him seem even more youthful than he probably was. His grin, with head cocked to one side, was both enquiring and endearing – it gave him a cheeky quality. She decided she liked him. And she definitely liked Callum.

'Hello, Graham, hello, Callum. What a pleasure to meet you both.'

'Ooooof.' Graham suddenly lost his footing as a small towheaded dynamo barrelled in from the gallery door and slammed into his leg. 'And this little hurricane is Liam. Liam's older than Callum by eighteen months.'

'Thirsty!' Liam said, arms still in a firm grip around his dad's legs.

'Well let's have a chocolate milkshake then,' Graham said, and smiled at the boy. 'Would you like to join us?' Graham asked Jessica and indicated the cafe. 'Apparently this is a wonderful spot for a snack, and I'd love to thank you for saving my son.'

Jessica smiled, wondering how to reveal that she was in fact the owner. But this concern was quickly overshadowed with another quandary: was it appropriate to sit down for a drink with a very attractive father?

As if he read her mind, Graham followed up the invitation with a subtle disclaimer. 'The boys don't get to be around female company too often; you would be doing me a favour.'

Oh, he's single, she thought, and eagerly accepted his offer. Four months later Graham and his boys moved in with her and a wonderful new life began.

She drew in a deep shuddering breath and noticed that her car was now enveloped in darkness. She needed some strength and inspiration to keep going. There was only one place to turn. She picked up her mobile and rang her dad.

His phone bleeped, the cork popped and the intercom buzzed simultaneously. 'Ya gotta love the busy city life,' Richard laughed to himself. 'Come on up,' he said into the intercom, then placed the bottle on the bench and pressed *accept* on his mobile.

'Hello, baby girl,' Richard boomed into the phone. He still hadn't worked out that mobile phones didn't need to be yelled at. 'Please tell me I can order the hit-man . . . okay, I'll hold off for now, but let me know, and *pow* – marketing-manager brains all over the Saab windscreen . . . What do you mean? . . . Okay, okay, too graphic.'

Still chatting, Richard opened the front door to let Genevieve in. She air-kissed him and, dropping her bag on the hall table, went to pour the open bottle of champagne. As usual, Genevieve was impeccably dressed; she always managed to be both classic yet fashionably up-to-the-minute in her style. Her Camilla Franks sequined caftan top was in the bright colours of tropical North Queensland and her bright orange Fendi buckle-toe pumps peeped out from under her straight-leg Bogner pants, which had been tailor-fitted to show her slim frame.

'So how are you, darling girl? How'd the store go today? . . . A mouse huh? Got traps set? Good girl . . . Yes, he's a good man . . . You been on a date with him yet? . . . All right, I'll stop playing Cupid, he's just such a great bloke though . . . Have you done all your setting up for tourist season? . . . I bet it looks lovely. Well done, you're a marvel, girl, you really are . . . Has the council approved the plans for the back deck reno? . . . God they're slow.'

Richard raised a finger to hold off on the glass of bubbles Genevieve was offering.

'Yeah, Angus is good, bloody busy though, never gets a chance to see the kids. Had a complaining email from Caro today . . . Yes, you're right, she does her best . . . She's still a pain in the arse though . . . This weekend? Can't, darling, Genevieve and I are off to Port Douglas for a few days. There's a new golf course at Peppers Balé I need to try . . . Yes, sorry about that, but never mind – Christmas is around the corner and I hope to grab a couple of weeks down there then . . . Must go, you're amazing and brilliant, hang in there, can't wait to see you . . . love you too. Bye, honey.'

'Hello, Gen,' Richard finally greeted his guest with a proper kiss. 'How are you?'

'Hello, darling; fine thanks.' Gen tossed her bouncy blonde highlights. 'How's Jessica?'

'Not great, poor love. She didn't say anything but I can tell by her voice. I really need to get down there and see her. It's a big ask, running the cafe and managing the property. She does a great job. At least she has Nick doing the bulk of the work on the estate now.'

'You must be proud of her; she's a lovely woman,' Genevieve said and perched on the edge of the couch.

'I am, I really am, I just wish she'd find a fella – someone to take care of her.'

'Well, she'll find someone when the time's right.'

'I know. It was the same after Eva died; it took me ages to get back out there again. I guess I just need to give her time to work things out.'

Genevieve nodded. 'She has to do it in her own time. Nick's obviously a great friend and that's what she needs right now.'

She stood and placed her glass on the side table. 'Just popping in to powder my nose before we head out to dinner.'

'And such a pretty nose it is too,' he said.

He looked after her in wonder. He was a lucky, lucky man. He had met Genevieve six months earlier when Beef Bargains had been presented with a new television advertising campaign. He hadn't taken in any of the information about demographic trends, media spread or research results because he'd been transfixed by the feisty fifty-year-old creative director's enthusiasm, broad smile and swinging hips.

Richard had pursued her under the guise of following up some important figures. As a board member it really wasn't his role, which was something they both knew, but conveniently forgot as they giggled over chardonnay at Nobu the following week.

He'd had dates and brief relationships since Eva passed away twenty years before, but there had been nothing so completely overwhelming as his current love affair with Genevieve. They were on the same wavelength; they had the same hobbies – although her skiing skills were a bit on the adventurous side for him. He loved every minute of her company and, at sixty-six, he was starting to feel that he had to make every minute count. So he was about to ask her to move in with him. Maybe even to marry him. Who knew what the future held? He just wanted to be sure Genevieve was in it. She could be a schemer, though, but he loved being kept on his toes. She always had a plan going; just last week she'd tried to manipulate him into investing in a new apartment tower a friend of hers was financing, and before that she'd spent weeks angling to get a look at his share portfolio. He grinned as he pulled on his navy blue reefer jacket, pocketing keys, mobile and wallet, and cheerfully brushed away her attempts to manage his money while finding her determined efforts quite amusing. He winked at her as she placed the glasses in the dish-drawer and watched fondly as she quickly reorganised his wine glass cupboard to better suit her own sense of style.

He was sure Gen would love to encourage Jessica to move out so she could redecorate the homestead, perhaps turn Jessica's crazy garden into something more structured. He grinned at the fun of playing financial games with his partner. She was far more the challenging adversary than the gentle lover and he relished every minute. Others might find it mercenary or unhealthy to be in a relationship where his partner was keen to know all his business affairs and net worth, but it kept Richard's blood pumping: he loved second-guessing her and sidestepping around her attempts to manipulate him. And he had to admit, he was completely dazzled by her sultry looks.

He was looking forward to the evening he had planned for them. He was taking his beautiful Genevieve to the Japanese restaurant across the road, then off to see a show at Her Majesty's Theatre, a short stroll away, then onto the Melbourne Supper Club for after-show drinks.

They grabbed their jackets and headed out. As he was closing the door behind them he glanced up at the portrait of Jessica hanging on the wall of the foyer. A shadow of concern passed over him.

~ 6 ~

The large sheet threatened to curl back onto itself but a carefully placed paperweight at each corner kept it flat.

The plans were good. In fact, better than good. They were brilliant. Sure, there was the irritating administration of town planning and infrastructure, but it could be bypassed by greasing the greedy shire palms with several thou.

The 'country-style' houses were French provincial in design. Perfect. Box on a block. No shape was cheaper to build.

The two-acre blocks were troublesome: it meant only room for forty homes. If the surveyor could be convinced to be a little creative with the boundaries, at least another two could be squeezed in. Land like this didn't become available that often and with the council's new push for medium-density housing in the area, it was just a money-maker waiting to happen.

After all, why waste that view on a few hundred cows?

~ 7 ~

The mid-morning brunch traffic was queued out the door. The chef had been slinging bacon and eggs in various formats since the first customers had arrived ready for breakfast at eight a.m.

Tourist season was fully underway. Although the summer holidays hadn't actually started, the warmer weather was beating down, the townies were flooding in for the weekend and Jessica had five front-of-house staff on as well as two cooks and two apprentices in the kitchen.

'Are you sure you're going to be okay for an hour or so?' Jessica asked her manager, Linda.

'Yes, of course we'll be fine. You go to your Pony Club customers,' the older woman assured her.

'Just keep an eye on Trixie, she's still finding her feet,' Jess warned as she picked up baskets overflowing with home-baked treats.

'What a diplomatic way of putting it,' Linda replied with a gleam in her eye. 'Table for six, sir?' She turned to a customer. 'Of course. Would you mind waiting five minutes while we set one up for you?'

Jessica drove into the car park at the Pony Club. A stab of pain in her stomach reminded her how much Liam and Callum had loved it there. Callum had been too small to ride, but he'd been her little helper as she sold her muffins and friands.

Liam loved the dressage, and he was such a natural. She really hoped he'd continued with his riding. She thought of his father. Somehow she doubted it.

It had broken her spirit entirely to finally decide to sell Tango. She'd considered keeping him in the top paddock, but seeing him every day was too painful. Liam had only been four when he'd had his first ride. It had been at Rainbow and Songbird's house, at one of the kids' parties. Although Liam had vehemently declined the offer of a pony ride, Jessica knew him well enough to realise that was just nerves. She knew how he shied away from anything new and different. She also knew all about his inner bravado, his adventurous side (not to mention his love of old western movies) and knew that if he could just find the courage he'd have a great time. It had taken all afternoon to convince him to try. He'd spent the day walking up and down beside the pony, chatting to Songbird in his barely coherent little-boy prattle.

Tears of pride had welled in Jess's eyes as she noticed him take the reins and walk the pony a short way himself. Eventually, without any encouragement from her at all, he'd asked if he could have a turn. She couldn't have been more proud of her little guy at that moment. And the grin across his face for the entire ten minutes of the ride lit up her heart. He was hooked. It wasn't long before they found the steady and calm Tango for him, and he began to have riding lessons each week, before moving on to join Pony Club after a few months. Jessica didn't mind the early starts, the competitions and the pre-dawn drives every weekend. It was worth it because Liam had discovered a passion.

She took a deep breath and sidled past the floats and four-wheel drives to the clubhouse. The city mums were all decked out in gleaming leather riding boots and spotless pastel Ralph Lauren polo shirts.

Jess always enjoyed it when the city tourists flocked into town for the summer: not only was it great for business, it also broadened her social life as well. Of course some of the Pony Club mums were complete princesses who liked to parade around in jodhpurs and never touch any horseflesh, but they were always good fun. If she moved to the city she'd get to see more of them, she mused.

Jimmy had called again last night to tell her that Mimsy wanted to meet with her, so they'd set a date for early the following month. She still hadn't spoken to anyone but Tori about the job in any detail, but she was pretty sure she was going to accept it.

'Jess, daaaahling!' boomed Cat. 'You're a sight for sore eyes. Look at you, laden with goodies. Here, let me help you.'

'Hi, Cat, hi, Pip, hello, Fi, morning, Pet, Pen, Flick, Sav, Cyn, Vi.'

The equestrian mums brayed a chorus of hellos and huddled around to sift through Jess's offerings, thrusting money at her.

'Jess, darling,' said Fi, grasping a clutch of mud muffins for her gang of children. 'I haven't seen you since . . . well, you know. We've been travelling quite a bit this year and this is the first time we've been down in simply ages . . . I just wanted to offer my sympathies,' she babbled in her high-speed staccato manner. She slammed her Fendi shades down to hide her embarrassment. 'How are you doing?'

'Hanging in there,' Jess replied. 'I'm fine, really.'

'We miss little Liam. Such a seat . . . I've never seen such elegance in a little boy. My Missy and Gracie just adored him.' Aware she was pouring salt on a wound, Fi abruptly changed subjects.

'Jessica, look at you: you look beautiful,' said Tori, who had just walked up from the stables with one of her riding boots green with fresh manure. 'I love your Chanel earrings, darling. Are they new?'

'Hello, sweetie, yes, they were a birthday gift from my gorgeous dad,' Jessica said and smiled down at the muck dripping from her friend's footwear. 'That's a nice scent, new from Paris is it?'

'Yes, Calvin Klein's latest, Eau de Equine. You like?' she said with a laugh, and she raised the offending boot to offer Jessica a smell.

'Look, I'll pass thanks, pet. Muffin? I think they've left a few.'

'Oooh, yes please. Do you have time for a Nescafé? I must tell you about the gorgeous bits and pieces I snapped up in Red Hill during the week.'

'Yeah, sure,' Jessica replied. 'Linda's got the shop under control.'

They went into the club's kitchen and Tori busied herself with the kettle.

'Sorry I didn't get a chance to see you properly when you were down mid-week,' Jessica said.

'That's okay. Here you go. I'm afraid it's not up to the General Store standards.'

'I'll cope; it's caffeine, isn't it?' Jessica replied. When Jess had fallen in love with Graham and gained an instant family, she had relied on Tori for advice and support. Tori had been more than a great part-time neighbour: she'd become a true friend. Their two families had spent weekends with the kids rough-and-tumbling in and out of the adjoining properties, getting loads of exercise as they ran the one hundred and fifty metres between each kitchen door, enjoying access to two biscuit tins and two sets of sympathetic ears. Jess's boys used to count the days till the weekend when the family next door would arrive.

'Oh, look who's here, it's your sister-in-law.' Tori brought Jess back from her daydream with a nudge as Caro passed by the window.

'That's right, she's joined the Pony Club, hasn't she? Well, Charlotte has, anyway.'

'She's taken over completely, you know how bossy she is,' Tori grumbled as she unwrapped her raspberry muffin.

'Oh, she's all right, that's her coping mechanism. She's nervous unless she feels well entrenched in a social group.'

'Ladies.' Caro smiled tightly as she entered the room and gave each woman a brief peck on their left cheek. 'Tori, I'm glad you're here,' she said. 'I wanted to discuss the urn. Who do I see to ensure the urn is on and boiling well ahead of the one p.m. break?'

'Well, we take turns setting up for lunch. The roster's on the noticeboard,' Tori said, pointing it out.

'Yes, but it's not a very efficient roster, is it?' Caro clucked. 'It doesn't spell out precisely what tasks each rostered-on member is expected to perform. I think I'll update it and pin it up for next week so there is absolutely no room for error.' She unpinned the laminated card from the board.

'And,' she said, clearing coffee cups and dirty sugar spoons from the sink, 'I've decided to have a little social gathering for all the Pony Club parents here at the club rooms in a few weeks' time. I've noticed there are a number of new members who float around and don't know anybody and it's time we got together.' She flicked a distasteful-looking Chux into the rubbish bin and rummaged under the sink for a clean one.

'What a lovely idea.' Jessica smiled at her sister-in-law in encouragement, which prevented Tori from butting in.

'Well, *ciao*, I'm off to run it past the other members,' Caro said, heading out to the tack room.

'Bloody hell, that Caro! Don't you think she's taking it a bit far?' Tori said. 'She's only a new member herself.'

'That's probably why she's doing it,' Jessica mused, as she watched Caro approach two women slinging tack a few metres away. 'Well, I have to head back to the store, but I'd love to catch up later if you're free?' Jessica asked and placed her cup in the sink.

'Yes, sure,' Tori said, 'I'd love to have a chat. There's some stuff I need to talk about too.'

'Really?' Jessica asked as she picked up her basket. 'Is everything okay?'

Tori's face tightened and her eyes filled. 'Um, well, not really, darling, but do you mind if we talk about it tonight? I have to get back to the kids just now.'

Jess was immediately alarmed. 'Sure, sweetheart,' she said, putting an arm around her friend. 'I'll be home after seven. Come over when you're ready.'

'Thanks, love, I'll see you then,' Tori said, pulling her

sunglasses over her face and heading back out to the Pony Club paddock. Jess watched her leave, filled with concern for her friend and anxious to find out what was making her so miserable.

8

Nick stuck his head in through the open rickety front door; its glossy green paint was chipped and scratched. Each mark represented a moment in the diverse inhabitants' lives; the time the kids had scratched their names into the door, the indignant hoof scrapes from a hungry goat sniffing out a tofu feast; and the thousand bangs and scuffs of everyday family life that were preserved in the veneer.

'Hello!' Nick called down the hall, surprised to find Rainbow and Songbird's house so quiet. It was strangely peaceful, considering that Songbird had been quite specific that she and Rainbow had wanted to show him something amazing they were working on.

Eugene's haughty face peered around the living-room door as if to indicate his displeasure at being interrupted.

'Where's the gang, old boy?' Nick enquired. Eugene simply rolled back his lips and flashed his yellowed teeth.

Happy squeals and whoops from the backyard caught Nick's attention, so he bid the alpaca a polite farewell and headed round the back.

Rainbow and Songbird's dilapidated house sat on an acre-and-a-half of scrubby land at the edge of Stumpy Gully. The building was perched almost on the front boundary, which gave the family plenty of room for a backyard-cum-paddock at the rear. Rainbow's much-loved vegie garden filled the front yard, while the alpacas – Eugene, Digger and Ralphie – had free reign over the backyard – though they were much more partial to Rainbow and Songbird's futon.

Nick could see the two women at the back fence, squealing and hugging each other. Rainbow was jumping from foot to foot with excitement. The children were on the other side of the property on mountain bikes, flying off the jumps that made up their makeshift bike track.

He meandered down the paddock, familiar with the rough terrain that he'd helped the girls to fence last winter. The soil was poor, a weak grey colour, and hard as concrete after a decade-long drought. The clumps of dry grass were pale and lifeless. He had to be careful he didn't trip negotiating the uneven rocks.

'What's the hooting and hollering all about, ladies?' he called. 'You discovered oil or something?'

'Yes!' Rainbow bellowed back. 'But black oil!'

Songbird shook her head and muttered something to her.

'Oh, I mean black gold!' Rainbow giggled.

As he reached them Nick saw the girls were standing next to an area of soil the size and shape of a backyard swimming pool. The soil was mixed with straw and to Nick's surprise appeared to be steaming. 'What's this?' he asked. 'A new compost heap?'

'Not quite, mate,' Songbird said. 'Rainbow and I are on to something huge here; it's a bit bigger than rotting vegies, that's for sure.'

Rainbow hugged her in delight as she went on.

'But we can't do it on our own. We need help, and you're our man,' she gave Nick an ironic wink.

'Ooh, I do feel honoured,' Nick teased. 'But what is it exactly?'

'Terra preta,' Songbird boomed proudly. 'It's fucking brilliant!' She couldn't resist the triumphant grin that creased her leathery face.

'We're going to save the planet!' Rainbow squealed and embraced Songbird rapturously again.

'Settle, petal,' Songbird said, shaking her off like a naughty puppy. 'Take a breath or you'll hyperventilate.'

'This?' Nick said looking at the rectangle of dirt and straw. 'This is going to save the planet? How? And what's terra preta?'

'El Dorado!' Rainbow beamed and said, 'This is El Dorado.'

'She been smoking?' Nick asked Songbird.

Songbird chuckled. 'Come on; we'll pour you a wine and explain it all.'

The trio headed towards the house as Songbird explained. 'Apparently the ancient Amazonian Indians had shit soil,' she began. 'So they made good, fertile soil by making bio-char. They made a hole like we did –'

'How deep's the hole?'

'Couple of metres . . . then they filled it with compost, timber scraps, fish guts, shit, animal carcasses, anything and everything organic. Then they set fire to it, right? Covered it with straw and soil and left it to burn.'

'Like a luau pit? Cooking a pig over a few days?'

'Exactly!' Rainbow said, excitedly applauding Nick's quick grasp of the subject.

Songbird continued. 'Then, after weeks of this process, the soil attracts bacteria, which grows, as well as worms, bugs and other creatures that filter it through their systems. It turns into this most way-out, rich black stuff you cannot believe. And fertile, man – you could grow a politician a conscience in this stuff!'

'So you're making really good compost; that's great – but what's so new about that?' Nick asked.

'But there's more, there's more, there's more, this is where we save the plaaaaa-net, tra la la la,' Rainbow sang as she skipped around them.

Songbird ignored her mate's antics and went on. 'Instead of the slash-and-burn method that we use today, which completely roots the environment and sends greenhouse gasses hurtling towards the ozone layer, the slash-and-char method not only keeps the carbon in the ground but – and get this – sucks it out of the atmosphere!'

'You can't be serious?' Nick said. 'I thought only trees could do that.'

'No, dude, it's true. It's because it's slow-burning organic material in an oxygen-deprived environment under massive heat and pressure.'

Nick looked at her and shook his head. 'Jesus, Songbird, you sound like a textbook; you must have been seriously reading up on this.'

She nodded soberly.

'That's amazing. It could be really, really important,' Nick said, trying to digest the information.

'And just now we checked the pit for the first time since we set it alight last week. It's been burning slowly underground for all that time, which means . . .'

Rainbow interrupted with a delighted screech, 'Which means it's working! Yahoozalee!'

'Which means it's working,' Songbird repeated, giving Rainbow a fond look.

They sat at a table on the back courtyard while Rainbow grabbed a bottle of wine and glasses from indoors.

'So basically, Nick,' Rainbow trilled as she filled the mismatched glasses, 'what we have here is a system that can increase plant growth, improve soil structure, reduce soil acidity, lower evil greenhouse gas emissions, reduce the need for poison-ous fertilisers, reduce nutrient leaching and fully improve soil water retention; all while cooking up delicious, healthy micro-organisms and fungi – AND sucking carbon back!'

The pretty blonde hippie hardly stopped for breath as she went on. 'These soils not only contain higher concentrations of nutrients such as nitrogen, phosphorus, potassium and calcium, but also greater amounts of stable soil organic matter.' Rainbow finished her spiel with a dainty pirouette and then dropped to a deep curtsey.

Nick was gobsmacked at Rainbow's scientific explanation. He turned, wide-eyed, to Songbird.

'Yeah,' she nodded, 'I still get surprised even though I've known her thirty years.'

'Oooh, pretty – look!' Rainbow cried and skipped off in pursuit of a passing butterfly.

9

Jess grasped the dust cloth tightly between her fingers and marched down the hall to fling open a door that had been closed for months. Inside, the red-white-and-blue quilt she'd made three years earlier lay crisp and neat across the base of the single bed.

A gingham teddy perched cheekily on the pillow. One glass eye was crooked and it made him look disappointed, as if he'd been hoping for a different visitor.

Only a few toys remained; mostly vintage things her brother had grown up with. The shelf above the small white desk show-cased things nautical: a sailboat, a miniature life-preserver, an antique boat in a bottle.

Dr Suess's *Hop on Pop* lay on the white wicker armchair in the corner. She knew the book word-for-word after reading it over and over in the four years she'd been a stepmother. The boys had called Richard 'Pop'. He missed them too.

She shook the memories from her head, bustled in and dusted the bookshelves, the desktop, the headboard and windowsills, refusing to linger over the photos on the pin board.

It was probably time to clean the rooms out altogether and turn them into guestrooms, but she couldn't face it yet. Maybe they'd come back one day; even just for the night, and they'd think she'd forgotten them. No, she'd leave the rooms set up for now. Just in case.

The phone rang, jolting her back to reality. She ran to the kitchen and grabbed it on the fourth ring.

'Hello? Oh hi, Caro.'

Jess had hoped for a pleasant diversion from her sad thoughts, but knew from experience that a phone call from Caro was hard work.

She clicked the phone on to speaker, and pulled out the long duster to attack the plantation shutters in the kitchen – no point in wasting a perfectly good cleaning urge.

'Hi, Jess, can you hear me?' Caro's voice crackled from the base.

'Yep, how are you?' Jess said, climbing the stepladder to start above the sink.

'Fine. You?'

'Yeah, great. How are the kids?'

'Hamish is brilliant, as always, brought home a sterling project mark today. Charlotte's a little minx. Has her father around her little finger at the moment.'

'Good on her,' Jess grinned. She liked Charlotte's forthright manner. 'Angus well?' Jess hadn't seen her brother for ages. He was always flat-chat at work. She reached up higher to get a recalcitrant spider and its elaborate home. God, those webs spring up overnight, she thought.

'How would I know? I haven't seen him in months. He eats and sleeps here, but that's about it. He's at the office or in court or interstate constantly. And of course I'm running around after him, doing all the little SMS lists he sends me. Pick up this, organise that. It's just a nightmare. The kids are miserable.'

'Charlotte still has time to wind him round her finger though?'

'Well, yes, they do see him occasionally. He still drops them at school on Wednesdays. And I only just found out that all year he's been going in and helping with their readers and music lessons. I didn't even know!'

Jess stepped down a level to address the dust on the window-sills.

'How lovely. What a good dad.'

'Yes, wouldn't it be nice if he could find the same sort of time for his wife? I couldn't tell you the last time we did something together.'

Jess shook her head in silent frustration. She happened to know Angus and Caro went out just a few nights before. Her sister-in-law used exaggeration like salt, to spice up any conversation.

'So, how *was* last Thursday night?' she asked and turned around to perch on the kitchen bench in order to reach the window ledges.

'What? Oh, when Angus and I had dinner with your father? It was fine; your dad's well. As dynamic as ever. Very keen on that Genevieve. Actually that's why I'm calling.'

'Oh, is something wrong?' Jess's duster paused.

'Well, I am a bit concerned actually . . .' she began.

Jess climbed down the stepladder. 'Is something happening with Dad?' Jess's throat felt tight.

'I don't like to bring this up, Jessica, but I feel I must tell you that Genevieve is flashing around *another* new piece of jewellery.'

Jess's tension dissolved, to be quickly replaced with a hot flash of anger.

'You're concerned that Genevieve has a new bit of bling?' She was incredulous at her sister-in-law.

'Not just bling, darling, it's the new Bulgari ring. It's worth absolutely thousands.'

'What has this got to do with us, Caro?' Jess had had enough of this conversation.

'Jessica, don't you understand the implications of this?'

'Ummm, no, I guess not.' Jess's voice was muffled as she searched out a Chux from the back of the cupboard under the sink.

'You know they're in Port Douglas, don't you?'

From jewellery to Port Douglas? Maybe Caro was having too many chardys with lunch these days. 'Yes, Dad said they were taking a mini-break.'

'A break?' Caro crowed. 'The man's semi-retired, what kind of break could he possibly need? Didn't he buy her the Tiffany tag pendant for her birthday?'

'Err, I can't remember,' Jess said vaguely, her attention more focused on the mould behind her tap.

'Jessica, your father is spending all of his money on this . . . this . . . woman.'

'So what?' Jessica snapped. 'It's his money, he's worked hard for it.'

Caro sniffed. 'I'd have thought that the fact that your father is frittering away the family estate might have been of concern to you,' she said haughtily.

Jessica rolled her eyes and put her hands on her hips to speak firmly to the handset in its holder. 'Caro, I'm sure you're over-reacting, there's nothing serious going on here. What's wrong with some gift-giving in a normal loving relationship?'

'Oh, Jessica, open your eyes. Don't you see that as soon as she becomes Mrs Richard Wainwright she'll be in control of the estate? She'll be a part-owner.'

'Well, I hadn't thought of that, but I still think you're over-thinking it.'

'Someone has to, Jessica. Surely you don't want the family fortune all spent on fripperies and girlfriends. Not to mention the risk to the future of the family estate. What would your mother have said to this kind of behaviour?'

An invisible line had just been crossed. Jess threw her cloth into the sink, picked up the phone and spoke slowly and firmly. 'Caro, I think it's time we said goodbye.'

'Well, this won't be the end of it. He's gone crazy: jewellery, expensive dinners, OTT holidays – it's neverending. You're down there in the country, you don't see what I'm seeing. I'll keep tabs on the situation and keep you informed.'

'Goodbye, Caro,' was all Jess could manage before stabbing the disconnect button.

She leaned heavily against the kitchen bench and peeled off her pink rubber gloves, seething with anger. How dare Caro bring her mother into this? She'd never even met Eva Wainwright, for God's sake, and to use her memory to manipulate her own greedy ends was unforgivable.

Jess thought about her mum every day. It had been twenty years since she died, but the ache of missing her had never dissipated.

She turned to gaze out the window as evening crept silently across the property that had once been her parents' home.

What *would* her mother have said about her dad getting on with his life? She thought back to the last time she had seen her mum. It was at a party on the homestead's back deck; a party for Eva. The family had just sold the lavender fields on the east edge of the property, with their adjoining cafe and distillery. It would mean an end to the long hours Eva had worked for years to make the business a success.

She had been giddy with the excitement of being a retiree at just forty-eight. It was a stunning summer evening, balmy and still. She'd had several of her special 'Lavender Bubblies' and was regaling the group with her 'must do' list as a lady of leisure. Her dreams were getting sillier and sillier and they were all in hysterics imagining the gregarious Eva Wainwright living for a month in Coober Pedy, mining for opals, but she insisted she just loved those dear little underground homes.

Then she'd died. Just like that. Without warning. Cruelly and stupidly, as if fate were listening to her plans and decided to stomp on her dreams for fun.

It was an aneurism. That very night; she didn't even get the dignity of finishing her own celebration, Jess thought bitterly.

The crowd had thinned about midnight and only family was left. Someone noticed Eva was missing. Richard went to look for her, joking she'd probably done a runner and snuck off to bed early. He'd found her on the bathroom floor.

When she'd fallen, a bottle of lavender essential oil had crashed to the ground with her and the sweet stink had filled the house. Jessica remembered the smell filling her nostrils just as her father came back, ashen, to the deck.

What *would* her mother have said? Jessica mused. Probably, 'Go for it, darl.'

~10~

Tori tapped at the screen door. She was holding a bottle of pink moscato in one hand, and a platter of antipasto in the other.

'Yum,' Jess said as she opened the door and took the wine. 'I love a guest who comes prepared.'

'Well, I figure you must get sick of everyone expecting you to be the queen of catering all the time, so I thought we'd break into some of my Christmas stash a bit early,' Tori replied as she made herself at home on a stool at Jess's broad kitchen bench. 'Oooh, looks like you've been busy here. What are you making?' she asked.

'Oh, it's just something I was putting together for the boys,' Jess said, picking up the scrapbook she'd been working on. 'It's photos of us all together, and captions so the boys can remember their country life,' she said, flipping the pages. 'Look, that's last Christmas at Rainbow and Songbird's: Nick dressed up as Santa and gave out lollies to all the kids.' She laughed at the memory.

'This is gorgeous, sweetheart, they'll love it,' Tori said, poring over the thick cardboard book with its handwritten captions, dozens of photos and bright borders. 'Do you think you might be able to give it to them in person?' she asked, closing the book and passing it back to Jess.

'I doubt it,' Jess answered sadly. 'I rang Graham again last night, but he still won't even return my calls.'

'Bastard,' Tori spat. 'Oh thanks, love,' as she took the glass of pink bubbly from Jessica.

'I agree.' Jess took a gulp of her wine. 'Ooh, this is lovely,' she said. 'Now tell me what's going on with you, girl. I haven't been able to stop thinking about you all afternoon.' She indicated the pile of paper, photos, scissors and glue scattered across the bench. 'You talk and I'll clean; I've been on a bit of a roll tonight.'

Tori picked at the sun-dried tomatoes on the platter before her. 'Okay,' she finally said and sighed deeply. 'It's Joseph and me. It's . . . ah . . . well, I think we're in trouble.'

Jess's arms were heaped with craft items and photo albums. She looked around for a place to set them down, taking a step one way and then another before finally dumping them back on the bench and walking over to embrace her friend.

'Shit, Tori, when you said serious I had no idea you meant seriously serious.' She sat on the stool next to her and looked into Tori's face with concern. 'What happened?' she asked.

'It's just come to an end. I am so frustrated with everything; we both are. We can't seem to be together without screaming at each other. And worst of all is . . . well, I don't even think I love him anymore. And I doubt he has any feelings left for me either.'

'Oh hell. Since when?' Jess asked.

'Well it's all so humiliating,' Tori paused for a mouthful of wine. 'It seems to stem from money troubles, embarrassingly enough. I mean, could it be any more clichéd and suburban?' Her eyes swam with tears.

'I just can't believe it, sweetheart,' Jess sympathised, rubbing Tori's arm. 'You guys have always been so great together.'

'I know,' she wailed. 'But now he's constantly hassling me about spending, and it's not as if I buy every designer bag that comes out, I'm really quite restrained, you know,' her eyes widened at the injustice of it all. 'Although I did just buy this fabulous Chanel bag last month in LA when I took the children to Disneyland; isn't it to die for?' She dropped the bag back onto the sofa in defeat.

'Our relationship has just become so stale and awful, there's nothing but squabbles. And with everyone talking about this stupid economic crisis – well, it's just too boring, isn't it?'

'Have you tried counselling?' Jessica asked and moved to retrieve the wine from the fridge.

'He's suggested it a few times, but I figure why bother? It's not going to help. I don't know if I even want to work on the relationship. I just don't know what to do. Please don't tell anyone.'

'Of course not,' Jess promised, topping up both their glasses.

'You know what? I really don't want to talk about it any more, it's so hideous,' Tori said.

'No worries,' Jessica said, 'but I'm here whenever you need me, okay?'

'Thanks, love,' Tori nodded, plucking a slice of baked eggplant from the platter. 'And I'm sorry for dumping all this on you. You have enough relationship angst of your own to deal with.'

Jess went back to sorting out her scrapbooking supplies. 'That's okay, sweetie, your stuff doesn't make mine any harder; we all have things to deal with.' She screwed the lid tightly onto her glue pot. 'Sometimes I just wish I hadn't been so sucked in by him, you know, but then I think that at least by trusting him I got those wonderful years with Liam and Callum.' She sighed. 'I can't decide what would have been worse; never having them to begin with, or losing them the way I have.'

'Darling, it's an impossible situation and there's really no point thinking about all the what-ifs,' Tori counselled.

'I know you're right,' Jess said as she screwed up scrap paper and threw it in the recycling bin. 'He was such a phoney, you know,' she said suddenly. 'That's what it was. He was such a good salesman as a wine rep that it spilled over to his private life. He would do or say anything to get his own way.'

'Oh, for sure,' Tori said. 'Like when he told Nick he barracked for St Kilda and managed to get him around to work all day during last year's finals when Nick had originally said no.'

'Yeah, that's right. I was so surprised about that. I couldn't work out why Nick wasn't going to the game. But he said, "Anything for a Saints fan." Then when I told him that Graham was a Kiwi who didn't even follow AFL he just stormed off. He never returned another of Graham's calls.'

'Wow, what a dog.' Tori shook her head.

'Come on, let's go and sit out on the deck,' Jessica suggested. 'It's a beautiful night.'

Outside a blanket of stars sparkled from above and a gentle breeze flirted with the gums. 'Here, this'll keep you warm,' Jess said and threw a mohair rug to Tori, who slipped it around her shoulders.

They settled into the outdoor furniture with their drinks, the snacks on a table between them, and Jess continued her story.

'It wasn't as if there was one big moment where everything fell apart between us, you know; it was more like a whole lot of little things that slowly eroded our relationship.'

'I know absolutely what you mean,' Tori replied. She pulled the rug closer around her. 'It's like there's just a long horrible rumbling of nastiness.'

'Exactly,' Jessica nodded, tucking her feet under her body. 'But I was so in love with the boys that Graham sort of faded out of the picture. The boys and I were a team. Perhaps that's why he left, maybe he felt excluded from our little group.'

'Not at all, you all had fun together, I saw it,' Tori protested. 'You guys did all the picnics and camping and stuff that any other family does. But Graham was never bloody happy, was he? He was always grumpy about something.'

Jess slapped at a mosquito that was humming around her legs. 'You know, I reckon he has a real nasty streak – well, in fact I've discovered just how nasty in the past year, but back then I'd only see it every now and then. He would occasionally tease the boys, but not good-naturedly, you know, almost like he enjoyed upsetting them.'

'Really, how do you mean?' Tori replied. She sat upright with surprise.

'Oh, nothing abusive or anything, just things like saying, in a sing-song manner, "Liam's got a girlfriend," and you know how sensitive little Liam is, he *hated* it. He'd beg his dad to stop until he was in tears. But Graham kept doing it. Sometimes he acted just like an annoying little brother, not a father at all.'

'That's just plain strange,' Tori said.

'Yeah, I know,' Jess said 'Hey, this marinated capsicum is gorgeous. Where'd you get it from? It might even be better than mine.'

Tori threw her head back with laughter. 'That's because it is yours, darling! I had the store send me some up for the season and I threw it on the platter with some other bits from The Essential Ingredient.'

Jess cracked up with laughter. 'Thank God I didn't say it was awful then,' she cried. 'Oh god, that feels good,' she said and wiped tears from her cheeks. 'It's nice to laugh.'

'We both need it,' Tori said, raising her glass. 'It's been a tough year.'

'It sure has,' Jess said. Her laughter turned to seriousness again. 'I tried so hard to make it work with Graham. I wish it hadn't ended, especially not the way it did. It was so ugly, so cruel.'

'The man is a creep,' Tori said, patting Jess's knee.

'You're right,' Jessica admitted, 'and he got worse so subtly, so slowly that I barely noticed. It crept up on me until suddenly I looked at him one day and thought, I don't even like you. But the boys made it worth putting up with his crap; well, to a point anyway. I always thought if we broke up I'd have joint custody of the boys.'

'Yeah, what's up with that?' Tori asked. 'No joy there at all?'

'The lawyers tell me I can't fight for the kids. I was just a girl-friend in the eye of the law as we didn't *officially* live together.'

'That's insane! He and his kids lived in your house for more than three years! You housed him! He owes you rent at least.'

'But there's no proof of that, can you believe it? He owned, and still owns, a house in Williamstown that he'd been renting out for cash – he's so dodgy – so he told the courts that it had always been his principal place of residence. We never had any formal documentation about rent or mortgage or anything. I'm such an idiot,' she said as she put her head in her hands.

'No, not an idiot; just trusting and too generous – beautiful traits,' said Tori, grabbing her friend by the hand.

'I've spent a fortune on lawyers but apparently the only option is to keep the relationship civil and appeal to him as a human being and try to make arrangements to see the boys privately, which I don't see happening any time soon. He's doing his best to just delete me from their lives, like I never existed.' Her face creased with pain. 'I get to speak to them once a month when their Aunty Samantha has them for the afternoon, so that's a blessing. But it breaks my heart when Liam cries and asks why he can't see me anymore. It's almost not worth it.'

'And there's nothing you can do?'

'Believe me,' Jess said, staring at the endless stars twinkling above, 'I have been through this so many times. If there was I would have done it by now.'

The car parks were full. The shops were teeming with well-groomed families in Country Road weekend wear. The main street was choked with flashy four-wheel drives and shiny European sports cars, and basic provisions were dwindling in the shops. The townies were back.

The township of Stumpy Gully was groaning under the weight of its tripled summer population. The summer holidays had begun and the city had emptied a good chunk of its population into the small towns dotted around the picturesque coast.

The visitors were easy to spot: their riding boots were shiny and dust-free, their Driza-Bones were unfaded and their children used hair products to keep their complicated styles in place.

The city ladies breezed up and down the main street placing orders with the bakery, butcher and florist to stock up for their holiday break. Their manicures were immaculate, designer sunglasses held back well-coiffed locks, and their designer weekend wear was clearly monogrammed with the appropriate designers; Tommy Hilfiger, Ralph Lauren and even Burberry gumboots.

'Dahling-how-are-yous' echoed through the car park as the visitors joyfully ran into other holiday-makers they'd seen only a few days before in the big smoke.

The locals rolled their eyes and swapped amused smiles as the city dwellers played at country life, singing out happily to each other in the shops:

'You must pop into the estate: I'm whipping up a pomegranate tart.'

'Do come to the property: we've had the gardener put in the most divine Stephanie Alexander kitchen garden.'

'We've had the living room done in French Provincial with a dash of Shabby Chic, it's just too *Country Life*!'

The shopkeepers stored up their favourite overheard quotes and shared them among themselves after hours.

Jess often felt torn between her friendships with the locals and the visitors; it was a tricky balance at times. This morning a throng of townies was at her store and she was dividing her time between work and sharing a coffee with Tori.

'So, what's on for this New Year's festivities?' Tori asked her as she scanned the menu.

'Sorted, darling!' A voice from above their heads boomed.

'Cat!' the two women exclaimed and stood to greet the new arrival with a round of air kisses and compliments. Cat heaved her bottom onto a chair and groaned in relief at taking the weight off her feet.

'Fi's doing a masquerade ball on her estate New Year's Eve. And I'm bringing in the nanny army for the children at mine.'

'Fantastic,' Jessica said. 'Sounds like heaps of fun!'

'Yep, the fun's at Fi's and the kids are at Cat's,' Cat boomed with laughter at her play on words. 'Cap, lovey, and don't spare the full cream!' she boomed over the heads of the patrons to the busy barista. 'Fi's actually on her way in now; she's out in the car park trying to negotiate a space for that beastly truck of hers.'

'Oh, she didn't buy the Hummer, did she?' Tori asked with a look of distaste. 'They're so, I don't know . . . pedestrian.'

'How can a car be pedestrian, you goose?' Cat replied. 'Yes, bloody great barge of a thing: she's already taken out the front bumper. On my stone gate post, no less. The gate survived, thank Christ. A small nick just improves the rural look of the entrance. Can't say that about her entrance though.' Cat indicated the front door as Fi stood holding it open for her four small boys. They barrelled in mid-wrestle, mid-argument and mid-squeal.

Fi stood with a tight grin on her face before following the rabble inside. She was wearing a long, sixties-inspired maxi-dress. Bony shoulders and clavicle poked past the spaghetti straps. Teetering cork espadrilles and a wide paisley headband completed the vintage look; her long blonde hair was high-lighted to perfection.

Fi deftly dispatched the four boys to the kids' table, slapped orange juices in front of them and ordered four toasted sand-wiches, all within ten seconds.

No wonder she was so thin, Jessica noted. If that woman even found time to go to the loo, let alone eat, it would be a miracle. Fi and her second husband, Anthony, had planned their first two boys, but the third unplanned pregnancy resulted in a pair of wild twin boys, which, when combined with Fi's two daughters from her first marriage, Missy and Gracie, meant the woman was run off her feet constantly. Yet she was the type to revel in the challenge – always working on a new charity committee, function or project – which was why it came as no surprise to anyone that she had volunteered to host the New Year's Eve function at her place.

'Girls, mwah,' she moued in the general direction of the table. She even shorthanded air kisses, Jess thought.

'It's on, at my place, huge masquerade ball. Everyone's coming. Harley, put that down. You must do the decorating, Jess – Tom, take that out of your ear this instant. Tori, you look great. Latte please. Did Cat tell you she's having the kids at hers?'

'Just starting to, lovey, before your family hurricane blew in.'

'It'll be brilliant. Tell them.' Fi downed her latte the second it was placed in front of her before a child-related event could prevent her ingesting the caffeine. It was probably why she never bothered ordering food, Jess thought: there was no chance she'd get to eat it. Even the laid-back Jess was on edge when she spent too much time in Fi's company.

Cat raised her speaking volume a few notches to compete with the cacophony from the children's table. 'We're turning the old stables into bunk rooms. We've got a jumping castle, a kiddie band, the local foodies are catering all the nibbly bits –'

Fi leaned forward to interrupt. 'And the best thing is Gracie's school friend is doing a nanny course and is bringing a truckload of trainee nannies down with her to supervise the entire shebang. It'll be like school camp. But with X-Box.'

'See, it'll be great!' Cat said.

'Fab,' Fi agreed. 'Hugh, pick that up. Tom, put that down. Must be off: they're turning.' She downed the glass of water in front of her and stood, swinging her Prada sac over her slight frame and collecting her charges as they darted left and right to avoid her grasp. 'Honestly, it's like herding cats. Get in the car you little monkeys.' With Fendi shades firmly in place, she eventually left and the entire cafe breathed a sigh of relief.

'Crazy!' Cat's booming tone soon disrupted the silence.

~12~

Jessica placed the last latte glass, polished and gleaming, atop the espresso machine ready for the next morning's attack, and sighed.

She usually loved the solitude of closing time, when only faint echoes of the busy day remained in the store and the amber glow of twilight warmed the walls. But today she continued to fight the feeling of dissatisfaction and despondency that had been haunting her lately. Outside the sun was sinking below the horizon and the sea was calm and still.

As Jess flicked a mop across the floorboards she remembered how decrepit the store had been when she had first taken it over. She and her dad had gone along to the auction ten years before out of curiosity more than anything, but as she'd wandered around the tired, sagging weatherboard shack that housed the local post office and sold basic bread and milk supplies, Jess had suddenly been seized with a sense of possibility.

'Dad, I could do this you know,' she'd said, squeezing his arm with excitement.

'Hmmm . . . do what?' Richard had asked, distracted by a discussion he was having with the estate agent about the local market.

'I could turn this into somewhere really special; a place where people could meet, eat good food and relax. It has so much scope, so much character; this is something I could really get my teeth into. Oh Dad, do you think, maybe, well . . . what do you think?' she had gushed, her shining eyes and flushed cheeks telling her father how badly she had fallen in love with her vision of a new General Store. And because it was the first time since she had finished design school that he had seen her so passionate about anything, Richard had raised his arm again and again as the auction price increased until suddenly Jess was hugging him delightedly and shrieking with joy and the General Store was theirs. They became a father and daughter team: fifty-fifty business partners.

She'd opened for business four months later. Rainbow and Songbird, and of course Nick, had worked long hours with her to clean and wash the dusty interior of the store, and she'd started out with simple offerings of coffee and cake, but soon her dreams of lime-washed boards, windows overlooking the slice of bay that peeped from behind the banksias, walls of shelving to hold locally made jams and preserves, vintage knick-knacks and work from local artisans filled the space. The long love-worn wooden counter from a country haberdashery became her front counter. She hired a chef and a manager and rummaged in op shops across the Peninsula, hunting out mismatched English china, souvenir teaspoons and retro jugs and glasses to give the store its eclectic feel.

Nick had worked for weeks with her that first summer, building the deck that became a favourite of locals and townies, who coveted the 1960s patio furniture with the best view of the bay.

Inside the store was bright, airy and open, the salt of the sea mixing with the local fare and attracting plenty of customers. Jess's design flair was stamped throughout the interior from tiny touches, such as pottery bowls of sea-smoothed glass collected on the beach that lay just metres from the store's front door, to the larger features, like the enormous pier bollards that marked out the parking area around the side. And her years of helping her mum in the Lavender Lunches restaurant paid off tenfold in the General Store's early days as she multi-tasked the pokey little corner store's way to a viable business. Her cook, Andrea, was a god-send but it was Jessica's stylish decor, merchandising and warmth with the customers that kept the punters flowing in the front door.

It was here, in her cafe and produce store, that Jess felt more fully at home than almost anywhere in the world; this was hers, her vision and hopes all realised within four walls. All the dreams and passion she had ever had for interior design that she could never seem to find the right outlet for after school seemed to come together in this simple beach shack – which these days proudly boasted a gleaming commercial kitchen that could cater a stylish wedding. Two years after the cafe was humming along and the produce store section began to support itself, Jessica had opened the art gallery. The short glass corridor led from the cafe section into a large white room where Jessica proudly showcased local talent, with a small corner dedicated to her own pieces.

Bold beach scenes in whites and neutrals in oil on enormous canvas, by local painter Helen Greenwill, were a big favourite – the tourists couldn't get enough of the things to feature over the stone fireplaces in their beach houses. Patrick Lardner, whose work was so well known and so highly priced that he was really a national treasure, even exhibited his bold, naive works on the odd occasion; more as a favour to Jessica than anything.

The other artists who exhibited in the General Store Gallery ranged from hobbyists to professionals – it didn't matter to Jess if they were well known or not.

But, even with her gallery, even with the store, now it was time to leave. She'd done enough here. She'd proved herself and now a bigger challenge lay before her. She recognised there was a void within her that was unable to be filled by the beautiful cafe. It had been filled by the boys and was now yawning; empty and painful deep inside.

Before Graham, she'd considered moving on to a new challenge. But then he'd walked into her life and had given her an instant family. In retrospect, up until then she felt she'd lived her entire life in black and white, and suddenly – with two warm bodies squeezed up against her on the couch as she read them stories – it was infused with colour.

Graham was sweet and fun – at first – but even the growing distance between them hadn't bothered her that much; hearing the boys call her 'Mumma' was bliss. For four years she was the centre of a family and along with the commercial and creative satisfaction of running her store and creating artworks for the gallery, she felt complete.

She was happy to take over the reins as full-time mum while Graham worked long days as the marketing manager for the National Vignerons' Association. He was often on the road, and he stayed in the city overnight at least once a week.

She rarely missed him; after all she had her gorgeous boys to keep her busy and fulfilled, and increasingly when Graham did come home he'd find fault with her, her dinners or her house-keeping, and she began to enjoy his absences.

Jessica relished the dawn wrestles with her boys, their vora-cious appetite not only for food, but also for entertainment and attention. She was thrown into the parenting deep end and she revelled in every second. In those precious moments with the boys, as she stroked their foreheads while they slept, kissed their plump cheeks or sang silly songs with them, it made her feel connected to her own mother, as though an invisible thread had wound down through time and joined them as mothers. For the first time since losing Eva, Jess felt a void had been filled.

Of course she knew that Graham was becoming distant; that their bond was straining, weakening. And she worried. She didn't want relationship issues to rock this special family boat she was cruising in. When he was around she tried to engage him in his family, talk to him about his life, act every bit the interested, thoughtful partner.

But they left anyway.

Graham met someone new and took the boys – her boys – to Melbourne to live with the new woman (his assistant, stereo-typically).

It happened so fast. One day she was worrying about Liam's lost library books and planning Callum's sixth birthday party – and the next they were gone. It was as if the whole thing had never happened. Sometimes she woke at night and had to convince herself that it hadn't all been just a dream. She would

stumble half-asleep in the dark house to the boys' bedroom
to touch their toys, their few remaining clothes, just to prove
to herself that it was real, that she hadn't conjured the whole
thing in her mind.

It was months since she'd last seen them; Graham wanted to
erase her from their lives; pretend she'd never existed. 'Let the
boys have a clean start,' he'd barked down the phone at her a
few weeks ago when she'd begged one more time to just visit;
just to hold them for a few minutes, to feel their heartbeats
against her and know that they were okay.

'You're stuffing up their lives,' Graham had told her. 'They
have a new stepmother now, you'll only confuse them.'

His cruel words still stung and she wondered if maybe he was
right; maybe she should just give up, let them adjust to their new
life. She had the chance for a new life now too, and she was
going to grab it with both hands and be a success. Jess stopped
mopping the floor, wiped the tears from her eyes and pulled her
mobile from her pocket. She flicked through her contacts and
tapped on Jimmy's name.

~13~

The shrill squawk of the wattlebird rejoicing in the grevillea's bright blooms didn't break into Tori's retail-induced trance as she pulled into the driveway of her country house. She was too excited by the bounty in her boot.

She'd popped back to Malvern this morning to drop the children with her parents for a few days, and then planned to call into the house to pick up Dustin's flippers and snorkel before heading off to Chadstone for some Christmas shopping.

She was surprised to find Joseph at home, sorting paperwork at the kitchen table. To her dismay he had immediately brought up the subject of money.

'What do you plan to buy the children for Christmas?' he'd asked.

'Um, well I thought an iTouch each would be useful and practical,' she'd stammered.

'There just isn't money for that sort of extravagance,' Joseph had said, his face turning a deep red. 'You have to stop spending.' He flipped the papers in front of him angrily.

'But it's Christmas,' she'd cried. 'What sort of Christmas will Priscilla and Dustin have if there isn't something fabulous for them under the tree?'

'They can have some presents, of course,' Joseph said and shoved papers into a briefcase already overflowing with documents and files.

'I suppose they could make do with sharing a Nintendo Wii,' Tori had conceded with a sniff.

To her shock, Joseph had exploded with anger. 'No, no, no!'

he'd yelled. 'No Nintendo, no iTouch, no bloody money. What is wrong with you, woman?' He'd grabbed his bulging briefcase and stormed out of the house, leaving Tori in tears.

It was hardly the way to start a shopping trip, but she'd decided the best thing to do was to pull herself together for the sake of the children; it was her duty to give them the best *budget* Christmas she could. She'd set off with her platinum Amex and the thrill of retail therapy taking the sting out of the early morning altercation.

Now she squealed with excitement as she saw the mountains of crisp multicoloured shopping bags crushed into her boot. She loved Christmas. It was the most exciting time of the year. There were so many retail opportunities. She prided herself on her beautiful Christmas tree display: each year her tree sported a new look. This season was to be turquoise and silver, to tone in with the seaside theme.

She was proud of herself for shaking off the morning's ugliness created by Joseph's mercenary attitude. All it had taken was some lateral thinking. If she couldn't afford quality items, she'd decided, she'd do quantity instead.

So what if they couldn't get a Nintendo Wii? She'd upgraded their X-Box experience instead and bought them each four new games. It was practically recycling, she thought proudly. She should get herself one of those hemp T-shirts, she was becoming so green, she thought with a chuckle.

Fuelling her children's reading habit was an educational rather than frivolous expense, so she'd felt quite justified in acquiring the entire range of twenty *Fairy Magic* novels for Priscilla and forking out two hundred dollars for some DK learning books for Dustin. After all, what price knowledge?, she thought, lugging the small library of books from the boot.

Then there was clothing; she'd spent a deliriously happy hour in Esprit and David Jones buying frocks and accessories for Priscilla and a little suit for Dustin to wear to Christmas lunch, along with more than enough casual wear to see them through the season. But clothes were essentials – so they didn't count.

Then she'd had a ball in Toys R Us buying cheap little stocking fillers, Nintendo DS games, Barbie dolls and Brio.

She breathed a happy, sated sigh. Her little darlings would have a wonderful morning opening the loot from Santa and she would feel like a perfect mother.

As she pulled more bags from the boot a slight twinge of unease hit her. She may have bought more than she'd realised. What was the Australian Geographic bag? She couldn't remember that store; she'd been in such a frenzy. Oh, yes, that's right, a telescope and a child's geology set. Oh, and night-vision goggles. Well anything from Australian Geographic was educational, no one could argue with that.

Hmm . . . a Darrell Lea bag? She peeped inside. Oh yes, more stocking stuffers, fifty-dollar showbags. Well that was all right, food definitely didn't count, that came out of the grocery budget. All was well.

Now she needed an iced tea and maybe one of Jess's fabulous frittatas, and a spot of PSA – Post Shopping Analysis. Sometimes just talking about her purchases was as much fun as the actual buying, Tori thought, as she jumped into the car and headed to the General Store.

'So, how goes Operation Country Christmas?' Jess asked once they were installed at a table with cool drinks in front of them.

'Absolutely brilliantly!' Tori said in excitement. She filled Jess in with a condensed version of that morning's shopping trip.

Jess was surprised at how her friend seemed to have shaken off the sadness of her troubled marriage that had had her in tears just a few nights before. Shopping seemed to transform Tori into a different person; a slightly manic one.

'And I'm saving, saving, saving,' bragged Tori. 'I'm so proud of my little budget conscious moves. I'm not buying those one-hundred-dollar Christmas crackers this year from De La Fleur,' she announced with aplomb.

'One hundred dollars? What, per cracker? What in the hell's in them?'

'Oh, I don't remember, but it's good. I think the jokes are written by Jerry Seinfeld or something. I'm getting the ten-dollar crackers instead.'

'Tori, that's two hundred dollars on a moment's fun and a lifetime of landfill. Why don't you make them yourself? It's just a loo roll and silver paper, a homemade key chain and a funny story about a family member. You can get the kids to make the festive hats. It's so much more meaningful. And so easy to do.'

'Oh, Jess, you know I can barely thread a needle. You're the crafty one. I don't know how you even think up that kind of stuff. Honestly, you're amazing.' Tori sipped her tea and stared at the thin line of sea in the distance. 'No, I'm proud of my decision, it's a huge saving. Of course, we can't be silly though with this budgeting thing: it's still Christmas. There are essentials to buy, like a reindeer, for example. Blitzen broke last year when those kookaburras mistook his tail for a snake. Obviously I can't have the lawn display without Blitzen. And yes, a reindeer costs a grand, but like I was saying, it's an essential. And tomorrow's the Christmas craft market: there's tons of fun festive stuff there I need.' She practically started shivering in anticipation.

'Tori,' Jess leaned forward and put her hand on the other woman's knee to get her full attention, 'sweetheart, I'm a bit worried about you with this spending thing.'

'You're starting to sound like Joseph, Jess. Anyway, given the financial crisis situation it's perfect timing to put on a brave face and throw a big, fun, down-home, country shebang. I've got the catering sorted, the decor all planned, I need to order flowers and the eye fillet, and of course the crayfish and oysters, but it'll be fun doing a humble, DIY kind of function.'

'Ummm, you know DIY means Do It Yourself, don't you, love?'

'Well, of course,' Tori emptied her glass with a flourish. 'I'm supervising, darling. Very tricky business being a delegator. Well, must fly, I've got a little man coming to quote on polishing the monstera leaves.'

The upbeat tempo of folk music drifted through the stalls at the Stumpy Gully craft market. Delicious early-morning smells of brewed coffee and egg-and-bacon rolls filled the air. Above, patches of blue sky flashed between the leaves of the gum trees that filled the racetrack market site.

Locals and townies meandered along the dusty paths, enjoying the free samples of fresh berries, pâtés and home-cooked fudge offered by stallholders and searching for unique arts and crafts to complete their Christmas shopping.

A flock of rainbow lorikeets squawked past, insistent that the crowds appreciate their lurid beauty. Kookaburras laughed at them, and a fluffy baby kooka hopped from branch to branch, its head tilted to keep a watchful eye on the sausage sizzle.

The eucalyptus litter, mulched in piles under the smooth grey trunks, was steaming from last night's rainfall, releasing a musty gum fragrance that wound its way among the stalls, competing with the aroma of samosas and enhancing the floral fragrance from the many soaps and bath salts.

The Christmas market was Rainbow and Songbird's big day. They had been knitting furiously for the past month, turning Eugene's wool into a colourful assortment of berets, throws, leggings and wraps. It was just one of the many markets they attended each year, selling their funky woollen designs at exorbitant prices, but this pre-Christmas market was their most important, thanks to the thousands of cashed-up tourists who attended, desperate for that eclectic little piece that would mark

them as unique, unusual and different at school pick-up during
the winter months.

Eugene, naked and shivering, had stared at his owners
reproachfully that morning as they'd set off in their Smart Car
packed with wares. 'Can't he come?' Rainbow had begged.
'He'll be lonely.'

'No chance,' Songbird had replied as she skilfully reversed
onto Stumpy Gully Road. 'You know he bites.'

The Smart Car was a recent acquisition; and one the women
were both thrilled with. They got around the little town on
bikes most of the time, but the car got them to markets in style
and comfort.

Now that their stall was set up, the two women sat back
and surveyed the passing throng from behind their knitting
needles. They'd discovered very early on in their market career
that the tourists were even keener to spend when they could
actually see the work being made. 'These amazing-looking
hippie women make the goods right in front of your eyes. It's
so earthy, so organic . . .' Songbird had once heard a market-
goer exclaim to her companion. From then on Songbird and
Rainbow made sure they kept knitting needles in their hands
to give the punters a show and increase their sales, although
due to the huge demand for their product they now had a
team of local grandmothers who knitted the bulk of their
wares.

'Wow, girls, you've outdone yourselves. Eugene must be on
steroids!'

Rainbow looked up at the familiar voice. 'Jess!' she called out.
'Songbird, Jess is here.' She threw down her knitting to greet
her friend with a warm hug. 'I love your skirt!' she declared. 'Is
it hemp?'

Jessica's taupe and crimson skirt was full and swishy, made
up of a series of vintage patches. She hip-twisted to let it flare
out and laughed at her hippie friend. 'No, it's a vintage Issey
Miyake,' she said. 'I've had it for years.'

'Well it's "toooo divine".'

Jess laughed at Rainbow's mimicking of an upper class Gucci Mama.

'Thanks, pet,' Jessica said with a smile, flicking her Luna Gallery raspberry shawl over one shoulder. 'How are you, Songbird?' Jessica asked. Songbird was wrestling with a knitting catastrophe.

'Can't talk,' she muttered, 'swearing.'

Jessica smiled and turned back to Rainbow. 'So, how's it going?'

'We're great,' Rainbow said. 'Business is booming: we've put on another two knitters to do our designs, which makes five.'

'Are they still complaining about the patterns?' Jess asked.

'Of course,' Rainbow grinned. 'One nanna keeps trying to talk us into doing a range of baby layettes and booties in pastel wool. It's hilarious, but she does such an amazing job: just look at this stitching.' She indicated a rasta-style hat with rows of vibrant colour.

'So neat,' Jess said, nodding. 'We must have another exhibition of your work. You have some wonderful new styles now.'

'Maybe after the Christmas rush,' Rainbow said, then winked slyly and added, 'and we'll make sure all the pieces we give you are Rainbow and Songbird originals!'

'Deal,' Jess said.

She had met Rainbow and Songbird, or Kylie and Susan as they had been known back then, when they were all students at the tiny local high school. Kylie and Susan had been inseparable best friends since they'd met in Year Seven. Susan, now Songbird, had come to Rainbow's defence when a bunch of Year Nine girls had begun teasing the frightened teenager, surrounding her in a circle of mocking faces.

'Oi, bugger off,' Songbird had called, pushing her way into the circle and putting an arm around the quivering Rainbow. 'She's my mate. If you mess with her, you mess with me,' the nuggety girl had snarled, fists clenched and spit flying from her mouth. The bullies had slunk away and left the beginnings of a firm friendship in their wake.

Both women had married, had children and divorced before they realised that they were happiest when they were together. They'd pooled their assets, blended their six children into one big, chaotic family and had never been happier.

Jessica had helped plan their weddings, divorce parties and finally their civil union on the beach the previous year.

'That bitch sister-in-law of yours is here,' Songbird grumbled, finally throwing her knitting down in exasperation.

'Songbird, don't be such a nasty pastie,' Rainbow said.

'Is she?' Jessica asked, moving to the side of the stall to make room for four well-dressed women who were exclaiming over the alpaca wares. 'She must have driven down this morning. Did she stop to chat?'

'Chat! Criticise more like,' Songbird spat, ignoring the surprised faces of her customers.

'Apparently our alpaca wool isn't as soft as bloody mohair . . . bloody cheek.'

'Oh dear, what a dreadful thing to say,' one of the shoppers interjected. 'Clearly this fibre is far better than mohair. I have extremely delicate skin and,' – she brushed a purple knitted glove gently against her cheek – 'this is far superior in softness to mohair, I can assure you.'

Songbird snorted rudely.

'That is so sweet of you,' Rainbow said, sliding quickly in front of her partner. 'We just love our alpaca.'

Songbird shook her head and rolled her eyes theatrically at Jess, who had to walk away to hide her laughter.

'Bye, girls,' she called with a wave over her shoulder. 'Good luck today.'

'Thanks, Jess,' Songbird tinkled. 'Oh by the way, Caro said she was desperate for caffeine, so you'll probably find her in the coffee aisle. I'm sure we'll have a great day.'

'Yeah, if the effing townies can bear to part with their precious cash,' Songbird muttered to herself.

★

Caro Wainwright tapped her Prada riding boot impatiently. Dust rose from the ground and swirled about the immaculate leather. 'Shit,' Caro said and immediately stood still to lessen the damage. She sighed to herself as the coffee queue slowly moved forward.

There were some things about country life she just couldn't stand, and waiting ten minutes for a simple latte was one of them. Her lovely Gloria Jeans at Chadstone knew how to do it: take order, take payment, deliver coffee. No bother, no fuss. No chitchat with each and every customer about the weather, their mother's arthritis or their sister's baby, for heaven's sake. Pop a Gloria Jeans in town, and country life would be far more comfortable.

'Caro, darling, hello!'

'Oh, Jess dear, hello.' The women air-kissed and Caro stood back, relieved at the distraction from the queue, to appraise her sister-in-law. 'Honestly, Jess, I know it's just a country market, but you really do need to get up to High Street, Armadale, more often: you look like you've rolled around in an op shop. That Miyake piece is decades out of fashion, and what's with the wool scarf on a summer's day? And is that a Chanel Baguette? I can't believe those bags are back again, though yours looks a bit well-loved.'

Jess smiled at Caro's customary tactlessness and said, 'I love your blazer, Caro. Have you got a meeting today?'

Caro had been a formidable real estate agent before becoming a mum, and now kept her hand in by buying and selling properties privately.

'A meeting?' she repeated. 'Don't be silly, dear, it's Ralph Lauren; my country look. Although I really ought to get my finger in the pie down here. It's positively rocketing. Let's drop in on the local real estate agency on the way home. How have you been?'

'Quite busy. I opened the store this morning and did the breakfast shift, so it's already been a full day for me.'

Caro stared at her blankly. 'I mean really, how are you, Jessica? How are you feeling?'

'Oh, good, fine, getting there.' Jessica didn't feel like delving into her true feelings in the middle of the coffee queue. 'So, where are the children?'

'On the jumping castle. Now, I just spoke to your father, he'll be at the house for lunch so I thought I'd buy some organic bits and pieces and do a cold meal. Is that okay with you?'

'Sure, Caro, you know the house is for all of us to enjoy. Angus coming down?'

'This evening: he has a client golf day or something. I saw your hippie friends. They have frightful concoctions on sale, haven't they? Do they ever sell anything?

'Oh, you'd be surprised, that look's quite popular down here, and with the tourists.'

'Yes, I'm sure it is.' Caro sniffed in the direction of a local woman who was standing in front of her decked out in what appeared to be an alpaca wool beret and fingerless gloves. 'But it's hardly designer label, is it?'

'Perhaps that's not important to some people,' Jessica suggested, smiling.

'Ha, don't make me laugh,' Caro replied. 'Now, I'm worried about you. Frantically worried.' She turned to place her order. 'Decaf latte please, skim milk, and not scalding like you normally do it.' She frowned at Doris, the coffee lady from the local CFA, to make sure her message was clear, but fortunately her recent Botox injection turned her frown into a blank look and Doris just smiled and nodded.

She turned back to her sister-in-law. 'What was I saying? Oh that's right, I'm worried about you. I told you that Graham was no good from the beginning.'

'No you didn't.' Jess shifted uncomfortably as a group of Pony Club mums wandered past. 'Can we do this later, Caro?' she suggested.

'Oh, didn't I tell you what I thought about Graham?' Caro continued, ignoring Jess's concern. 'Well I certainly thought it. How dare he leave you for another woman after you raised those children of his? I've been thinking about it, you should really send him an invoice for nanny duties. Four years at eighty thou a year is a fair figure. Angus could handle the case for you.'

'Here you go, love.' Doris passed over a steaming latte. 'Something for you, Jess?'

'No thanks, Doris.' Jess blushed, sure the woman had heard Caro's rant.

She pulled her sister-in-law over to a bench under the gums.

'Look, Caro, it's over. Good God, I've told you this for almost a year now, why won't you let it go? I really would prefer to put it all behind me and just move on. Is that okay? Can you help me with that?'

'Humph, if you insist, but it's just not right.'

'Life sucks I guess,' Jess said to end the topic. 'Now, how are the kids?'

'Oh, it's terrible darling, just awful,' Caro said, tipping artificial sweetener into her coffee and stirring vigorously. 'There is a hideous bully who is making little Hamish's life absolute anguish at the moment. Such a dreadful boy.'

Jess nodded absently, distracted by the sight of Hamish, whom she spied over Caro's head trying to bounce smaller children off the jumping castle. It was hard to imagine the strapping ten-year-old in the role of playground victim.

'Well, he's very, ummm, assertive,' Jess reassured Caro. 'I'm sure he can look after himself.'

Hamish was now holding a little boy's cap above his head as the smaller child fought to get it back.

Caro went on. 'I said to the principal, "If you can't guarantee my son's psychological wellbeing I will just have to —"'

'Hamish,' Jess called sharply, unable to watch him taunt the other child any longer. 'Come here and . . . ah . . . give Aunty Jess a kiss.'

Hamish dropped the cap and ran over as fast as his solid legs would carry him.

'Hello, Jess,' he said, wrapping his arms around her waist, his sweaty hair in her face. 'Mum, I'm hungry. Can I have some money?'

'You're insatiable,' Caro said with a grin and selected a twenty-dollar note from the thick wad in her purse. 'He'll eat me out of house and home,' she laughed indulgently as he pushed in front of harassed mothers in the *poffertjes* queue.

'Well, I'm off for a wander.' Jess stood and shook out her shawl. 'See you at the house this afternoon.'

'Ciao, darling.' Caro shaded her eyes with her hand as she looked up at Jess. 'We'll have a lovely lunch and sort you right out, you'll see.'

Jess trailed around the colourful stalls, enjoying the spicy aroma from the satay vendor, blended with the familiar sizzle of the scouts' barbecue and the gentle waft of incense from the Tibetan craft stall. She was relieved to be free of Caro: her sister-in-law meant well, but she could be hard work sometimes.

Smiling and waving at the familiar faces soaking up the late spring sunshine, as she walked past a flower stall Jess suddenly felt a jolt of sadness. Her boys had loved this market. It was a family ritual to get up early on market days, eat breakfast beneath the dangling gum branches, stock up on fresh-baked goods and locally grown fruit and vegies. The last time they'd been here the boys had pooled their pocket money and bought her a bunch of fragrant sweet peas from this stall, their little faces flushed with the excitement of the gift.

The joy of the memory was quickly replaced with the pain of missing them. Was she even a mother anymore? She had loved them, she still loved them; her heart ached to hold them.

She stopped walking and stood frozen, lost and directionless. Suddenly an arm slipped through hers and she was being gently led forwards.

'Come on, Jess,' Nick said. 'How about a cuppa? I've got a thermos in my ute.'

Mute, Jess allowed herself to be steered through the bright morning away from the pain and dislocation that sat jagged and painful inside her.

'Thanks, Nick,' she said, grateful for his presence and support. He nodded, but kept his head down and his hand thrust in the pocket of his khaki shorts as he propelled her gently towards the car park.

'It's okay, Red. You looked like you could use a friend,' he said, his blue eyes meeting hers briefly.

'It was the boys,' she said quietly.

'I figured.' They picked their way over the bumpy paddock that served as market car park.

'I'm sorry, Nick, I know we've been over this so many times . . .' she started.

He stopped abruptly between a sleek midnight blue Mercedes and a rusty Landcruiser. He pulled Jess in front of him. 'And you'll probably need to keep talking about it again and again until you can make peace with it in your head, and that's okay.' He was grasping her hands tightly and Jess saw the pain flicker across his own eyes.

'It's okay for me to talk about my stuff, but you never talk about yours,' she said hoarsely.

He immediately dropped her hands. 'Some things are better left alone.'

Jess shook her head and they made their way to his ute in silence.

Caro – arms laden with shopping, grizzly children in tow – observed Jessica and Nick stand face-to-face in the grassy car park and she tilted her head to one side. What was that about? she wondered. Could a relationship between them be beneficial to the family? Caro walked towards the highly polished Cayenne, unlocked it and dumped her stuff in the boot.

To Caro, family was everything and she had worked hard to get the one she wanted. When they'd met at university, she had been determined to marry Angus Wainwright. He was wealthy, connected, from a good, strong, well-known family and owned acreage. (As a country girl, she well knew the value of acreage.) And besides, she'd really, really liked him. She remembered something about weak knees. They'd met in first year: he was studying Law and she was doing an Arts degree. Although she'd attended a private school, the young Caroline Phillips wasn't from a wealthy family. Her family lived in a remote country town and Caro had boarded in the city since Grade Four. She never really got to know her older sisters, who both married young and moved away; one to a Queensland macadamia nut farm and the other to pursue a corporate career alongside her husband in Sydney. Once the older girls were married off, her parents felt that their parenting duties were over, and had little interest in their 'surprise baby', Caro, who had muscled her way in fifteen years after they thought they had completed their family. Her mother had been delighted with what she had thought was menopause, but distraught when she'd discovered she was actually pregnant at the age of forty-seven.

Caro had vague memories of coming home for holidays to parents who were constantly working: fencing, shearing, watering, feeding. She would get a tired smile from her mother, and an occasional conversation with her dad. She presumed they were proud of her; she had no evidence to the contrary. She never looked back on her childhood with regret or sadness. What was the point?

These days she was fiercely protective of the beautiful family life she had built so carefully. She would never risk feeling as lonely and isolated as she had as a child.

She looked over at Jessica, now perched on the tray of Nick's ute, her head on his shoulder and clearly in the middle of a deep and meaningful conversation.

Caro started the ignition with a roar and gripped the steering wheel with determination. She had plans for this family and she hadn't decided yet if Nick Johnson would fit into that picture.

~ 15 ~

Richard felt a familiar rumble of excitement in his guts as he turned onto Old Quarry Road.

What a place, what a view! He never got sick of it. The uninterrupted expanse of paddocks flanked by hills that reached to the edges of the sky. He was almost home. He wound down his window to breathe in the familiar aroma of the lemon-scented gums.

Richard had been raised on this property. His family had bought it when he was a boy and he'd moved down with his three brothers, parents and grandparents. He'd gone to boarding school with his brothers, but it was nearby so he came home every Friday night. The weekends were a glorious ruckus of catching up with all the local news, enormous meals and helping the old man with a bit of farm work. Local mates would drop in to kick the footy, family would drive up from town for a house party and the barbecue sizzled from dawn to dusk.

He and Eva had met at a produce export company in Melbourne. After they had married and were expecting their first baby, Richard's elderly parents had asked them to come back home and help run the property. They'd been thrilled with the opportunity and together had turned Springforth into a vibrant business and a basis for their busy family and social life.

A similar, if somewhat more gentle, lifestyle continued at the property nowadays and Richard always looked forward to coming back. He just wished Genevieve had been free to join him this weekend: she liked to roam the property, soaking up its ambience and admiring its many aspects. Mind you, he thought ruefully, Gen's absence would save him having to deal with Caro's frostiness towards his girlfriend.

He swung his Mercedes into the long driveway and crawled along the gravel to savour the landscape. A few sleepy heifers chewed slowly and gazed at him passing by. As he pulled up in the circular driveway in front of the house, he gave three quick toots to announce his arrival.

'Pop!' A welcoming committee of two small people came racing around the corner. Richard put out his arms and hugged his grandchildren as one. 'Hello, Hamish, what a big strong lad you've become, and little Charlotte, what a pretty frock.'

The two stood smiling expectantly, waiting for their grandfather's regular routine to begin.

'I suppose you guys want money?' he asked, as he always did. 'But I'm all out,' and he pulled out his pockets in an exaggerated pantomime to demonstrate their emptiness.

'Pop!' The children squealed in delight.

'I'm completely broke!' he replied with a smile. 'What about your money? You've got money. Don't you keep it in your pocket?'

Hamish beamed madly while Charlotte cackled in hysterics.

'You don't keep it in your pockets? Well, where do you keep it then?'

Charlotte could barely contain her mirth and bounced up and down as she giggled.

'Hang on, what's this?' Richard appeared confused as he peered at the side of Charlotte's head. He reached forward and tickled her on the ear, then drew his hand back and, with a flourish, presented her with a two-dollar coin.

'In your ear! What a crazy spot to keep your money. And what about you, Hamish, are you as silly as your sister?'

Again his hand moved into the child's ear and pulled out a gold coin.

'You're both as mad as hatters. You should keep your money in a bank, not in your ears!'

The children, clutching their windfall, ran back inside the house, and Richard followed.

'Dad!' Jessica came from the kitchen, wiping her hands on her floral pinny.

'Hello, my girl,' Richard said and embraced his only daughter.

'Hello, Richard,' Caro was close behind and offered her powdered cheek for Richard's peck. He ignored it and gave her a big squeeze as well.

'Something smells good!' Richard said and led the way into the kitchen.

'Oh, that's the pumpkin roasting for the spinach, fetta, pine nut and pumpkin salad for lunch. I know it's your favourite,' Caro said as she took the sizzling golden vegetable from the oven to cool.

'Mmm,' Richard murmured and looked nervously at Jessica.

'And roast beef,' Jess quickly reassured him as she brandished the carving knife over the cooled piece of eye fillet.

'Mmm!' Richard repeated, this time with infinitely more enthusiasm.

'No Genevieve?' Caro asked from the kitchen bench as she vigorously stirred a jug of margaritas.

'No, she has family stuff on,' Richard replied.

'Shame, we just don't get to see her enough,' she said.

Jessica shook her head; her sister-in-law would make a terrible actress.

They settled out on the deck that overlooked the property. Richard accepted his salt-encrusted drink from Caro with thanks. 'How's business, Caro? Still wheeling and dealing?'

Caro looked smug. 'Yes, faaabulous, Richard.' She placed the jug onto the table. 'Carnegie is a little gold mine. I knew it would be. I'd predicted that place would go off for years. I've just done a twenty-four per cent increase in profit in six months.

Richard grinned. She was a tiger, and he admired that. She'd always get what she wanted. He sat back on the Adirondack chair and let out a huge sigh that dispersed all the stresses of his week in the city. A huge smile came over his face as he surveyed his land.

'It looks fantastic, Jess. Nick's doing a great job.'

'Yes, he is. He's coming for lunch to see you, by the way.'

'Excellent, I'd love to thank him. Best thing we did, getting rid of that other guy and putting Nick on last year.'

'He certainly knows what he's doing. I think he wants to talk to you about the rear fence on the top paddock.'

'Oh, yes, I know what he'll want. That's fine: it needs electrifying if we're going to have Billy the bull back next season. He's a bugger of a thing. Nick seems so much better nowadays. He was in such as state after the baby died, wasn't he? Does he ever talk about it?'

'Yeah, he was a mess,' Jess nodded. 'He still won't talk to me about it. I feel rotten that I wasn't there for him, but he just disappeared. I didn't even know about the break-up till months later. I don't even know that many details because we'd drifted apart at that stage. I mean, I wasn't even asked to the wedding so I just figured he had a whole new group of friends.'

'Hmm, tragic business,' Caro said.

Richard sat and enjoyed the sun on his face and the view of the bay in the distance, nestled between the two hills in from his bottom paddock. Having Jessica live here to keep the homestead humming was a great arrangement, he thought happily. The hundred hectares had been in his family for sixty years now and he was proud that it paid its own way with Wagyu beef cattle.

He watched Hamish and Charlotte chasing each other around the front lawn and smiled with satisfaction. He had visions of his grandchildren bringing their grandchildren here one day. It would be his legacy to his descendants. Generations of Wainwrights would touch this soil, make a living from it, walk on it and love it as much as he did.

'So, Richard,' Caro interrupted his thoughts.

'Yes, Caro,' he replied, somewhat distracted.

'What are your plans for the property?'

'Well, there's that top electric fence we were just talking about –'

'No, no – the future of the property. It's a lot of land, you know.'

'You're right, and it's tricky to manage with just that one shed. I'm thinking of building a large barn, just up the back behind the rain tanks. And getting a new tractor with a thresher so Nick doesn't have to rent one each season. I'm also considering a highly confidential agricultural proposal at the moment.'

Caro flicked her fingers impatiently. 'No, no, the long-term plans, I mean. You are aware rural land in this region is worth thirty-five thousand per hectare? You could get nine mil or even more, considering the views.'

Jessica gasped and quickly looked at her father to see his reaction.

During his career, Richard had captained his industry and become director of boards for many reasons, including his high intellect, superior negotiating skills, and balls of steel. But Richard Wainwright's peers would acknowledge his greatest strength around the boardroom table was his poker face.

He turned to his daughter-in-law, the serene smile still playing on his face.

'I don't think so,' he said simply. He took a sip of his drink and looked back at the view.

'But –' Caro tried.

'I said, I don't think so!' Richard repeated pleasantly with his eyes closed and the same peaceful countenance. But Jessica, knowing her dear old dad as well as she did, heard the underlying icy tone and silently warned Caro to shut the hell up.

'Well, I just think we have the right to know the property's future, that's all,' Caro said in a small voice, taking a large gulp of her drink.

~ 16 ~

Rainbow and Songbird's kids had spent a busy morning picking
through the mini-skip from next door's building site and creating
an array of recycled Christmas ornaments. Tin-can baubles, foil
tinsel and plasterboard angels hung from the fallen gum tree branch
that was now their Christmas tree.

'Kiani, that's absolutely fantastic. Songbird,' Rainbow called,
'come and see the Christmas wreath Kiani's made.'

Songbird, spade in hand, rounded the corner of the weatherboard house to where Rainbow and Kiani were admiring the
artwork.

Kiani had found an old toilet seat and, after a thorough wipe
down with vinegar and bi-carb, had wound wire around and
around the u-shape. She'd then attached metal offcuts to the
shape and made stars by binding together twigs and painting
them silver. Fresh sprigs of poinsettia gave the wreath colour.

'Girl, you've outdone yourself. That's freaking fantastic.'
Songbird ruffled the elfin haircut of her eldest and went back to
the compost heap.

'Remy and Tyson helped, too,' Kiani said, eager for credit to
go where it was due, 'but Darren, Taylor and Sunshine were just
too annoying so I told them to go hunt for koalas.'

'Good idea.' Songbird laughed at her initiative, then turned
back to the job at hand.

Rainbow followed her and picked up another spade to help
turn the compost. The women worked away at the pile of muck
in companionable silence, flicking and turning it in the early
morning sunshine.

Rainbow suddenly downed tools as she remembered something. 'I called Jessica this morning. Did you know she was going to bail tonight?'

Songbird looked up. 'What? Why?'

'She didn't think that we would want her since she doesn't have any kids to bring this year. She said she thought it was a BYO-kids-or-don't-come deal.'

'Stupid cow. Did you set her straight?'

'Yeah! Of course.'

Jess had shared Christmas Eve eve with Rainbow and Songbird for the past four years. Her boys had revelled in the junkyard atmosphere of the hippies' relaxed backyard, and their festive get-together had quickly become a much-enjoyed tradition.

'I'm worried about her, Songbird. She's still not quite right. We need to look after her.'

'Course we do, but she'll be right, mate. She's a tough chick, it'll take more than this to get her.'

'I still can't believe that Graham could walk away like that,' Rainbow said as she flicked fresh manure onto the heap.

'Don't worry, as I've always said: karma will get the fucker.' Songbird was well known in the community for her words of wisdom and philosophy.

Two small boys ran through the yard, trailing shredded silver insulation lining. 'Taylor and Tyson, what are you doing?' Songbird asked, with a scowl.

'We're being falling stars, Mum!' Taylor shouted back as they zigzagged through the compost and ricocheted off the manure pile.

'Meteors, you mean!' Rainbow called to the disappearing silver streaks.

'Yeah, meteors, Mum!' Tyson yelled back.

'We're doing the astronomy module at the moment,' Rainbow told Songbird.

'Yeah. I start the human body next week, don't I?'

'Yep, that should be so exciting.' As keen advocates of home schooling, the couple found that their children – especially the boys – learned faster if they got to experience their learning.

'Tyson!' Rainbow yelled and stopped turning compost as the child darted by again. Tyson stopped and turned back. His enormous green eyes peeped out from under his dirty blond dreadlocks. 'Yeah, Mum?'

'Name the planets.'

Tyson grinned and dropped his outstretched flying arms into a karate starting stance for his favourite solar system kata.

'Mercury!' he shouted and his arms crossed in front of his little body, arms finishing in fists. 'Venus!' His right knee came up and landed in front, the left arm crossing over then forward into a palm heel. 'Earth!' The palm heel dropped down and the left leg came forward in a quick kick. 'Mars!' Each planet announcement came attached to a sharply executed karate move. When he got to Neptune he finished with a neat little bow, hands and feet together.

'What about Pluto?' Songbird asked with a smile.

'Pluto's not a planet!' he called out and zoomed off with his stepbrother.

The two mothers smiled at each other and continued their work.

'They're here!' Sunshine yelled out. She'd been standing at the front fence awaiting Jessica's arrival. Four-year-olds Darren and Sunshine squealed in excitement. 'Let's get this party started,' they sang as they scrambled from the sandpit.

Jessica had stopped to pick up another friend, Petal, the local beautician, and her three children, Jasmine, Rose and Willow. She was glad to do it, as she still couldn't get used to arriving at a kids' party solo.

'Hi, girls,' Petal said with a broad grin as she hugged her friends.

Jessica was next in line and got an especially big hug from Songbird, who slipped a bit of healing reiki in her touch to give Jess strength.

'Sorry about the mix-up, girls,' Jessica explained as they moved into the kitchen to deposit their offerings of wine and snacks. 'I didn't know if it'd still be on . . . you know, given the circumstances.'

'You're a dumb bitch, you know,' growled Songbird as she rifled through the cupboard for a bowl to dump the carrot chips into. 'Who do you think we are?'

'Songbird means –' Rainbow started.

'I said what I meant,' Songbird interrupted.

Jess laughed; she could well interpret Songbird's gruff manner by now.

They loaded up with organic hummus, julienned vegies and preservative-free white wine and made their way out to the backyard.

The children were shrieking with delight as they all joined in on an impromptu game of Geology Jump; loosely based on leapfrog, it was an invention of Songbird's during the 'Mother Earth' teaching module.

'So, how goes it?' Songbird asked Jessica. 'Any progress with Graham?'

'No, he still won't return my calls,' Jess said tightly.

'I remember those days.' Rainbow said. 'Bloody Jim was really difficult in the beginning. Men are awful when it comes to custody; it's not about the kids at all, in their mind. Suddenly, it's as if the children are property that you're trying to steal or something. Remember how he fought me in court until he finally got two days a week, and then he'd spend those two days at the office and have a nanny care for them? It made me so angry.'

'That's just crap,' Petal sympathised.

'Not half as bad as what Songbird went through. Tell 'em, Songbird.'

'Straight after the separation, Trev decided he just *had* to have the kids,' Songbird said, and she took a drag from her rollie. 'His life depended on it, apparently. You should have heard the sob stories at the mediation and through the lawyers. It was pathetic.

Cost a freaking bomb. And the arguments in front of the kids! It was awful. Then when he finally got them fifty per cent of the time, he spent the whole the time on the phone to me whinging about them.'

'God, you must have missed them so much,' Jess said, shaking her head in sympathy.

'I did. Then he'd guts-ache if he wanted to go out and I couldn't drop everything and run over to pick them up. In the end he just stopped coming to collect them and now I have to phone *him* and remind him that he's a father who has responsibilities, for Chrissakes.'

'Moron,' Petal said. 'It would have saved a lot of money and time, and pain I'm sure, if he'd just let you have them from the start.'

'Yeah, exactly,' Rainbow said, 'but they don't care about the kids; it's just about winning; and trying to weasel out of paying maintenance, of course.'

'I just want to see my boys. He can keep his money and his new lover; it was pretty much over between us anyway,' Jess said. 'But I never thought he could do something like this to me.'

'Hang in there, doll, it'll happen,' Songbird said. 'It just takes time.'

'And a good lawyer,' Petal added.

'I'd prefer to avoid any more of that for the boys' sake,' Jess said and sighed, her face pale and wan. 'And I'm not their biological parent, so my rights are really blurry.'

'You love them,' Rainbow said, gently patting Jess's arm, 'that must count for something.'

'Mums, we're hungry!' Kiani yelled, breaking the sadness of the moment.

'Okay, you can have your first course,' Rainbow called back. The children squealed and raced each other to the orchard, where they were each allowed to pick two pieces of fruit before lunch was served.

★

Lunch was a joyous grab-fest with Eugene enthusiastically joining the fray, fighting the kids for the salad. The adults and children sat around the outdoor table, which was an old door supported by two reclaimed builders' trestles. Rainbow leaned behind her chair and grabbed handfuls of cherry tomatoes and sprigs of basil, dumping them in an old hubcap they had cleaned and repurposed as the salad bowl. Petal had brought her famous vegetarian lasagne and Jess had baked her trademark gingerbread people dressed in bikinis and board shorts.

'Cute!' Kiani squeaked. 'Mine's got a bellybutton ring.'

'Thanks for the biscuits, Jess,' Taylor said.

'You're welcome,' Jess said and smiled at his serious little face.

'Where are Liam and Callum? I miss them.'

'Yes, I do too. They're with their dad today.'

'Oh, okay, yeah. I have to go to my dad's tomorrow. Don't worry, they'll be back soon,' he reassured her, and ran off. Jess hoped that his famous skill for premonition was accurate today.

After they had eaten, it was present time. As Rainbow reached into a red linen sack to bring out a handful of gift-wrapped delights, Jessica watched the children's upturned faces. She remembered past Christmases so well. She would be so churned up with excitement by the time she went to bed each Christmas Eve that she'd be unable to sleep. The thought and effort that had gone into the perfect Christmas presents, the decoration, the evidence of Santa's visit took Jess weeks of planning. Every year had been more exciting than the one before. The idyllic Christmases of her youth came rushing back each time she filled a stocking or decorated another corner of the house. The boys would get increasingly excited as each day passed, and they loved checking their advent calendars each dawn for that day's surprise – Jessica had tailor-made the calendars so each day revealed a different small gift or treat.

Then last Christmas had happened. She'd never truly enjoy Christmas ever again, Jess thought bitterly as she watched her friends' kids rip into their gifts.

'Water pistols!' the children yelled as the wrapping disintegrated.

Jessica stared at Rainbow and Songbird in amazement. 'Guns?'

Songbird explained, 'They're made from recycled timber and the reservoirs are old drinking yoghurt pots.' She looked over at the children filling up their guns from the water trough with glee. 'They're *supposed* to be used for shooting the rabbits away from the vegie garden and the Indian mynahs away from the native birds. But I'm sure the occasional war game could be overlooked.'

'Kill each other with love!' Rainbow warned as the children ran off, shrieking as they squirted each other.

~17~

It was the night before Christmas. The house was finally quiet after the festive family dinner. Jess threw the tablecloth into the laundry, and while she was there she checked the mousetrap and found one very still, furry creature. A quick, well-practised flick out the door into the compost heap disposed of the little corpse. The Buddhist sympathiser in her cringed while the homemaker in her breathed a sigh of relief that the cereal stored in the bottom of the pantry would see another day.

She glanced in at Charlotte and Hamish, snuggled up in their beds. They were finally asleep, exhausted after the big day. No doubt they were dreaming of the excitement that Christmas morning would bring. Carrots and milk sat by the fireplace awaiting Santa and his reindeer.

It had been a warm afternoon, but the forecast was for an unseasonably cool evening, which had now transpired. Caro and Genevieve were washing up, and the men had adjourned to the verandah. Heading into her room, Jess picked up her tie-dyed kerchief from the foot of the bed, wrapped it around her head and grabbed her Lee Mathews cardigan. She found her dad's favourite woolly earflap cap to take out to him. Stupid Victoria. Completely unreliable weather, she grumbled to herself. At least Christmas Day was expected to be sunny, for a change.

The farmhouse was large and rambling. It had endured many renovations over its life but had finally settled into its current form: two wings off the central entry and living areas. The east wing housed a formal study and three double bedrooms – the master, which Eva and Richard had shared and which was still

Richard's, done in Ralph Lauren red and navy checks, and two guestrooms. This was known as the grown-up wing. Jessica had promoted herself from the bedroom she'd grown up in to the prettiest of the guest suites. It was a delight in French Provincial chic with a timber four-poster bed, rustic furniture, and patchwork and linen in a soothing array of creamy tones.

Angus and Caro used the other suite – a more sophisticated room in chocolate velvet and fawn metallics, with minimalist lines and a natural stone ensuite bathroom. Jessica had kept Caro's subdued but luxurious tastes in mind when she'd decorated it a few years before.

The west wing was for the children: three bedrooms – including Callum and Liam's old rooms – and a big rambling playroom came off the farm-style, pine kitchen. Copper-based saucepans hung from an overhead rack, clay pots housed timber implements, and jars of dried herbs rested on the wide windowsills.

Passing back through the central living room en route to the deck beyond, Jess replaced a stray gift that had fallen from one of the bulging stockings, and felt a pang of sadness as she thought of the cheery red felt personalised stockings she had made for her boys, which now sat empty in her bedside drawer.

She scooped up a piece of gift wrap that lurked under the coffee table from the one present each of the children had been allowed to open earlier. She smiled as she remembered Hamish's excitement when he'd ripped the paper away from Richard's extravagant gift: a battery-powered ride-on motorbike.

Her nephew had been speechless with delight and had sat on it for the rest of the night, roaring down an imaginary racetrack. Jess knew that there were two similar toys in the garage, wrapped and waiting for Richard's other two grandsons, in case a miracle happened and Graham decided to relent and let the boys come to visit their other family.

Jessica had worked hard at the General Store until she knocked off just after lunch – she needed to keep busy for as long as she could. She'd come home and made a half-hearted effort to get things organised, but she knew that Caro would swoop in and take over anyway, so she'd left the linen unfolded, the food in the fridge unprepared and the table unset, then sat on the deck staring at the view. It seemed there was nothing she could do to calm her jangled nerves and stop thinking obsessively of how this time last year was the last truly happy day she could remember.

She and the boys had spent that day dropping homemade shortbread and gingerbread gifts into their neighbours, friends and local shopkeepers. By late afternoon, Liam had been over-tired and over-excited as the Christmas tension mounted. He was sick of going from place to place delivering Christmas treats, and wanted to know why Santa wasn't there now, and why they had to wait 'forever' until they could have their presents.

Jess winced to herself as she remembered how she had snapped at him. She was tired and strung out too, and Graham had been acting strangely for weeks. He hardly spoke to her and only laughed sarcastically and walked away if she tried to start up a conversation about their relationship.

If she'd known then that it would be her last day of carefree time with her boys, she might have held them longer, or just sat quietly and looked at their beautiful faces. And now, somehow, a whole year had passed. When Jess walked into the kitchen she caught the last snippets of conversation between Genevieve and Caro.

'So he threw an almighty tantrum last night at bedtime,' Caro was saying. 'It was just awful. He was purple, I could barely hear what in the hell his problem was.'

'Oh, dear,' Genevieve said as she wiped another bowl and stacked it on the pile on the bench. 'What was wrong?'

'Well, I made the mistake of telling them we were heading down here first thing this morning and Hamish just started wailing and howling. I finally worked out what was wrong: he hadn't told Santa yet what he wanted for Christmas.'

'Oh no!' Genevieve said. 'What did you do?'

Caro took her soapy hands out of the sink and turned to include Jess in her story. 'I suggested email, phone messages, everything, but no, it had to be the real deal. And he was so upset. Well, I was feeling a bit guilty about wriggling out of the whole lining-up-for-Santa catastrophe anyway, so by then I felt terrible.'

'But you've just got to do the Santa thing, Caro,' Jess said.

'Yes, all right, thank you!' Caro snapped. 'So, rather than settling in with an eggnog and my *White Christmas* DVD, I gritted my teeth, threw them into the car – still in their pyjamas – and headed off to Malvern Central.'

'You didn't?' Jess said, amazed at such an unlikely burst of spontaneity from Caro.

'I bloody did!' Caro said.

'You're a good mum,' Genevieve said.

'Yes, but wait for it,' Caro went on. 'Can you imagine the queue for Santa at seven p.m. on the twenty-third of December? We waited an hour! It was hideous. Charlotte was tired and whingey, and the brats in front of us kept pulling faces at Hamish. I had to do a well-placed stiletto warning on one particularly pushy queue jumper. Then finally it was our turn.'

'So what did he want for Christmas after all that?' Genevieve asked.

'Well, after staring mutely at what I must say was a very bedraggled-looking Santa, do you know what Hamish said?'

'What?' the women asked in unison.

'He said he wanted "a surprise"!'

'NO!' Genevieve and Jessica burst out laughing.

'Kids, it's lucky they're so cute or you'd kill 'em!' Jess said, wiping tears from her eyes.

Leaving Caro and Genevieve to finish the dishes, Jess went outside to join the men.

Nick's voice greeted her as she approached. '. . . So then he said, "If anybody here believes in telekinesis, raise my right hand."'

Nick sat back, grinning at his own punchline, while Richard's guffaw bounced down the darkened hill. Angus smiled, more at seeing his father so relaxed than at the old joke. It was good of Nick to drop by and visit before heading over to his parents' house for his own Christmas celebrations. Angus glanced up at his sister's entrance and hoped it was more than kindness on Nick's part that had brought him here on that evening.

'Hello, darling girl,' Richard said. 'Oh, you're a wonder, you are. Just what I needed,' and he gratefully took his favourite woolly cap and shoved it onto his head, taking on the look of a brave arctic explorer. 'It doesn't ever warm up down here until late January, does it?'

Jessica smiled and took a seat next to her dad.

'So, how are those two getting on in there?' he asked, indicating the kitchen.

'Really well, actually. Caro's sharing some raising-children war stories,' Jess said.

'Excellent,' Richard replied. 'Gen means a lot to me, guys. I'm rapt that you've welcomed her into the family so warmly.'

'Dad, she's fantastic. You two are a perfect match,' Angus said. 'It's great to see you so happy.'

Richard looked at his son and beamed. 'Yeah, she's a keeper. I've got to keep an eye on her, though – she thinks she's got me wrapped around her little finger,' he chuckled good-naturedly, 'and she might be right.'

At that moment, Genevieve and Caro appeared with more drinks.

'Nightcap?' Caro asked, a bottle of Bailey's in hand.

Enthusiastic responses quickly filled the air as Caro passed around balloons of ice and liqueur.

The group settled contentedly with their drinks and enjoyed the sounds of the evening. The roar of the surf leapt up to meet the sound of the cicadas. A tawny frogmouth hooted in the distance; a cow answered the call of its calf.

'I know it's crazy, but I keep expecting to hear jingle bells from the horizon,' Jess said. 'It's a magic night, Christmas Eve, isn't it?'

'You do know Santa's not real, don't you?' Caro asked.

'Caro, do you have to say it out loud?' Nick reprimanded her. 'Can't you just let Jess enjoy the fantasy?'

Jess smiled. 'It's okay, Nick, I do know that it's only the Tooth Fairy who's real,' she reassured him.

'Speaking of fairies, Jess, I just love your Christmas angel sculpture in the front room,' Genevieve said. 'You could do a lot with your art, you know.'

'Hmmm,' Jess said slowly. 'Well, actually I am thinking about doing more with it next year. I have a meeting with Mimsy Baxter coming up and I think she wants me to work at Still Life.'

Caro leapt from her seat in excitement. 'How wonderful! What an opportunity: you could move to the city and really give your career a chance to explode.'

'Hang on there, Caro, slow down,' Nick said. 'I doubt Red is thinking of moving to town.'

'Actually, Nick,' Jess said, 'I've already said yes to the job, so if Mimsy wants me I'll be moving to the city early next year.'

Richard, Angus and Nick all gasped. Jess usually discussed such big decisions with them all.

Caro, however, could barely contain her enthusiasm. 'Tremendous, brilliant, well done! You'll get the job and have a marvellous career in the city for decades to come. I'm so thrilled for you. And until you find your feet you're more than welcome to stay at our place. I'll help you with my network; I'll send you tons of business. They'll love you.'

Richard glanced at Caro's animated face. What was she up to?, he wondered.

'Well, it's a big change,' Angus said, moving to give his sister a hug, 'and it will feel very strange to come down to Springforth and not have you here, but I reckon it could be a wonderful new start for you, sis.' He raised his glass. 'I'm proud of you.'

'Cheers,' they all echoed, lifting their glasses into the air. All except Nick, who sat staring at Jess, his eyes boring into her.

'Thanks guys,' she smiled, excitement flooding her as she looked at the happy faces of her family. She glanced at Nick and decided to ignore his surliness. 'I can't wait,' she said firmly, and drained the last of the sweet liquid from her glass.

★

'What do you think is going on with Caro?' Richard asked Genevieve as they were preparing for bed later that night. 'She seems overly enthusiastic about Jessica moving to town. It's not like her to be so keen for change; she normally digs her heels in if we suggest any change to family life.'

Genevieve smiled calmly and placed her hairbrush back into her toilet bag. 'Richard, don't you see, it's for the best. Jessica needs to break free of your property, your business, your life. It was you looking after her, then Graham doing it, and now it's back to you again. She needs to be the master of her own world – she's almost forty – and I just think Caro recognises that.'

'I guess you're right,' Richard conceded. 'Maybe I am just being over-protective.'

'I'd be disappointed if you weren't,' she told him affectionately, and she reached up to give him a kiss on the cheek.

~18~

The cows grazing contentedly in the paddocks the next day were oblivious to the Christmas mayhem at the farmhouse. Jess stood on the deck, looking out over the sweeping lawn to the swing-set, where Hamish and Charlotte begged their dad to push them 'higher, higher'.

Jess had expected to feel sad today – it was inevitable given that the day marked the first anniversary of losing her family – but there was another feeling too: hard to name, it was uncomfortable and stifling; it seemed to fill her chest and make it hard to breathe.

Her brother's deep-throated laugh filled the air as he wrestled with his children on the lawn and Jess's face twisted painfully, her thoughts carrying her back to the Christmas morning of a year ago.

Jess had been so excited knowing how thrilled the boys would be when they saw their gifts under the tree in the morning. Callum and Liam had whooped into the bedroom at five a.m., bubbling with the news of the wicked new mountain bikes that Santa had left for them.

Giggling in delight, she cuddled their tousled heads to her; she had searched for weeks to get the exact bikes they had asked for and this moment of pure pleasure made all the effort worthwhile.

While the boys tried to rouse Graham from his grumpy slumber, Jess had gone to make some coffee. Graham was useless before he'd had three or four caffeine shots in the morning.

But he'd surprised her, shuffling into the kitchen a few minutes later, yawning and scratching his stubble.

'Hey, sleepy head, Merry Christmas,' Jess had said, smiling, but something in his body language made her stop short of delivering the hug she was about to give him.

He'd sighed. 'Look, we have to talk.'

Surely he was joking, she'd thought. She'd tried to get him to talk for months; to sort out their relationship – and he'd finally decided to talk *today*, Christmas Day?

She had tried to listen but his words buzzed around her head like blowflies as she'd stood gripping the edge of the sink.

'Not suited . . . tried to tell you before . . . time to move on . . .'

Staring at the kitchen cloth, its pitted surface grey and ugly from too much domestic duty, she made a mental note to pick up a new one next time she was in town.

But then Graham had shaken her from her reverie with one stinging sentence: 'I've met someone else.'

Everything ended there.

When the boys had run in a moment later, keen to tackle the pile of presents in the lounge room, Callum had looked up and asked, 'Why are you crying, Mumma?' It was only then she'd noticed her Santa T-shirt was damp at the neckline.

She gasped, bringing herself back to the here and now. She squinted into the early morning sun, her tears blurring the blue sky. This new pain was pushing down on her harder and she couldn't seem to take a breath; she felt paralysed, frozen in place by the intensity of the emotion.

The morning had been the usual mayhem of Christmas madness, with gifts, over-excited children, croissants and champagne. She was sad, and had the familiar sense of loss and grief hanging over her; but why was she feeling so tense and sick?

She closed her eyes and tried to calm her breathing. She fought to identify the new sensation. As her heart beat less frantically and her pulse slowed, she used a technique that Rainbow had taught her: using colours as a guide to emotions.

She asked her inner self to flood her consciousness with the colour she was feeling and instantly green shot into her mind like laser light. A lurid, acid green.

Her eyes flipped open in fright and there in front of her again was the sight of Angus playing contentedly with his children. Oh my God, she thought, I'm jealous. It was an uncomfortable realisation.

She drew her cashmere cardigan around herself tightly and turned back to the house. She'd never been a jealous person before.

Shaking, Jessica sat at the kitchen table and rested her head in her hands. 'Bloody spoilt rotten little children,' Caro spat, as she strode into the kitchen and flung open the fridge. 'They don't know how lucky they are. Mobile phones at that age! Honestly it's a disgrace. And I wouldn't have done it, you know, if it weren't for the fact that the Ferguson children were getting phones for Christmas. There's no way I could bear the moaning when my two got to school and found out that the Fergusons got mobile phones and they didn't. Never mind. Coffee?'

'Um, herbal tea, if you don't mind,' Jess said quietly.

'What's wrong?' Caro demanded. 'You're not your usual nauseously joyful yuletide self.'

'I'm just shaky after, you know, last year.'

'Yes, yes, of course. I can't believe the bastard did it on Christmas Day. Here, let's have some more festive bubbles. I know it's only eight a.m. but if we add orange juice and call in the public-holiday-rule, we might just get away with it.'

Caro poured the drinks and sat down next to her sister-in-law, her voice lowered to a whisper. 'I've got something that might cheer you up. I've done the funniest thing. You know how I've got Genevieve for Kris Kringle? Well I've given her the 'free gift with purchase' – a little gold make-up bag with goodies – I got from Estée Lauder when I bought my cleanser last week! How funny's that?'

Jess shook her head, brow wrinkled. 'I don't get it.'

'It's the free gift with purchase! Sixty bucks' worth, for nix! And I'm giving it to her like it's some big luxurious present.'

Caro chuckled at her own bitchy cleverness. 'She'll think I'm being really nice, but I'm not!'

'Oh . . . right.' The sip of champagne suddenly stuck in Jess's throat. She stood and took it to the sink. 'I don't feel like alcohol right now. I think I'll have that chamomile tea instead.' She poured the boiling water into her cup and headed off to her room, leaving Caro to plot and scheme.

As the day went on, Jessica started to feel more like herself, any tinge of green now a safe distance away. She was able to laugh along with the others during the Christmas cracker jokes, she took photos of funny faces and enjoyed the compliments on her festive decoration. It took an effort to keep it up, but she figured she was doing pretty well.

As the late-afternoon Noel naps were starting up and the dishwasher was humming with its enormous load after lunch, Jess walked in on Genevieve in the bathroom. 'Oh, sorry,' she apologised and went to back out.

'Don't be silly, I'm just touching up my make-up,' Genevieve replied. 'Come in.'

Jess began to straighten the towels and noticed Genevieve was using an identical gold make-up purse to the one Caro had just given her. It seemed Caro's nasty scheme wouldn't go unnoticed.

'Nice make-up bag,' Jess commented.

'Yes, I love it, it was really great to get a second one from Caro. You always need a back-up, I say.'

Jess waited, but Genevieve didn't add a bitchy comment or any touch of sarcasm, although she would be entitled to; especially as she had given each of the family a personal and thoughtful gift instead of sticking with the Kris Kringle formula. When Genevieve had unwrapped her gift from Richard – a pair of emerald earrings – Caro had actually stormed out of the room.

'Right-o, I'll leave you in privacy,' Genevieve said as she snapped the lid back on her lipstick.

'Genevieve,' Jess said.

'Yes, darling?' Genevieve replied, one hand on the doorknob.

'Thank you so much for being so great for my dad.'

'Oh, believe me, the pleasure is mine,' Genevieve replied with a cheeky grin.

'I'm sorry if you're not feeling *completely* welcomed into this family.'

'I work in advertising, Jessica, it takes more than a few nasty asides to get to me. And Jess, by the way, you're doing such a wonderful job. It must be hell for you. I just want you to know how proud your dad is of you and how very worried he is.'

'Really? Gosh, I didn't think he'd be worried. I haven't wanted to let on how I'm feeling.'

'He knows. He's very connected to you.'

Jessica hesitated; killing moments by folding and refolding the facecloth. 'Can I ask you a personal question?' Jessica's words finally rushed out.

'Of course,' Genevieve said and, closing the lid of the loo, sat down and planted an obliging expression on her face.

'Did you ever regret not having children? Following your career instead?'

Genevieve smiled, threw her head back and took in a big breath, which she blew out in a gust. 'Don't you find it interesting how fascinated others are in a childless woman's reasons?'

'I know what you mean!' Jessica exclaimed. 'I've felt pressure to procreate ever since my first serious boyfriend. I've heard all the comments, from "Wouldn't your kids be beautiful?" to "Hadn't you better have children before your ovaries dry up?".'

Genevieve laughed. 'Let me guess, that last one was from Caro?'

'Yes, you must be psychic!'

'Now that would be a handy skill to have,' Genevieve said. 'But seriously, I have regretted not having children often, but then I look at the life I have, at the career I've made for myself in a male-dominated world and I'm proud of my achievements.

I think we all want what we haven't got. But I guess my answer
to you would be yes, but with concessions.'

'But it's not like a career decision or a suburb choice, Gen,'
Jessica said and perched on the edge of the bath. 'Having babies
is so much more. It's a biological urge; it's something you just
have to do. I get so cross with women who can just spit out
bambini as if they're merely baking a cake and then complain
about how grizzly their kids are and how they never have time
to themselves. I think, don't you know how lucky you are?' Jess
crossed her eyes and made a face at herself in the mirror, making
Genevieve laugh.

'Then I feel like I've become a bitter old spinster, and I hate
myself for it,' she grabbed the brush off the bathroom vanity unit
and attacked her curls savagely. 'And it's almost worse having
had the boys already, you know? Because I've been a mother.
I know the highs and the lows, I know about sleepless nights
and teething, and I know the joy of Christmas morning and the
pride at school concerts when your kid is the best. I miss my
boys so much, but I also miss being a mum. I really feel I've
missed the boat.' Her hair crackled with electricity as she turned
to face the older woman. 'I'm so scared, Gen.'

Genevieve couldn't help laughing gently as she threw her
arms around Jess. 'Oh, you goose. Look at you. You're barely
thirty-seven: you have your whole life ahead of you. Who
knows what's around the corner? You're about to launch into a
tremendous career change. You will have lots and lots of chances
in life. But,' – Genevieve's face softened – 'I do understand that
today is tricky. And it's okay to feel crap.'

'Knock knock,' Richard yelled. He hammered on the door.
'You girls are taking going to the toot in pairs to a whole
new level!'

The women laughed, and Jess stepped away from Genevieve
to splash her face with water at the sink. 'Coming, Dad,' she
called. 'Thanks, Gen.'

'Merry Christmas, darling. I'm here whenever you need me.'
Genevieve checked her lips in the mirror once more, spritzed

on some Chanel No. 5 and then lightly patted Jess's shoulder as she left the room.

Jess stood enjoying the swirl of warmth she felt inside; it felt good, really good, and it reminded her of something: this was how it felt to be mothered. She'd forgotten how wonderful it was. She'd never seen Gen as the maternal type, but suddenly she saw a whole new possibility for their relationship. The thought made her smile.

~19~

Jessica was struggling to breathe. As she waited in the assistant's office at Still Life, she sat on her hands and tried to focus on just moving air in and out of her lungs.

At least she was in a beautiful environment, and that always helped her relax. She tucked her legs under the chair to stop her knees from shaking and surveyed the office. The look was tonally neutral, but they were very beautiful, precise and carefully chosen neutrals. There were beiges that evoked the colour of sand, greys that spoke of gum tree trunks, and blacks with the sheen and lustre of panther fur.

The sumptuous tones soothed Jessica's nerves and she felt her breath returning to normal. How could she not love working in this environment? She wanted this job more than ever now.

She'd dressed with painstaking care this morning, aware that today her body would be her canvas. She paired her favourite Comme des Garçons tulle skirt with an aqua cotton knit that had striped flowers blossoming down the left arm. It fastened with enormous cloth covered buttons, each a different fabric to the next. Metallic pink ballet flats completed her look.

Finally, after an interminable forty-five-minute wait, she was ushered into Mimsy's office by an efficient assistant who looked a little like a prison guard for the fashion police; dark hair slicked back, her outfit consisted of a gunmetal short-sleeved turtleneck, matching gunmetal cotton trousers, silver cage high heels, and large silver bangles on each wrist, which alluded to handcuffs. The enormous collection of Thomas Sabo trinkets around her neck reminded Jessica of a warden's keys.

The door clicked closed behind her and Jessica stood soaking up Mimsy Baxter's inner domain, a largely monochromatic world punctuated with splashes of spot colour.

Although she was pushing sixty Mimsy had the white face, sleek black hair and scarlet lips of a geisha. She held up one finger to indicate she'd soon be finished with her phone call.

Jessica scanned the room, happy for the chance to soak up her surroundings. A white leather wing-back armchair nestled up to a charcoal couch. A slate flokati rug sat beneath a black enamel coffee table. The albums on the table were slate, the coffee set, steaming and waiting, was silver, and the tray ebony. Oyster cushions, mother-of-pearl picture frames and ivory blinds softened the severity of the room.

In the centre of the room sat a sculpture that was undoubt-edly one of Mimsy's own creations. The stunning deep red piece was in metal lacquered to a high shine. Stylised flames climbed up each other, from a mound of red Australian desert soil, to reach a point where they started to bend away. The metal work defied gravity as it bent away from its upward reach. It was dangerous, intentionally unbalanced and threatening. Jessica was moved by the beauty of the piece but unnerved by it as well. It was missing something crucial.

'Sit.'

Snapping back to the present, Jessica realised Mimsy had finished her call and was standing and gathering her paperwork. She moved towards the couch. The corner of the diminutive woman's lips curved upwards a fraction as she met Jessica's eyes. Oh, she's smiling, Jess realised, and returned the gesture, putting out her hand.

'Hello, Mimsy, it's a pleasure to meet you.'

'Hello Jessica, likewise. Please sit.'

Jessica did as she was bidden, as Mimsy's black eyes stared at her intently through silver-rimmed glasses. Her outfit was obvi-ously Akira Isogawa: asymmetric lines in a stiff cotton, again in shades of grey. Mimsy was known for being fiercely proud of her one-quarter Japanese heritage and her design and personal dress sense reflected this.

Mimsy took the white leather armchair, facing Jessica on the sofa.

'You like it?' She indicated the red sculpture with her chin.

'Yes.' Jessica was being honest. She liked it very much.

'What do you say about it?' Mimsy flicked distractedly through her papers as if she couldn't give a toss about Jessica's opinion.

'Well, to me, it seems to represent earth, wind and fire, but it's unsettling because it doesn't have the balance of water.'

'Yes, I call it "Drought".'

Jessica cheered inwardly. She knew there was really no right or wrong in art appreciation, but it didn't hurt to have correctly interpreted Mimsy's intention for the piece.

Mimsy poured two cups of tea, sat back and regarded Jessica.

'So?' she said.

'Ah . . . oh, right,' Jessica said, assuming this was Mimsy's interview technique. She explained, as concisely as possible, her past experience in art and design, mentioning some of the artists she worked with in her gallery. Taking her folio out of her bag, Jess showed Mimsy some examples of her own work. Her cute kitchen art seemed to interest Mimsy; vintage cutlery bent into sculptures; anodised teapots nestled into one another to make an S-shaped wall hanging; the flags made from old calendar tea towels, flying out the front of her store.

She nearly hadn't brought those photos because she was worried that the work fell into the crafty category.

'I see you have a sense of humour,' Mimsy observed. 'A sense of the quirky. This is good. I like funny.' She said this with such seriousness Jessica nearly burst out laughing.

'Good.' Mimsy stood up. 'Jimmy will be in touch. Goodbye.'

Mimsy turned back to her desk and, clearly dismissed, Jess stammered a farewell, collected her folio and found her way back out through the studio. She was a little confused. Had she got the job?

She drove home, her mind racing. She wanted the job, but there was so much to consider, so much she would have to organise if she got it. She hoped Jimmy would let her knew soon so she could start things moving. She felt a small twinge of panic: getting the job would mean an enormous lifestyle change. The General Store was a successful business and she could stay in contact with her manager Linda via email and phone calls. She might have to hire an assistant for her, but Jess was sure Linda could run things efficiently. Nevertheless, the idea of putting the business completely in someone else's hands did make her a bit nervous. The General Store's quaint look and cosy atmosphere belied its profitable turnover. Just because it looked like Nana's kitchen didn't mean it wasn't a successful business.

During the busy summer period the General Store was the second-most successful business in town, after the winery. On a good day it served more than three hundred cafe guests, about two hundred shop customers and at least one hundred take-away sandwiches and coffees from the side window to the beach-goers.

It was thanks to a large and talented staff that the business operated so efficiently and profitably. On a busy summer Saturday Jessica had ten staff in the kitchen and another ten at front-of-house with three more sharing the shop and the take-away window duties.

The profits had really taken off when the business had secured a liquor license three years earlier. Sourcing her drinks menu only from the local breweries and wineries really gave the General Store the edge, as it was the only business on the Peninsula whose wine list showcased every single vineyard and brewery, no matter how tiny and boutique it was.

Jessica had learned early on, from her father, that to run an efficient business you needed to hire people smarter than you. Her executive chef was the best in the business and she trained the chefs who worked with her; the store's business manager gave Jess a monthly budget for capital improvement to avoid overspending and her maître d' was even better at learning names, habits and foibles of important customers than she was.

She had to admit that the General Store would roll on very nicely without her. She looked out the Patrol's window as traffic and concrete gave way to gums and hills. Still, she thought with a sigh, she would miss the local landscape.

~ 20 ~

Jess took a gulp of sea air as Nick parked his ute in the car park. The breeze smelt of summer, seaweed and gourmet sausages cooking on the nearby barbie.

'Mmm, I'm starving,' Nick said, catching a whiff of dinner. 'Come on, Red.' He gave Jess a playful nudge as she stopped to pull on her thongs.

'Hang on, I'm coming,' she protested, swiping him away and laughing.

Down on the beach, the waves barely licked the sand, the slight breeze of the day had dropped and the water was a mirror reflecting the orange dusk as the sun set behind the hills of the old Cole land.

The tide was still out and dozens of children were clambering over the rock pools, investigating the ecosystem each little pond housed.

Des Parker was manning the brick barbecue built on a strip of grass between the car park and the beach, while his wife, Merle, threaded in and out of the crowd to make sure everyone had drinks and nibbles. The Parkers had owned the local supermarket for decades and were stalwarts of the community. Des was the head of the town branch of the Country Fire Authority and Merle was the go-to-person for anyone in town who needed help or support. The Parkers' home sat on the edge of the beach, just a few doors up from Nick's place, and their annual New Year's Eve party for locals sprawled out from the deck to the sandy foreshore. Tonight it seemed the whole community was there.

'Goodness knows who's looking after the townies,' Nick joked as he gratefully accepted a cold beer from Merle and gave her a quick peck on the cheek.

The Parkers had raised three boys in the two-bedroom fibro shack that sat perched on the edge of a sand dune. The house had slowly been extended as their family grew and now the home and their little supermarket were worth twenty times what the couple had paid in the seventies, but they weren't interested in moving. As Des said, 'As long as the sun comes up every day and the dolphins come to visit once a week, I'm as happy as a joey in a jumper.'

'Hi, girls,' Jess called to Rainbow and Songbird, who were supervising their tribe as they fossicked in the shallow water.

Sarah from the organic greengrocer's had hitched her long flowing crochet dress up so she could wade with them, laughing as she was splashed. Steve from the milk bar and his girlfriend were over at the trestle table, which was groaning under the weight of homemade delicacies, and chatting to other local business owners about how the year had been and how the tourist season was shaping up.

Tradesmen, farmers, shopkeepers, the publican and the karate teacher (who also ran the local radio station) were all there. Alfred Dunville, who owned the local winery, attended every year carrying a case of his latest Pinot Noir. Many of the party helped him pick grapes during harvest and greeted him (and his case of wine) with glee.

Des clanged his ship bell and everyone turned his way.

'Firstly, Merle and I would like to acknowledge that this get-together is being held on the traditional land of the Bunnerong people,' he stated. 'Secondly, we would like to thank you all for coming to our place tonight. It's great to see you all together. We're so lucky to live in such a beaut community. Grub's up!'

Jessica laughed with the women she was standing with. That was probably more than he'd said all week.

'Dolphins!' called one of the children.

The group turned back and stared out to sea in delight.

Although dolphins were regular visitors, the magic of their arrival never faded. Tonight they had a calf with them and the pale grey infant showed off to the crowd by leaping into the air and flicking itself about. A couple of the children leapt into the water to swim alongside them. The graceful creatures welcomed their playmates and mimicked the kids' swimming strokes.

Jessica wriggled her toes into the wet sand and happily watched the aquatic show. She had done her best during her interview with Mimsy and now she was determined not to think about the job again until she knew for sure what was going to happen.

'You look happy,' Merle commented as the dolphins finally swam off to another beach.

Jess turned to her and laughed guiltily. 'Actually I was just thinking how nice it will be to have the house to myself again when the family goes home in a couple of days!'

'There's nothing wrong with that,' Merle said with a smile. 'Of course you want your own life back: that's perfectly normal, dear. I'm sure your sister-in-law is a bit of a trial sometimes.'

Jess agreed wholeheartedly with Merle, but her loyalty kept her from kicking off a bout of Caro-bashing.

'Oh, she means well,' she said. 'She loves Angus and the kids, and that's all that matters in the end.'

Merle laughed, 'I'm sure she does love your brother, but sometimes I wonder how he copes really. He was always such a laid-back boy.'

Jess grinned wickedly. 'Well, let's just say he travels a lot.'

Merle chortled as Jess walked away to meet up with Rainbow and Songbird who were headed for the well-stocked buffet table.

As the three women loaded their plates, Rainbow seemed more giggly than usual, and even Songbird had an out-of-character beam on her face. Jessica looked around for Nick, sure he'd want to join them for dinner. But Nick was talking to a slim young woman in a white dress, who Jess didn't immediately recognise. Nick burst into laughter as if the woman had said something hilarious. Jessica frowned. He tilted his head and grinned that irritatingly lovely grin of his which Jessica could just tell the woman was finding most attractive. Then the woman turned so Jessica could see her face. Oh, Jess did know her after all – she was the daughter of the vineyard owner and was newly married. Shouldn't she be off talking to her husband then? Jess continued to glower. Why was it that every single bloody female in town was attracted to Nick?

She studied him from afar, perfectly aware of why he was so damn attractive. He was very tall, for a start: six four, with that fatal all-Aussie surfer boy look going on. Even in his late thirties he still had young-boy charm, complete with freckles and hair that always needed the salt washed out. It was starting to thin a little, but it was wild, dirty blond and bleached almost pure white on the ends where it was regularly traumatised by the surf and sun.

Jess gazed at Nick's wiry, muscular build, his long lean torso and legs to match. He had his back to her, giving her a view of his cute little bum. She took in his broad shoulders and his strong forearms, mesmerised for a minute by the idea of being held in them. She shook herself back to reality and realised with a burning embarrassment that he had turned around and was staring straight at her. She choked on a mouthful of bread roll. Nick laughed and pointed straight at her, then he and the girl waved cheerily.

Damn him, she thought. His grey-blue eyes were sparkling with mirth at having caught her checking him out.

She turned back to her food, but within seconds he was beside her, tickling her bare arm with one finger.

'Did you want something?' he asked teasingly.

'No,' Jess managed, again caught unawares with a mouthful of food. 'I was admiring Fiona's dress; it's gorgeous,' she said.

'Right,' Nick laughed and leaned over her to kiss Rainbow and Songbird hello, his shirt lifting to give Jess an enticing glimpse of his brown tummy with its smattering of golden hair. With a quick wink her way, he was gone again.

'You all right, love?' Rainbow giggled. 'You look a bit shook up.'

'I'm fine,' Jess answered as she watched Nick wander over to another gorgeous woman – Joanna from the hairdresser, a stunning Amazonian woman with slicked back hair and a flawless face. Jess knew she was gay, but she was obviously still enjoying Nick's attentions.

'Great tucker,' Songbird announced out of nowhere, which caused Rainbow to explode into giggles. 'That wasn't even funny, you fruitloop,' Songbird growled at her mate.

'Have you guys been smoking?' Jess asked.

'Just a little joint,' Songbird said. Her grin widened to encompass most of her face. 'We're growing some great shit at the moment with this new soil we're making. It's outta control.'

'Want a little toke?' Rainbow asked.

'Or maybe have one of Rainbow's brownies later, they'll work a treat,' suggested Songbird.

'Oh, you haven't laced the brownies, have you? You two are reprehensible! No, I have to go to Fi's party later. I should be on my best behaviour.'

'Ooh, lah-di-dah!' Rainbow said. 'Swanky! Hope you're changing: they'll throw you out if you turn up in that.' Rainbow pointed at Jessica's homemade denim cut-off hot pants. She'd sewn on floral pockets and added flared ruffles around the legs.

'I've got a hot pink sari with gold embroidery. Should be all right.'

'Sounds gorgeous. Who's your date?'

'No one special,' Jess said, still stinging from Nick's social antics.

'Hang on a minute, I resent that!' Nick said as he rejoined the group. He was carrying an elaborately decorated pink cocktail that had skewered fruit, paper umbrellas and straws bursting from the rim.

'Whoops, sprung!' Rainbow teased Jess.

'You know what I mean!' Jessica said, backtracking quickly.

'Yeah, yeah, suck up to me now. I'm just boring old Nick the handbag, I know.'

A paper plate with a generous square of chocolate was in his other hand. 'I don't know why the rations, but the brownies up at the buffet table had a little sign saying "Strictly one per person".' He picked up the dessert and started munching.

'I think they must be very special,' Jessica said, with a wink at Songbird and Rainbow. As Nick ate, Jess eyed his outfit critically. 'Is that what you're wearing to Fi's party?' she asked.

'What?' he said.

'That — those ratty shorts and that old Hawaiian shirt?'

'Old . . . old . . . ?' Nick put out his hand and pretended to choke. 'You with your designer labels and your vintage eclectic blah blah you're always going on about, which, God knows, I listen to with interest for hours on end —'

'Oh my God, you so don't! You blank out and change the subject —'

'This,' Nick interrupted, 'I'll have you uninformed fashion-ignorant types know, is a genuine *Magnum PI* Hawaiian shirt. Genuine. Look . . .' He reached behind his head and grabbed the collar, pulling it up for all to view. 'Made in Hawaii. Do you know what this is worth on eBay?'

'No, what?' Jessica asked, arms folded.

'Oh, I don't know either . . . I'm asking.' He grinned.

'What do you mean by "genuine", anyway?' Jessica asked, her hands on her hips now, lips pursed. Rainbow and Songbird continued eating, ignoring the playful banter.

'I don't know, but that's what it said on the label when I bought it online.'

'You got ripped off, you know,'

'I did not!' Suddenly Nick started to look a little pale. 'Whoa! What's that all about . . . freaky!' Nick staggered to a sitting position on the sand next to Rainbow and Songbird. 'Oh, you girls, what have you done to the brownies?'

Songbird said, 'Feeling mellow, dude? How's your Hawaiian shirt looking now?'

Nick looked down, then back up with a beatific grin. 'Psychedelic!' he said.

~21~

Fi's clifftop home glittered like a fairyland. With little regard for energy conservation, light spilled from each window onto the lush lawn, which was suspiciously green despite the current drought.

From the two-storeyed, architecturally designed house came the sound of jazz, drifting through the balmy summer air to greet Nick and Jess as they arrived at the party. Jess had changed into her pink silk gold-sequined sari and had even convinced her ridiculous locks to stay restrained in a long braid. Nick had, as usual, completely ignored Jessica's outfit guidance and still wore his tatty shorts and floral shirt.

'You know she rang me last week on her way down,' Nick said as Jess killed the engine. Neither of them wanted to leave the calm, private atmosphere of the car.

'Who? Fi?' Jess asked.

'Yeah, she wanted me to hose down the gravel drive because she'd just had the X5 detailed and didn't want to raise dust clouds and damage the finish as she drove in.'

'Hasn't she heard of water restrictions?' Jess asked.

'Yes, but she insisted anyway: she said considering they were on rain tanks it didn't matter.'

'But hadn't you just filled her rain tanks with Melbourne water?'

'Exactly, but she said she paid through the nose for that water so she could do with it as she liked. Luckily a shower set in an hour before she arrived so it was damp looking when she got here.'

'Ah, problem solved then,' Jess smiled at him in the dark. 'You must have a direct line to the gods.'

'I wish,' Nick said ruefully. 'That would make life much easier.'

'In what way?' Jess asked.

'Oh, nothing, just being silly,' Nick said, the more sober part of his brain kicking into action.

They sat in comfortable silence for several minutes. In the dark the property was mysterious and romantic, the tall oaks casting shadows under the moon's glow.

'Well, let's do it!' Jess dredged up motivation and grabbed her bag.

'Yeah, can't wait,' Nick said with barely concealed disappointment.

A path of tea lights led to the side of the house where the party was in full swing on the back patio. The band was blasting out tunes and the dance floor was full of revellers.

Fi flew over as they walked in. 'You made it,' she cried, and embraced them. 'Everyone loves what you've done with the space, Jess. Thanks, darling, you're a hit. Must go circulate,' and she was gone in a flurry of linen and pearls.

'Hi, Pet, Pip, Dot, Vi, Flick, Kit.' Jess greeted each of the bespangled and bejewelled, highlighted forty-somethings with an air-kiss.

'How on earth do you remember who's who?' Nick's aside was muffled by the brass section.

'Years of practise,' Jess whispered back.

'Hello, gorgeous — love your sari.' Tori came up and the women double cheek-kissed.

'Thanks,' Jess said. 'Love your sheath dress — too sexy!'

'On sale, five hundred off! Am I not a bargain hunter? Here, got you both some bubbles,' she said, holding out two flutes of sparkling rosé.

'Oh, you have mine, Tori, I'm not one for champagne,' Nick said and ambled off in search of a beer.

'Chin chin!' Tori said and they raised their glasses.

Jessica could tell by the strain in her voice that her friend was trying to cover her sadness.

'Tori, how's it going? Have you spoken to him?' Jessica asked.

Tori's face fell. 'Oh Jess, it's so terrible. I think it might be completely over. We both seem to have given up. We're going to use the holidays as a trial separation.'

Jessica took Tori by the elbow and steered her to where the crowd was thinner. They sat at a small table on the darkened edge of the patio.

'But neither of you cheated; no one was beating up the other – surely it's worth working on for the sake of the kids?'

Tori looked at her and Jessica could see the black smudges of exhaustion beneath her foundation.

'I keep asking myself that, Jess. But is it? I might sound lazy, but really, after the first eight years of marriage it just got so hard. It's like living with a colleague you have to get along with for the sake of your career or to impress the boss, but you can't wait to see the back of them – and for no particular reason, Jess. I wish I could tell you he's cruel or nasty. But he's not. And he can't say I'm anything other than a model citizen. We're polite, civil and respectful. And the fights are more terse, tense, under-tones.'

'How are the kids?' Jess asked.

'Oh, Jess, the guilt.' Tori buried her face in her hands. 'The children don't even know yet: I haven't had the heart to tell them. They wondered where their dad was for Christmas Day but we were so busy with uncles, aunties and cousins they didn't really seem to care. He's away such a lot anyway. Now for them it's just summer holidays at the beach house as usual.'

At the sight of Nick returning with his beer they switched their conversation to a less personal topic.

'Got your bevie okay?' Tori asked, attempting a light-hearted tone.

'Yep, cheers,' Nick said and downed half the glass of beer in one gulp.

'We've just come from the locals' beach party,' Jess said and leant forward to squeeze Tori's forearm as a promise to return to the conversation later.

'Ah, boho by the bay. How was it?' Tori asked, her merry veneer returning.

'Bloody Rainbow and Songbird doctored the brownies,' Nick said, only just recovered from his dizzying dessert.

'It was utterly divine,' Jess told Tori. 'The dolphins came.'

'How beautiful. There's such great wildlife down here. You know there were a couple of koalas in Fi's one-and-only eucalyptus tree just before the party and she sprayed them in case they started their raucous mating calls during the party.'

'You are kidding!' Jess said. 'Why the hell has she got a country house when she doesn't like dust, native animals or native plants?'

'Well you know she's a minimalist at heart. It's Cat who's the classic: she's a hard-core Brit-o-phile,' Tori said.

'Yeah,' Nick interrupted, 'she doesn't mind the animals but she hasn't got a single native plant on her hundred acres.'

'But she's more Australian than any of us. Didn't her ancestors come out on the First Fleet?' Jess asked.

'Shhh,' Tori said, making an exaggerated play of looking for eavesdroppers, 'don't mention her criminal background. She'd be mortified. She's the only Aussie I know who isn't proud of being related to convicts.'

'By the way, you've done a remarkable job on the decorations,' Tori continued, looking around the extravagant outdoor room. 'It's so beautiful.'

'It has turned out well,' Jess agreed. 'I had an unlimited budget, so that makes it easier.' Jessica's red-and-gold theme was a triumph. It gave the space a sexy, glitzy feel with a touch of Moroccan sultriness. Hundreds of red chilli lights draped down from the patio roof, punctuated by crimson Chinese lanterns. Huge stems of crab claw reached into the outdoor room from each corner. A centerpiece of red lilies hugging gilt candles sat on each of the many small gold-draped tables. The red-raw silk high-backed chairs had a regal feel against the backdrop of a galaxy of dangling white pea lights.

'It's like a jazz club from Shanghai in the forties or something,' Tori said as she took it all in.

'That's exactly the look I was going for,' Jess admitted.

'Ah, she's a talent this one,' Nick said, draping his arm around Jess's shoulders. 'Says she's going to leave us, but I don't reckon she'll go through with it.'

Jess stiffened under his hold, but before she could answer he was distracted by the appearance of three young women dressed in slinky silk creations, each more low-cut than the last. 'Oh, good, Fi's sisters are here,' he said, almost rubbing his hands with glee. 'They're a riot. Excuse me girls.'

Tori and Jessica rolled their eyes as they watched Nick bow to the new arrivals and escort them to the bar.

'So you're going to have a go at a city career?' Tori turned her attention back to Jess.

'I think I am,' Jessica said. 'I had my interview two days ago and it sounds like I got the job although it hasn't been officially offered yet.'

'That's fantastic, I'm so proud of you.' Tori raised her glass and drained its contents. With perfect timing a waiter arrived with a tray of sparkling. They each took a glass and sat gazing into the party for a few minutes, lost in their thoughts as they swayed to the gentle jazz notes.

When the band switched to a dance number, Nick reappeared.

'Looks like you two need a bit more fun over here,' he said, offering Jess his hand. 'Dance with me, Red?'

'Sure,' Jess said and jumped to her feet.

'So what do you think about Jessica's new –'

'Shoes!' Jessica cut Tori off abruptly. She raised her eyebrows and glared at her friend to shut up about the job. Now was not the time to talk about it. It was a perfect night and she wanted to enjoy it without any tension. Tori gave a tiny nod of understanding and Jess responded with a grateful smile.

'Come on then, girl, let's do it,' Nick cried, swinging Jess out into the crowd with a flourish. His strong arms and graceful steps spun and flipped Jessica around the floor. Her vintage satin Indian shoes were the perfect footwear for twisting and turning as she followed his lead, anticipating his moves. Her smile was broad as he had her dipped in one moment and swept her around in a twirl the next. 'Choo Choo Ch'Boogie' wound up its big ending and they joined in, loudly cheering the band.

'Cutting in!' Fi slipped between the thin gap as Jess and Nick stood side by side.

'My turn next!' Cat boomed as she sashayed by with her husband Freddy. 'Freddy's got two left feet.' Freddy grinned and offered no argument to his wife's assessment of his skills.

Jessica graciously relinquished her dance partner and found Tori again. The two sat down with a bottle of champagne and made short work of it.

'It's late,' Tori said a few glasses later, squinting at her Omega with one eye closed.

As the exhilaration of the dancing subsided, Jess was filled with a sudden champagne-induced sadness. 'You're the greatest friend, Tori,' she cried. 'I can't believe your marriage is in danger.'

'*I* can't believe my marriage is in danger,' Tori replied.

'It sucks,' Jess said.

'I don't want to talk about it,' Tori said.

'I don't want to leave Nick behind,' Jess stage-whispered to Tori.

'I knew it was about Nick!' Tori accused her friend with a pointed finger. She reached out and grabbed the bottle and clumsily poured them each another drink; most of the bubbly went onto the ground, but some made it into their glasses.

'I know, I know, it's dreadful, terrible,' Jess said, throwing her head into her hands dramatically. 'But what can I do? He's so damn gorgeous, and . . . and . . . he listens to me all the bloody time, and that is so lovely, you know?'

'I know.' Tori nodded her head emphatically to enforce her grasp of the situation.

'But I don't want a relationship with him. No, no, no!'

Tori was confused. 'No?'

'No!' Jess shook her head violently.

'Ahh . . . no.' Tori nodded again to show she understood, but she wasn't all that sure she did. She looked up at the sky and wondered if it had always been that damn far away. 'Hang on then,' she said, looking back at Jess and feeling mighty dizzy. 'What *do* you want?'

'I just want to see him all the time and I don't want him to see anybody else. And I want my boys back, and I want a successful design career . . . and, well, I wouldn't mind a nibble of Nick's oblique muscle.'

'Right, of course,' Tori nodded. To her addled mind it all made complete sense.

The haunting strains of 'Always' filled the country air.

'I love this song,' Jess said, distracted by the music.

Nick came up behind her and grabbed her shoulders. She stood unsteadily and winked at Tori just as Nick twirled her to face him.

She felt her head clear as they danced the next few numbers. Soon she was less drunk, but still felt divinely loose and relaxed as Nick spun her around the floor. She didn't even think about the moves; she just followed his lead and let the music take them away. All the sadness and heaviness of the past year seemed to dissipate in that moment, and she was relieved to be free of the burden, even if for a short time.

She surrendered herself to Nick's capable arms, her body pressing against his and her eyes closing as she let him take control of her, of the moment. She relaxed into him more and lost herself in his warmth; only aware of the subtle scent of pine on his neck and the delight of his strong arms holding her so close.

A cool breeze rippled in from the sea and she shivered, suddenly conscious of how his body felt under her fingertips. His hand brushed lightly up and down her back and he murmured something wordless and gentle into her hair.

The music ended and they reluctantly stopped moving, but their arms remained around each other. Jess opened her eyes slowly and stared directly into Nick's. He held her gaze.

'Thanks for the dance,' Nick whispered.

'That's okay,' she whispered back and his lips came down to brush hers. The brush turned into a linger, then moved into an open-mouth kiss of such electricity Jessica's knees weakened beneath her. It lasted a mere five seconds. So brief that none of the other party-goers even noticed. But it felt like much longer to Jessica.

Nick pulled back from her with a look of shock.

'Ah, music . . . there's um . . . no more music,' he stammered, and he propelled her gently from the floor.

Jess's heart was beating a tattoo of shock and her cheeks felt hot; she avoided meeting Nick's eyes.

'Well, I'm off to the bar,' Nick said, his eyes firmly on the ground. 'Drink?'

'Er, yeah, great, ta, thanks. Umm, where'd Tori get to? I'll be back,' Jess stammered back, and they scurried in opposite directions.

Jessica went to the kitchen and ordered a coffee from the catering staff. She was confused and needed to clear her head. She did like Nick, a lot. Maybe pursuing a relationship with him was the right thing to do after all. But was that what he wanted or had he just been swept up by the moment? All his silly flirting with her was no indicator; he did that with all the girls. It was so hard to know when Nick was serious. Maybe she should find out.

A chorus of voices suddenly began the countdown, so Jess put her cup in the sink and headed back to the party. The New Year was welcomed with a chorus of happy voices and a joyous fanfare from the band, who were replaced by a local DJ, Eighties Daze, who cranked up the classics as midnight slipped into the early hours of the morning.

Tori, Fi and Jess danced in a circle to the 'Bus Stop', Michael Jackson, Prince and other musical flashbacks until they were flushed and breathless. Fi and Tori finally threw themselves panting and laughing on one of the several lounges scattered around the periphery of the party room. Jess had tried to keep an eye out for Nick while she was dancing, but she hadn't seen him for some time. She wandered into the house to check the enormous family room, the living room, the drawing room, the study, even the kids' playroom. But he was nowhere to be seen. She returned to the others who were cackling gaily.

'What did I miss?' Jess asked, sitting next to Tori.

'Not Binky's dress, that's for sure!' Fi chortled.

'Shut up!' Binky said crossly. 'Fluoro is back in, I keep telling you that!' Binky was what Pip called a CUB: a Cashed-Up Bogan. She and her husband owned an enormous brick beachfront house that stuck out like an ugly chain store jumper against the locals' fibro beach shacks. Binky was glitzy, ditzy and shallow, but hilarious fun at a party.

'Yes, if you're fourteen, and believe me you're more than double that . . . hang on . . . *triple* that!' The group laughed.

'Hang on a minute, no I'm not,' Binky stood to protest with hands on her non-existent hips. 'Wait on . . . yes I am . . . no I'm not . . . How old am I? How much is three times fourteen? Where's my iPhone?'

The other women laughed even louder.

'Oh stop it,' Binky said in irritation. 'I'm not ditzy, I've just got Bolly Brain.' She had another swig to prove it.

Fi leaned towards Jess. 'So you win for bringing the hottest date. Nick scrubs up a treat out of his stubbies and singlet.'

'I wouldn't mind seeing Nick out of his stubbies and singlet,' Cat boomed as she stood to top up the champagne flutes. Everyone pealed with laughter, imagining the conservative Cat ogling a naked Nick Johnson.

Jess squirmed; the one thing she didn't want to talk about right now was Nick. For two hours she'd been reliving the moment of their kiss, and feeling alternately horrified and thrilled. What had she been she thinking? Luckily no one seemed to have noticed.

'He's an odd one, that Nick Johnson,' Fi said. 'I really like him – have done ever since we bought down here – but that whole first marriage thing has an air of mystery about it.'

'Nick's been married?' Pip squeaked in wide-eyed thrall at the unexpected gossip. Pip and her former AFL-playing husband had only bought their property two years earlier, and she was still catching up on the community news.

'Yes, to his childhood sweetheart apparently, wasn't it?' Tori asked, turning to Jess for clarification.

Jess blushed, mortified to have to even think about Nick, let alone fuel gossip about him. 'Well, I wouldn't say childhood sweetheart. She went to high school with us. Her name was Imogen.'

'Ooh,' said Pip, 'what happened?'

Jess wanted to close the topic. 'I'm not sure. People break up all the time, for all sorts of reasons. Who wants nibbles?' She waved at the waiter who was walking past with a tray of mini hot dogs. The women all shook their heads, except Cat who took three.

'Oh, it was *massive*!' Fi said, oblivious to Jess's scowl. 'She was apparently madly in love with him and then they lost their baby when it was only four weeks old and *then* he walked out on her just six months later.

'No!' Several members of the audience gasped and leaned forward in their seats.

'It was a very difficult time for both of them,' Jess murmured. 'I don't think it's up to us to judge.' But no one was listening. It was frightfully dreary to have facts get in the way of a good story.

'She was devastated apparently, DEVASTATED,' Fi said, warming up to her tale. 'So distraught she had to move away.'

'Her parents moved to Adelaide so she decided to go with them,' Jess interjected on behalf of her friend. 'It wasn't all Nick, you know. You can't put all the blame on him,' she added crossly.

'Well why *did* he leave his wife, then?' Pip asked. Jess kept her mouth shut and stared into the bushes as if to indicate she wasn't prepared to spill the beans. The group turned to Fi.

'Fi, why did he leave Imogen?'

'Well, that's the best bit – and the worst bit,' Fi paused dramatically. 'Apparently he was having an affair!'

The group gasped and turned as one to Jess to verify this scandalous allegation.

'That's not true!' Jess cried, determined to defend Nick. 'He would never do something like that.'

'Sorry, love,' Fi said, and patted Jess on the knee. 'I know you think the world of him, but my sister-in-law is friends with Imogen's cousin; isn't it a small world? Anyhoo, she heard it from the horse's mouth, so to speak. She found out that he was seeing another woman and that's why she finally left him.'

Bile surged in Jess's throat. She couldn't believe it. Maybe she'd been wrong about Nick. She ran her fingers lightly over her lips. Maybe the kiss was just a bit of fun for him. Damn him.

~22~

'Hello, is that I.G. Homes? Yes, I am just phoning to confirm an appointment that I have with your draftsman for tomorrow morning. Yes, at the property known as Springforth.

'I just need to change the time. The tenant is vacating the property shortly so I'll call you next week when I know which day is free.

'Thank you. Goodbye.'

~23~

Jess checked her reflection in the rear-view mirror. She held both hands across her stomach in an attempt to quell the butter-flies that were fluttering inside her.

She was parked in front of the renovated cottage in Williams-town. The boys were inside and expecting her. It was surreal, she couldn't believe it was finally happening after she'd waited so long.

The drive to town that morning had seemed interminable. She was abuzz at seeing her boys but also completely rattled by the news she'd heard about Nick at the party two nights before.

Was it really true? Had Nick been having an affair? Was that why he left his wife just after their baby had died? It was too awful to be true. But he was a shocking flirt; maybe it was possible that he screwed around on Imogen.

But how could he? Driving along, she had shaken her head. Not Nick. Jess trusted him. He wasn't one of those guys; she knew it in her gut. But clearly she was no judge of men. Look at Graham. She would have sworn he was a decent man with integrity and character. So who was she to judge? Maybe she was blind to Nick too? He certainly enjoyed flirting; maybe there was more to it than harmless fun. Well, she was going to protect herself. No more Miss Innocent. As she had driven further from Stumpy Gully and closer to the city, her buzzing brain was soon distracted by thoughts of her boys.

It was over twelve months since she'd seen Callum and Liam. A year since that awful Christmas Day when Graham had put the suitcases, presents and boys in the car and had driven off. Just like that.

That day, Jess had stood and watched the plumes of dust rise from the Saab's tyres and felt as if she'd been in a car accident. It was surreal. Her family had simply driven out of her life. How could that happen? How could that even be real?

Now she wanted to do what was best for the boys – she didn't want to disrupt their new life, but it broke her heart to think how confused they must be. She didn't know what Graham had told them about their break-up. And try as she might, she just couldn't overcome her need to place a palm on their soft, plump cheeks, smell their soapy skin, and kiss their silken hair one more time. All her desperate efforts to see them for Christmas had failed, but, unexpectedly, Samantha had rung a day ago with the news that she was babysitting the boys one day during the week. Jess could sneak in to visit them.

'Graham's going to kill me when the boys dob,' Samantha had sighed.

'I know, I'm so sorry to put you into the middle of this,' Jess had replied.

'It doesn't matter. They need to see you,' Samantha had said, 'and it's just wrong that he's cut you off like this. He's such a dickhead. Umm, and sweetie, I hate to break this to you, but you do know Karen and Graham were married a few months back?'

Jessica had just laughed. Typical. Graham had always insisted he'd never get married again. Seems he just hadn't wanted to marry her.

So here she was, parked behind Samantha's Hyundai outside Graham and Karen's cottage.

Samantha opened the door to Jessica's shaky knock and grinned at her. 'They're so excited,' she said. 'I told them half an hour ago.' She led Jess through the first door off the hallway to where two cross-legged figures sat in front of the television.

'Hello, my beautiful boys,' Jess said. Both children flicked around as one. 'Mumma!' they screeched and scrambled to stand and run in one motion. They flung their arms around her and squeezed so hard that Jess toppled from her crouched position onto her bottom. The boys piled on top of her, both of them trying to reach her face.

'Why are you crying?' Callum demanded.

'What's wrong?' asked Liam, getting off Jess's supine body. 'Are you sad?'

'No, you silly chickens,' Jess said, laughing through her tears. 'I'm very, very happy to see you! Look at you both; you're so big! You got so big. Help me up.' The boys dragged Jess to her feet and she stood and looked down at them standing next to each other, grinning.

'Oh, Callum, sweetheart you've lost your first tooth, look at that. You look twice as cheeky now.'

'No, Mumma, that's my third tooth!' Callum said proudly.

His statement felt like a knife slicing her guts. It was agony to think she'd missed so many important milestones in their lives.

She smiled through her tears and said, 'And, Liam, you've got glasses, darling. My goodness, you look so clever. Come and sit down on the couch with me for big cuddles.' Jess nestled on the sofa while Samantha put the kettle on. An intense sense of deja vu struck as both boys tucked their shoulders under her arms and draped their legs across her legs automatically, just as they'd done hundreds of times before. Sadness grabbed at her throat.

'Now, I want every detail. How was prep, Callum? Big, grown-up schoolboy. I can't believe it.'

'I can read now,' Callum replied proudly.

'You can not,' his big brother scoffed.

'I can so, I can read fifty words.'

'Can you?' Jess said. 'That's so brilliant, you're so clever. What about you, Liam? How was the first year at your new school?'

'Okay, I guess,' Liam replied. 'But Mumma, I missed you so much. Why did we have to leave? Callum cried lots, you know; but that's cos he's a baby.'

'I'm not a baby,' Callum said indignantly. 'But I had bad dreams, Mumma, and I woked up. Why weren't you there when I wanted you?'

Jess covered her face with her hands. The pain was too much. The thought of the confusion and sadness the boys must have felt to be wrenched away overwhelmed her.

Callum prised two of her fingers from her tear-stained cheek and she felt his hot breath on her face.

'Was it cos I was bad, Mumma? I'm sorry I was naughty lots.'

'Oh, sweetheart.' Jess sat up and held them both tighter. 'You weren't naughty. You are both my beautiful, beautiful boys and I couldn't love you one bit more than I do – and that will always be the same. Sometimes mums and dads can't live together anymore, so they go to live in new places; but they never stop loving their children just as much as they always did. And do you know, I've missed you both every single day since you left, and I've thought of you every day too. I love you both bigger than the moon you know.'

'I love you bigger than Jupiter,' Callum chimed in with their well-practised routine.

'I love you bigger than the whole universe,' Liam added.

Jess laughed and hugged them to her. 'Now tell me about your holidays. Are you having fun?'

Now there was a topic of interest, and the two conversations spilled on top of each other as they gabbled about Scienceworks, play-dates with new school friends and, Jess was pleased to hear, even a horse-riding weekend.

She noticed the boys' chatter was liberally punctuated with Karen's name. She'd expected that to happen, but not for it to hurt so much. Samantha walked back in the room as Liam was saying, '. . . and Karen's sister has a water slide. It's so cool.'

'Callum, I don't think Jess wants to hear about Karen anymore,' Samantha said.

'No that's okay, I'm pleased they're enjoying themselves . . . Really,' Jess said and reached out for her tea as the boys tumbled onto the floor in a wrestle.

'How are you?' Samantha asked when the children were out of earshot, squealing in delight at the Christmas presents Jess had brought for them.

'Oh God, that was incredible,' Jess said. 'I can't believe how much they've both grown up. But excruciating as well – to have them ask why I haven't been to see them before was agony. How do you explain this mess to kids?'

Her eyes started to well again and Samantha pulled out a clean tissue from her jumper sleeve. 'Sorry,' Jess whispered. 'I just can't help it.'

'It's all right darling, I'd kill him if he took them away from me. That's why I've kept in contact with the bugger.'

At the sound of a car pulling up outside, Samantha looked up in wide-eyed fright. 'Oh, shit,' she said, 'that's them. They're not supposed to be back for hours.'

'Hi, Dad. Hi Karen,' the little voices trilled from the hallway. Samantha and Jessica stared at each other in horror, wishing the floor would swallow the entire couch.

'Hello, Samantha, thanks for minding the boys. Hello, Jess, fancy seeing you here.' Graham was as slick as oil as he entered the room. 'I don't believe you've met Karen. Karen, this is Jessica.'

At least Karen had the decency to act uncomfortable. She was a nice looking woman, in a plain kind of way. She had mousy hair and glasses and was wearing a simple beige linen shift dress: quite the opposite of Jess in her way-out lurid colors and flowing fabrics.

'Oh, right, um, yes . . . hello,' Karen said and folded and unfolded her hands. 'My, well, this *is* awkward. Okay then, tea, yes, kettle. Anybody want something? No? Never mind . . . I'll pop it on anyway.' With that she skittered off down the hall, but not before Jess saw Graham shoot her that irritated look with which she was so familiar.

'So what brings you to the big smoke?' Graham asked as if Jess had just popped in on her way by. 'Desperate to get a taste of big city action, I bet?'

'Oh, I just brought the boys their Christmas presents,' Jess explained. All three adults were standing in the room in a triangle. Samantha's eyes darted nervously from Graham to Jess.

'Well, aren't you thoughtful? But really entirely unnecessary. You didn't need to go to the bother.' Graham started collecting and screwing up the discarded gift-wrap. 'So, how's work? You still waitressing?'

'I still own the General Store, yes,' Jess replied.

'Excellent, good to see someone's maintaining our rural areas. They're in such a dreadful state, aren't they, what with the drought, the fires, the unemployment? I don't know how anyone stands living in the country.'

'Well, the Peninsula doesn't have fires or unemployment actually,' Jess began and remembered how he was like talking to a brick wall. She couldn't believe that she used to find this side of his personality commanding and attractive.

'Yes, dreadful state of affairs,' Graham continued as if she hadn't opened her mouth.

'How are the boys?' Jess said.

'Haven't you seen them yet? I thought that's why you were here?' Graham said in mock bafflement. His sister rolled her eyes and left the room to help Karen.

'Yes, I can see they're healthy. But are they happy? Are they, you know, well? I'd just like to know what their year's been like.'

Graham sat on the couch with one ankle perched on his knee and his arms folded behind his head, the very picture of cocky self-assuredness. 'Oh, just grand. Of course Callum's broken arm took much longer to heal –'

'Callum broke his arm?' Jess said in fright. 'When?'

'Oh, that's right, you were gone by then. He was climbing the back fence. He did his forearm, both bones, the little bugger. This time last year. I was interstate as luck would have it so Karen had to juggle the two of them.'

Jessica couldn't tell if she was going to faint or vomit. Her little baby, in hospital with a broken arm, with some bloody stranger looking after him. They could have called her. She would have sat by his bedside and read books and sung songs until he recovered. Well, she desperately tried to reassure herself, at least Samantha would have been there.

'And worst timing, Samantha was in Italy.' Did he just say that to fuck with her mind? Jess looked at Graham blankly. No, he was completely oblivious to the fact that she wanted the boys desperately and would have moved heaven and earth to care for them. Maybe he doesn't know because I've never told him, she suddenly thought.

'Graham, I was wondering if it was at all possible for me to see the boys occasionally. You know, now that the dust has settled.' She twisted her hands in desperation.

'For God's sake, Jessica, do you have to keep making life so bloody difficult?' Graham snapped.

Jessica failed to see how cooking his meals, giving him free rent for four years and loving his babies made his life so 'difficult', but she knew arguing wouldn't get her anywhere.

'Oh, Graham, I don't mean to be a pain, I'm not expecting you to come down to the farm or anything. I could come to town, just now and then. Please, Graham.'

Graham slipped his phone out of his pocket and checked it.

'I don't know, Jess, we've just got them settled. It's going along very nicely without you interfering.'

'Well, I could be your babysitter on call.' Jess knew she was clutching at straws but she was prepared to do whatever it took. 'For free of course, so that's a good deal isn't it, Graham?' She couldn't get his attention.

'Good God, look at the time. You must be desperate to get back and miss the worst of the traffic. We've taken up far too much of your time already,' he said, as if she hadn't spoken.

Graham picked up her handbag and in one motion had her at the open front door.

'Can I say goodbye to the boys?' she asked.

'Oh, I'm sure they'll be fine – I'll pass on your farewells.'

'But Graham, they'll be so disappointed if I don't say goodbye.'

'Oh, Jess, darling, I do believe you're overestimating your own importance in their lives. It's been a year, you know. Best regards to your family. *Ciao*.' And he shut the door just centimetres from her nose.

~24~

It had been a miserable couple of days since Jessica's visit to the boys. She'd been so frustrated and pissed off with Graham pushing her out the door and speaking to her like an idiot that she'd just let loose and screamed with frustration on the drive home. Finally, with her throat sore from yelling and her heart pounding with adrenaline, she decided she was going to fight the bastard. There was no way she was going to give up on being a part of the boys' life, no matter how difficult Graham tried to make it. Just making the decision made her feel stronger and more determined and she liked feeling that way.

Now she stood in front of her bedroom mirror and twirled. She felt gorgeous in her vintage fifties frock. Today was the annual Peninsula Polo Match and she was determined to get out and enjoy it. She didn't even care if she ran into Nick: she felt ready to face him now. One kiss shouldn't change the wonderful relationship they shared. She didn't know what the truth was about his past, but she had enough going on her life right now without getting into that as well.

Smiling at her reflection one last time, she grabbed her keys and clutch bag, and jumped in the Patrol.

Her mobile trilled as she was driving out Springforth's gates. She hit accept, then the speaker button. 'Hello, Jessica Wainright.'

'Hello, gorgeous!'

'Hi, Jimmy,' Jessica said and a smile crept over her face. 'How are you?'

'Fantastic; better for hearing your voice of course. Hey, I hear you whipped the specs off Mimsy the other week. She was dead impressed, my girl. I knew she would be.'

'Really? I wouldn't have guessed, she's not exactly exuberant with her praise is she?' Jessica replied.

'Yes, she's been working on that whole enigma thing for some time now. It's one of her specialties. She'd never let anyone know how she really felt.'

'Tell me about it. It's quite intimidating.'

'Well the job's confirmed. Mimsy's given us her blessing. You still on board?'

'Absolutely,' Jess answered, and punched the air with excitement. 'I cannot wait.'

'Brilliant, my style guru, I'll have the documents drawn up and see you at work on the eighteenth.'

Jessica hung up as she turned into the Polo Club car park. 'Woohoo,' she whooped aloud. 'I got a new job, I got a new job,' she chanted happily, beating time on the steering wheel and grinning crazily at herself in the rear-view mirror.

It was perfect timing: now she wouldn't have to face the Nick issue at all, her store was humming along nicely on its own and she was more than ready for a change. Perfect.

Her car crawled along in a queue of black Range Rovers, merlot Cayennes, navy X5s and forest green Land Rovers streaming into the paddock. The lumbering vehicles reversed into position and the dusty, shabby field was soon transformed into a five-star circus as boots were flipped open, trestle tables assembled and decorated and market umbrellas festooned with lengths of floral bunting.

Well-modulated greetings crisscrossed the car park and by the time the first couple of bottles of Domain Chandon were downed and the laughter became more hysterical, the raucous sulpher-crested cockatoos gave up competing with the noise and flew off.

The fashionable coastal town was enjoying its finest hour (according to visitors, anyway). The polo was on and people from miles around – both those with a passion for the sport and those with the name monogrammed on their shirts – attended in droves. It was the ultimate Peninsula social occasion for the well-heeled country visitor keen to elevate or cement their social status.

The air rang with names: 'Oh, we're at the Baileau marquee'; 'Oh, really, we're at Pratt'; 'Come and say hi to us at the Smorgon tent'; 'Oh, darling, I couldn't leave my dear friends the Murdochs.'

Despite the pretension, Jessica always enjoyed the polo, and today there was a sense of magic in the air that came with finally knowing where her future lay. As always, she and Linda had set up her mobile cafe on-site to soak up the fun of the day. They had the operation down to a fine art. Pretty chiffon fabric lined the marquee's interior, and the tables were draped in muslin and topped with jasmine flowers in cut-crystal vases. Jess's white-on-white theme delighted the polo elite, who loved being seen as they sat daintily at her tables, sipping lattes and waggling their fingertips at acquaintances. Fi, Cat, Tori, Caro, Cyn and Binky had left their children with their reluctant husbands and decided to enjoy a girls' day out, basing themselves at Jess's cafe. This suited Jess very well, as she could sit and enjoy the fun with her friends, while keeping an eye on her staff as they kept up with the coffee and food orders.'Darling, the cafe is delightful. How sweet!' Tori exclaimed as she swept in, air-kissing several other women as she glided past. Only Jess picked up on the slight twitch of sadness at the side of her friend's mouth, the deep crease in her forehead.

'Gorgeous, my dear. We need you up at Flemington with us next year,' Cat boomed.

'Well, funny you should mention that,' Jess said, serving from the platter of spring vegetable frittata the waitress had placed in the centre of the table as first course. 'I've decided I'm doing it: I am moving to the city.'

'What?' Cat, Cyn and Binky chorused in surprise. But Jessica was their country pet. She couldn't move to the city. Where would they get their pumpkin scones from during their winter sojourns?

'Yes, Mimsy Baxter loves her,' Caro said with something approaching pride. 'We've planned it all out. She's moving in with me until she finds her own place.'

'But what about the General Store?' Cyn whined. 'How will I know I can still get good coffee when you're gone?'

'It's okay,' Jess said, patting Cyn on her Tiffany solitaire. 'Linda is still managing it, as she's done for the past year. She makes a wonderful espresso.'

'But, as I've said before, how will you cope, darling? The city's quite challenging, you know. It will be a real culture shock, you know,' Binky said.

'Oh, don't talk nonsense, Binky,' said Caro. 'It's Melbourne, not Mars. You're quite mad.'

Jessica just laughed. 'I'll be fine, I'll Google images of trams and instructions on how to catch a taxi.' These women were being completely ludicrous. She'd lived in town when she'd studied, in the heart of the CBD actually, not to mention spending hours trawling inner city suburbs for art pieces and props.

'But what about hook turns, darling? I'm a native and they confuse the hell out of me!' Binky said.

'I have been to the big city before, Binky, I'll be fine.' Good Lord, Jessica thought as she took a bite of frittata. This group had completely pigeonholed her. Was she really such a country bumpkin?

Cyn brushed a crumb from her black ruched Easton Pearson skirt. 'I'm sorry, we shouldn't sound so negative. Do tell all; what's the job about?'

'Well it's a design role, actually, which is terrifying and exciting all at once. I'll be working as Mimsy Baxter's head designer.'

'Really?' Cyn, said.

'That is prestigious,' Cat added.

'Still Life is a really big and important company,' Cyn said.

'And Mimsy is, like, so famous. I met her once, you know,' Binky said.

'You must be really good . . .' Cyn drifted off.

'Of course she's good, you ninny!' Caro snapped at Cyn. 'She's better than good: she's wonderful. How can you look at the General Store and the gallery and not see it?'

'Oh, I'm colourblind and spatially challenged. I need a stylist just to dress myself,' Cyn giggled.

'Then keep your opinions to yourself, for goodness sake.'

Although it was perhaps a little aggressive for a ladies' lunch, Jessica could have hugged her sister-in-law for standing up for her.

As for Cyn, she tossed her titian locks, folded her arms and shut her mouth.

'Tell them about it,' Caro instructed Jess.

'Well, Jimmy McConnell is the Chief Operating Officer, so he'll be my direct boss, but Mimsy sets the direction.'

'Jimmy McConnell – I've heard of him. A real man about town,' Cyn said, not one to be absent from a conversation for too long. 'He's just split from his second wife.'

'He's really nice. He's been very supportive,' Jessica said. 'I knew him from school. We were friends back then.'

'What will you do with the farm?' Cat asked. 'It won't run itself.'

Jess bit back a sarcastic remark and instead answered, 'Nick will be looking after it. He knows what he's doing.'

'Actually I plan to be down here a lot more,' Caro interrupted. 'Angus and I need more family time. Of course, it's not actually Jessica's farm, it's her father's, so my little family might just have our turn for a while. And besides, I suddenly feel a real need to get my hands on that property: it has so much potential.'

'What do you mean?' Jessica asked, alarmed at Caro's comment. She felt a tad apprehensive about leaving the property in the care of Caro and Angus. She'd always thought that Nick would continue running things.

'Well, darling, you'll be a city girl now, with city friends, doing metro things like Chapel Street and Bridge Road on the weekends. You won't have time to play farmers. I thought I'd help you out a little by taking over the reins.'

'Oh, really?' Jessica said. 'Well, that's very nice of you.' She quietly chastised herself for being greedy. It was only fair that Caro and Angus had their chance to enjoy the property and she had to trust that Caro would manage it just as well as she had.

'Darling,' Tori stood and flattened down the creases in her frock. 'Fancy a walk to the ladies' with me?'

'Of course.' Jess suspected her friend wanted a private chat. 'Let me just grab my bag.'

They linked arms and carefully picked their way through the paddock, weaving between the open car boots and polo fans.

'Thanks, love,' Jess said. 'I needed a break from the grilling they were giving me.'

'My pleasure.' Tori nodded. 'I was hoping we could steal a quiet moment for a quick chat anyway.'

'How are things going at home?' Jess asked. She grabbed Tori's hand. 'You okay?' she asked.

Tori looked at her blankly and all emotion drained from her face. 'Well, it looks like our timing is crap.' She gave a brittle laugh. 'While you go off to start a new life in the city, I'll be moving down here permanently.'

'Does that mean you and Joseph have decided to break up?'

'Yep,' Tori said. Her voice was flat. 'It's a done deal I'm afraid.'

'Oh Tori.' Jess's instant reaction was to put her arms around her friend and hold her. Tori was stiff and unyielding in her arms. Jess studied her face: Tori's eyes were glassy. 'Tori, talk to me, tell me everything.'

'It happened last night. He came down and we talked. It was the world's weirdest break-up. I asked him gently, quietly, if he wanted to split. He said yes, it was probably for the best. I asked him if there was someone else.' Tori looked up, her grey eyes molten with pain. 'And, Jess, he looked at me as though the nasti-ness of the last six months was nothing compared to how much

I hurt him with that one sentence.' She folded her arms around herself protectively.

'I tried to take it back, but the damage was done. He said those sorts of comments were exactly the problem; it showed that I didn't even know him. And he's right, Jess.' She shuddered with emotion. 'I didn't know him. I wrote him a long letter explaining how I felt. I said how sorry I was that I hadn't been able to make it work and left it for him this morning. Then we had a bizarre SMS conversation about logistics this morning. I offered to stay down here after the holidays end. And then we'll just see what the next few months send us as a family.'

'Tori, you poor love.' Jessica grabbed some tissues from her bag to dry her own tears as Tori stared dry-eyed into the distance.

~ 25 ~

The morning's howling norwesterly had whipped the surf into a pounding frenzy that had tradies across the Peninsula pulling sickies, and smartly suited executives rescheduling their days' work to take advantage of the perfect swell.

Nick was no exception. He'd swapped his usual early-morning start at Springforth to hit the beach at dawn. Not that anybody would mind. Richard was happy with whatever hours Nick chose to work, as long as the job got done.

Walking back up the beach with his board under his arm, he felt exhilarated by the morning's exercise. A few hours in the pumping surf always cleared his mind and helped centre his thoughts – and there was certainly a lot going on in his head at the moment.

The kiss he had shared with Jess had been amazing, unexpected and overwhelming. She'd always been special to him but he'd resigned himself long ago to just being her friend; he'd thought it was the best he could hope for and had swallowed any dreams he had had for more. But the kiss changed everything. It told him that not only was there a powerful physical chemistry between them, it seemed she wanted him as much as he wanted her.

He shook the salty water from his hair and leaned his board against the front wall of his shabby fibro shack.

But everything had been so weird between them since the kiss; what if that one intense, glorious moment had ruined their friendship? He valued Jess too much to lose her altogether. He knew that she was thinking about moving to the city, and he had no right to ask her to stay, not unless he was honest about how he felt. He needed to show her he meant business; that he was really into her and was the right choice. Then she would realise that she couldn't possibly leave him.

He unzipped his wetsuit to the waist, pulling his muscular arms free of the sticky rubber, and rubbed his towel vigorously over his chest.

Inside, the house was already heating up for what was threatening to be another scorcher. He peeled off the bottom half of the wetsuit and flung it into a corner of the bathroom where it landed in a crumpled headless faint. His skin tingled with relief when he stepped into the powerful stream of hot water running from the shower.

Jess's face played in Nick's mind; her smile teasing his imagination and the memory of her lips on his, fuelling a desire to touch her and be with her so intense that it shocked him. He thought of her wide smile and generous cheeks and how much she hated being what she called a moonface. Of course, it was exactly this broad, round face that kept her looking so much younger than her thirty-seven years.

He remembered how her figure looked in the sari at the party; generous hips, and perfectly in proportion breasts to match. His thoughts lingered on her breasts a little longer as he remembered a red and white dotted bikini he'd seen her in the previous summer.

'This is crazy,' Nick said aloud to the empty room. He twisted off the taps and dried himself quickly, grabbing a clean T-shirt from the pile on the end of his bed.

He dragged his Levis on and buckled his favourite leather belt into place before moseying into the kitchen to flick on the kettle.

He loved this shack. Sure, it was no palace, but then it was eighty years old, and was probably well past its use-by date. Nick didn't care that there was constant upkeep on the old place, which leaked in a different spot each winter, had rising damp and a rusted, corrugated roof that was more patched than original.

The timber kitchen cupboards were lime green with bakelite handles. Pokey and deep, they were lined with cracked and peeling adhesive lining with a fruit and vegetable motif. Soon he'd need to spend some serious money updating the place. He loved his home too much to seriously consider moving; and where else would he find somewhere right on the beach like this?

Nick wandered into the lounge room in search of his favourite mug. The lounge suite was a hand-me-down from his parents. Brand new in the sixties, by the early nineties it had been old-fashioned and lame; yet another thing for Imogen to find hideous about her wedding nest. But today the Scandinavian style setting was retro chic; in fact, Jessica loved it. The slim, angled blond timber legs and arms of the suite were elegantly tapered, and aqua bouclé fabric covered the armchair and sofa cushions.

It was fifteen years now since he'd bought the shack, back when he and Imogen were first married and expecting. He had paid a hefty premium for the location, but it was a mere fraction of the land value now.

He'd felt very proud of himself at the time. Sure, he'd made a mistake by getting his girlfriend pregnant. But he had done the right thing: he'd married her and then he put a roof over her head, with what he thought was the best view in the world. At twenty-two years old it wasn't easy working enough odd jobs to service a mortgage, but he was determined to be husband, father and provider, so he'd done it. He'd saved enough for a deposit (with his parents helping out by matching him dollar for dollar) and then he kept up the repayments, even if it sometimes meant working fourteen to sixteen hour days.

Imogen had complained bitterly that she would have been more comfortable in a contemporary unit in the suburbs with all the mod cons, but Nick reckoned nothing could beat being lulled to sleep by the rhythm of the ocean and waking each morning to see the swell from his bedroom window. The view alone made up for the outdoor dunny. But in deference to Imogen's needs he had added an indoor toilet and bathroom as soon as they moved in − but that was the only concession to modern domestic living he'd been able to afford to make.

Now Nick was glad that he hadn't bowed to pressure and slapped in a cheap Ikea kitchen. It would have detracted from the time-warp look he had going on in here now.

Yesterday's newspaper was strewn across the coffee table, with sections spilling across the couch and onto the floor. He scooped it up and dumped it in the firewood basket, admiring the original stonework of the chimney as he always did. It was his favourite part of the house. A rosewood sideboard, again with elegantly tapered timber legs, sat under the window. A Newtone vase sat on top of the sideboard. He hadn't a clue what it was when he bought it at the secondhand shop he'd just liked the green hue and how it mottled so well with the brown base of the thing. It was Jessica who pointed out that he'd found a true Australian treasure.

The kettle boiled. He found his Hawthorn mug under the armchair, rinsed it out in the sink, then sniffed it suspiciously. He rinsed it one more time.

He grabbed a CD at random from the pile on the kitchen bench, put it in the player and cranked it. As he leaned back against the sink to sip his scalding coffee, the opening notes of the Hoodoo Gurus' 'What's My Scene' filled the shack and drifted down the beach to the few remaining surfers, who nodded along in time.

The music transported him back decades and he found his gaze shifting to a small framed picture on the wall. He'd played this CD over and over the night he'd celebrated the birth of a baby girl, his baby girl. His daughter.

The memory was painful. He glanced again at the picture. At the hand prints; tiny little hands. It seemed impossible a life could have been supported by something that minuscule, but he knew it had; he had seen the life force, the energy in her navy blue eyes.

He put his strong weathered hand next to the little fairy print and shook his head. Tears pricked at the back of his eyes and he exhaled loudly, puffing out his cheeks and shaking his head more vigorously.

'That was then, this is now,' Nick said out loud and steeled himself.

Life could be so cruel and take happiness away so suddenly. He had learned that a long time ago. Suddenly Jessica's face flitted in front of his eyes again.

He really needed to see her. He wanted her in his life and he needed to tell her how he felt – now that he had finally worked it out himself, he thought wryly. The idea of her moving was crazy; what was she thinking? This was her home, here with him and the people who loved and appreciated her. She needed a reason to stay; he had to let her know she had a future here.

Nick texted her: 'Brunch? I'm cooking' and started to throw some food and drinks into a recycled supermarket bag. He had a King Island brie in the fridge, but no crackers so he whipped up some toast. He was really good at toast. What else?

Was this a good idea? He suddenly second-guessed himself as the toast darkened in the grill behind him. What if she laughed at him? Or was so shocked that their friendship was wrecked forever?

Bugger! The room was filling with smoke and he had no clear idea if he was doing the right thing, but he kept preparing anyway. He took another look at the hand prints on the wall and felt resolved again.

He really needed one more time alone with Jess, one more chance to let her know. How could he have let it all fall apart so badly after New Year's Eve? He'd run off confused, horny and a bit drunk, just going for a quick walk to clear his head. But, with his mind whirring and the beach calling, he'd found himself back home. He should have gone back to the party. He should have carried the kiss through. She was probably hurt.

That was four days ago; he should have called her by now. He should have, but he'd been too scared of what might happen.

He knew now that he'd let her down by acting as if everything between them hadn't been irrevocably changed by that one charged moment.

They'd been through a lot of ups and downs in their decades of friendship. They hadn't seen each other at all for the ten years after Imogen and Nick had split. He didn't blame Jessica – after all, he'd been the one who cut her out of his life. Jess, her boyfriend, Pete, and Nick had all been good mates at school, but after he'd married Imogen she'd insisted he shun all their friends and focus just on her.

There were always mates to have a beer with at the pub on a Friday night, but he'd missed Jess, and the way she understood him.

God, she was beautiful. He decided to whip up a batch of pancakes; they were her favourite.

After he'd lost both his wife and his daughter he'd gone to ground. For a long time he was too broken and grief-stricken to be of any use to anyone. In those long years he'd just worked and surfed and tried to get his mind on track again. He'd kept his emotions locked up in a dark place that he would never let anyone access.

Then, finally, four years ago, he'd come out of the isolation and dark depression that had haunted him for a decade and the first person he'd run into was Jess, and within minutes it was as if they'd never been apart. She had just met Graham and was bubbling with new love and the thrill of her instant family. He'd been happy for her and they had fallen comfortably back into a close, supportive friendship that had sustained them both.

Of course it hadn't taken long for Nick to see what a user Graham was. It made his blood boil to see him live in Jessica's house, have her care for his kids like some kind of free au pair. He knew it was just one big use from start to finish. And he suspected Jessica did too, the way she changed the subject so abruptly every time it came up. He knew why she kept her head firmly wedged in the sand. It was those little tykes. They were just so important to her. He understood why she put up with Graham as long as she did. Kind of.

He was livid when he first found out Graham had ditched her, and then when it was apparent the boys were never coming home the furious impotence surged inside. Nick wanted to take action, do something, force Graham into shared custody, hire lawyers, rant, fight, punch. Jess was dying inside, and he missed the little guys too.

He finished cooking the pancakes and waited for them to cool. His phone tinged with an incoming SMS from Jess: 'OK. Where & when?'

'Bushman's beach, 20 mins,' he replied, noticing her text was less than enthusiastic; that was okay, he knew he had important ground to recover.

He slapped some of Jessica's own General Store jam on the pancakes, put them in an old ice-cream container, grabbed a bottle of wine, some plastic tumblers and a few apples.

Nick was more excited than he'd been for years; everything finally seemed clear. They would work it all out.

~ 26 ~

Jessica parked next to Nick's big ute and ambled down the short path to reach the isolated rocky beach. A storm was threatening; she could feel the electricity in the air. The overcast sky was oppressive, making the humid day feel all the more still and close. It was particularly stifling on the path, as very little breeze penetrated the ti-tree lined track. The scrappy bark peeling from the boughs of the melaleuca hung drooping as if it were too hot to cling to the tree any longer. Jessica smiled as she caught sight of a small possum, too hot for indoors, lying limply on the branch just near its nest's entrance, its small arms wide open, so like a human in its lethargy.

She emerged onto the foreshore with relief and the slight sea breeze cooled her flushed cheeks. The acrid stench of seaweed steaming in the heat stung her nostrils.

This part of their coastline was like another part of the world. The cliff face was red and held millennia of weather stories in its layers. Little sand softened the rugged landscape. The beach was all rock pools and inlets, too dangerous for surfing or swimming and guaranteed to be private. Jess knew it was one of Nick's favourite thinking spots.

His text had sent a shiver through her. They hadn't spoken since New Year's Eve and she was desperate to put things right between them. She wanted to get back to the way they'd always been. And she owed him a face-to-face explanation of her plan to move before he heard it on the local grapevine.

Nick was one of her closest friends and life seemed to make less sense without him. The kiss had been a mistake; a moment of passion fuelled by the sentimentality of the occasion, the music and alcohol. Hopefully they could put it all behind them, she thought, pleased with her sensible approach. But a tiny shred of something else nagged at her: maybe he wanted to meet her here for another reason; maybe he had felt what she had in that moment when their lips had met.

'For goodness sake,' she scolded herself. 'Enough with the schoolgirl fantasies already!'

The path broadened out to the sand and Jess saw that the beach was empty except for a single figure, staring out to sea, standing hunched against the wind on a flat rock.

Her heart seemed to beat faster, and she had to stop and take a deep breath. 'Nick,' she called.

'Jess, you're here!' He stood and walked towards her.

She picked her way across the uneven rocky ground. As they drew closer he smiled broadly, put his bag down and embraced her.

Her thoughts were scrambled. Were they back to normal as great friends, or was there something else between them now? She was too confused to tell so she simply gave into the warmth of his hug, holding him tight and close. Finally she mustered her composure and pulled away.

'So?' she said, pushing her sunglasses on top of her head. 'What's for lunch? I'm starving.'

He'd forgotten to bring a blanket so they sat on a small patch of sand at the base of the cliff. Protected from the wind, it was a warm, sheltered place to share the picnic.

'Oh, you've done well,' Jessica said in delight as Nick unpacked the food.

As they ate they chatted about light topics: the store, the local football team, his work on the estate. Nick poured them both a second glass of wine and they sat staring out to sea, letting their meals sit comfortably in their stomachs.

He looked over at her. She took his frank gaze. She wanted more than anything to delve into the scandalous gossip she'd heard from the women the other night at the party. But there was no way she was going to wreck such a special moment.

Nick would tell her when he was ready. It wasn't time yet. History had taught her that Nick Johnson, like a sea anemone, withdrew at lightning speed when prodded.

Nick leaned forward and brushed away the crazy curls that were fluttering in front of Jess's face. She watched his eyes and her playful smile dropped as she saw what was coming. Her heart fluttered; her stomach followed suit. Nick leaned in and kissed her fully on the mouth. Her lips opened to let him in, her arms wrapped around his neck. She lay back on the sand, bringing him with her. He couldn't touch enough of her body. His hands roamed, exploring her curves. She clasped her hands around his back, pulling him even closer.

'Oh, Jess,' he murmured into her hair. 'Don't go, please don't leave me.'

'Nick, Nick, Nick,' she said, not wanting to talk; not wanting to face the question he was asking; not wanting to think about the future. All she wanted was for the present to last forever, as it was, a perfect moment in time.

He looked at her, his eyes asking the question his lips had just begged.

'Don't, Nick,' she whispered. 'Just kiss me again.'

He moved in to oblige, murmuring softly, 'Darling, the city would eat up a little country bumpkin like you.'

She froze.

'Nick?' She said it gently. 'Do you really have that little faith in me? Don't you think I can do this?'

'It's not that, Jess. I'm sorry, I shouldn't have said it. It's just that I want you to stay here, with me.'

'What for, Nick?' She sat up and pulled her tank top straight. 'We're great friends, but that's all.'

She saw him flinch at her words.

'I can't stay here, Nick. I need to prove to you and Dad and everybody that I can go to the city, that I can take on this job. But most of all, I need to prove it to myself.'

'You have proven it – look at the General Store. You are a success. What more do you want, Jessica?'

'I don't know . . . more? How can I explain it? I just don't feel fulfilled here anymore.'

'I know what *you* want.' His words were like driving hail, cold and stinging in the heat of the afternoon. 'Jimmy McConnell.'

'How can you say that, Nick?' Jess stared at him, willing herself not to lose it and scream at him. 'Don't you understand? I need to take this chance to see where I can take my career. And I need to be close to the boys.' She stood up angrily. 'And anyway, you're not the guy I thought you were. I don't even know who you are. You've been keeping things from me.' She crossed her arms in front of her in anger.

'I've never lied to you. Never,' he told her.

'Graham never lied to me either,' she shouted. 'He just pretended to be something he wasn't, and how do I know that you're any different?' Now she was shaking with anger. 'How can I trust anyone ever again? How can I trust you when you kiss me one night and then avoid me for days afterwards? Did it mean nothing to you?'

Nick stalked towards the water's edge, where he picked up a rock and threw it into the surf. Jess stared at his clenched jaw. Clearly he had nothing to say.

Right, that was it, she thought. Enough was enough. Over before it had begun.

'I thought you would understand me better than anyone, but I guess I was wrong,' he said quietly.

She ran her fingers through her tangled locks in frustration. 'Nick, I don't think you know what you want, but I know that I can't be with someone who doesn't have faith in me.' She reached down to find her bag and put her thongs on.

'Jess, please don't go,' Nick implored, his hands outstretched towards her. 'Please stay, we can talk about it.'

'I'm done talking,' she said and walked across the rocks and up the beach path, leaving Nick alone on the beach. She was so fed up with men and their bullshit lines, their secrets and their insecurities.

Nick sat staring into the waves for more than an hour after Jess left. It was his own style of meditation; gazing at the surf until his thoughts stilled and his heart rate calmed. In his semi-trance the sound of the waves melded with the blood thrumming in his ears until he could no longer tell the two apart. He wasn't sure how he had managed to stuff up something as simple as telling Jessica how he felt.

~27~

The monthly summer country races were days for dressing up: bare feet were upgraded to thongs, the locals dusted off their *good* Akubras and their daggiest stubby holders were on parade.

The city folk roosted on the timber picnic benches in the cyclone-fenced members' area, which looked more chicken coop than privileged space, and pecked at their store-bought gourmet snacks, sipping their bubbles and sheltering from the harsh sun under their feathered hats.

In the decades Richard had been coming to the races he'd never signed up for membership. He couldn't see the point when he could relax under the enormous manna gums that peppered the car park, just metres from the bookies, the steak sandwich stall and the cold beer.

It had been Richard's idea to come down today and give Jessica a proper bon voyage from the Peninsula. He couldn't think of anywhere more fitting. He and Caro had planned it as a surprise, and now his daughter-in-law was unpacking several gourmet picnic platters from their esky. He put his hands behind his head and leaned back in his fold-up captain's chair, surveying the scene before him. Beside him Genevieve sat chatting with Tori about a designer sale in the city during the week. Several picnic blankets were spread out, a banquet spreading across each one. Songbird was fast asleep on the rug, and unaware that Taylor was using her open mouth as target practice for sultana shooting.

'Who's going to win in the next, Taylor?' Richard asked.

Without hesitation Taylor said, 'Wet star is a long way away.'

'What in the blazes does that mean?' Richard asked and grinned at the child. He'd always scoffed at the idea that the boy was psychic.

Taylor simply shrugged and ran off to find his siblings.

Richard took a quick look at the field in his race book. 'Wet star? That doesn't make any sense at all,' he muttered.

Angus sat opposite Richard, mirroring his father's body language. Richard noticed and smiled as he watched his son place his own straw panama on his head.

'Who do you like in the next, Dad?' Angus asked as he studied the form guide.

'My Little Pony has come in at the bookies. It's the favourite now.'

'Ahhh,' his son replied, scribbling down the information.

Richard noticed Nick's car pull up at the rear of the paddock. What a nice surprise for Jess, he thought.

Jessica was enjoying her last day as a local. The past week had been a blur of briefing Linda on the finer details of running the General Store, daytrips to the city to find a corporate wardrobe, packing up the clothes and books she wanted to take with her to Angus and Caro's, and trying to read as much as she could about Still Life and Mimsy Baxter so that she felt truly prepared when she started her new job.

Now there was time to enjoy the Peninsula sunshine and farewell as many of her friends as possible. Jess and Rainbow were wandering around the busy racecourse, weaving in between the many picnic blankets and camp chairs and stopping to chat with friends.

They met up with Steve from the milk bar and Sarah from the organic greengrocer's, who were sharing a barbecue of lentil burgers and T-bones.

'Hey Jess,' Steve greeted her. 'You off soon?'

'Yep, couple of days,' Jess answered. 'I'm doing the rounds today, saying goodbye.'

'Good luck.' Sarah gave her a warm hug. She stood back and wrinkled her nose as a sudden gust of wind swept across the grounds, whipping up dust. 'Oh, my goodness,' she said, 'what in the world is that smell?'

'Yeah, it's a bit ripe, isn't it?' Steve agreed. 'It's been like it for a few days now. Especially when the wind blows from the north.'

Rainbow looked around, then down into the wicker basket that hung from the crook of her arm and started scrabbling through it as Des ambled over to join the group, his thumbs stuck firmly in his jean pockets.

'Hello ladies, Steve,' he said. 'Are you talking about the pungent north winds we've been enjoying of late?' He looked pointedly at Rainbow. To the others he said, 'You do know where it's coming from, don't you?'

'Where?' Sarah asked.

'Rainbow, would you like to explain?' Des asked; a tease of a smile played on his face.

'Oh all right, I admit all.' Rainbow threw up her hands in surrender. 'It's coming from our place, it's the terra preta. Well, not the earth itself, that's fine, it's just the delivery of the fish guts and compost scraps. We just need to get it into the ground more quickly, that's all. And it's just been so hot lately . . .' she trailed off feebly.

'What? Do you mean this black gold that's going to change the environment is making the smell?' Steve asked.

'This magic stuff?' Sarah clarified. 'This magic dirt that's apparently sucking carbon back into the earth? That's what's so stinky? It's coming from your house. My God, the whole village reeks of it!'

'Jeez, Rainbow,' Jess whispered, 'where's Songbird when you need her?'

'I know, I know.' Rainbow wailed. 'I'm sooooo sorry!'

'Don't be sorry, you daft thing,' Jess said. 'What's short-term stink for long-term gain? You'll get a storage facility in place soon enough. We can't expect you to get it perfect on the first shot.'

'Yeah, absolutely,' Des said, 'it's all for a good cause. Merle's got a load of scraps from the fruit and veg section to drop off at your place later today. We're one hundred per cent behind you love.'

Sarah nodded. 'Sorry, Rainbow, I didn't know it was coming from your place.'

'Don't worry about it,' Steve said reassuringly to Rainbow. 'If anybody asks I'll just tell them it's Cat Bayard's estate and she's just had it blood 'n' boned.'

Rainbow breathed a sigh of relief. 'Oh thanks so much, guys, that's fantastic support. I really appreciate it, and I know Songbird does too.'

'You kidding?' Jessica said. 'The whole town's behind you. It will take more than a couple of strong-winded afternoons to turn us against your project.'

'It's very embarrassing that it's coming from my house, though,' Rainbow mused. 'It's like being stuck in a lift with twenty strangers after eating a bowl of lentils.'

After farewelling the group, Jess headed back to her family's spot and felt her stomach flip as she saw Nick had arrived.

Bugger, she thought. They had managed to avoid each other entirely since their picnic date a few days before. Oh well, she was going to have to face him sooner or later – she could hardly leave town without saying goodbye.

'Oh, Jess, you're back,' Tori said.

'Yep.' She tried to sound bright. 'Hi Nick,' she said and forced a smile to her face.

'Hi Jess,' Nick said. But his face was a lot softer than hers. He was obviously feeling badly about the other day.

'Here's to our Jess, best of luck with your big move,' Tori said, toasting her.

The others raised their glasses, Richard and Genevieve holding hands, Angus and Caro with hearty 'hear hears' and Rainbow and Songbird offering their best wishes. Tori looked downright miserable.

'Give us a run-down of what you think your first day will be like,' Rainbow said from her reclining position. 'Tea lady in the morning and general manager by lunchtime?'

'Oh, I'm not that sure, really,' Jessica replied.

Caro piped up brightly, 'We can ask Jimmy when he gets here.'

Nick sat bolt upright. 'Jimmy's coming?'

'Yes, of course. I thought it would be fitting: out with the old and dreary and in with the new and exciting,' Caro explained. No one missed the meaning in Caro's clumsy message. Richard shot her an angry look.

'Oh, lovely,' Genevieve said. 'I've known Jimmy McConnell for years. We worked at the same agency. He's a darling boy, very ambitious. Such charisma.'

'Well, you'd all better shush, because here he comes now,' Jess whispered nervously.

Jessica stood to greet her new boss. She smoothed down her straight, white cotton skirt and pulled her grey Tigerlily T-shirt taut over the waistline, quickly adjusting her lime citrine pendant. She didn't usually dress so plainly but she was practising her more staid city look.

'Hello Jimmy, it's nice of you to join us,' she said.

She had to admit he was damn cool. Very few men could pull off the kind of eclectic fashion that Jimmy achieved with such aplomb. His vintage bowling shirt hung over the top of a pair of loud checked shorts, while a charcoal pork pie hat pulled the two pieces together in a way that said, 'S'up.' Both wrists were bound in numerous braided leather bands. The ink that snaked from under the shirt-sleeves towards his elbow begged further examination.

Jessica expected him to give her a polite cheek-kiss, so was quite taken aback when he put both arms around her waist, picked her up, swung her around and mashed her lips with his own.

'Ahhh, now I've got you all to myself!' he purred.

Rainbow flicked her eyes nervously over at Nick and was sure she saw the blood vessels in his eyeballs popping.

'Oh, Jimmy, yes, right, hello,' Jess said, flustered, stammering through the introductions. When she came to Nick, a moment of heart-stopping anxiety made her mind go blank. He and Jimmy were shaking white-knuckle hands and looking at her as she said, 'This is Jimmy. Jimmy this is . . . um . . .' The silence was unbearable. Jimmy's grin got wider as Nick glared at his lifelong friend.

'Nick Johnson,' he snarled, then turned and stormed off to the tote.

'Friendly chap,' Jimmy said, and accepted a glass of champagne from Tori. 'Chin chin,' he said and raised his glass to the group.

The slick newcomer wasted no time in charming them all. He chatted real estate with Caro, promising he'd sell his Richmond loft apartment with her. He and Genevieve reminisced over the crazy advertising days of the nineties. Tori nearly got whiplash from trying to communicate her approval of Jimmy to Jessica through a series of elaborate winks and nudges.

Songbird and her son Taylor, never ones for quick decisions, sat together to one side, two sets of hazel eyes gently observing.

'Muuuum,' a nerve-scratching screech in the distance shattered the serenity. Tori rolled her eyes and pulled herself to her feet. 'Not again, this is the tenth time today. Coming, Priscilla! I honestly don't know what's got into them,' she said, shaking grass from her dress. 'Dustin lashes out violently at the smallest thing, and Priscilla goes to water if anyone so much as looks at her funny. It's driving me insane.'

She stalked over to remonstrate with her children and then came back shaking her head. 'Do you think it's the separation?' she asked Jess as she sat back down.

'Of course that's what it is,' Caro said, overhearing the conversation.

Tori rubbed her hand over her eyes, tiredness evident in the lines on her face.

Jessica felt for her friend. 'Have you talked about it with them?'

'Yes, I explained everything to them just a few days ago, that's when the behaviour started.' She sighed. 'We had a shopping trip yesterday. I thought it would cheer them up, but they didn't even seem interested.'

Caro snorted. 'Well of course they don't want stuff; they want their parents to love each other and be able to live together.'

'I know that,' Tori said angrily. 'I just thought an outing to the shops might distract them, that's all. I feel so guilty about all this.' She watched her children playing on the nearby playground. 'I think I'll go and treat them to some fairy floss.' She jumped up, grabbed her bag and dashed off.

The horses for the next race trotted past to take their places in the gates. The gum trees filtered the hot autumn sunshine perfectly, spilling gentle beams of warmth onto the picnicking punters as the group made their way down to the fence to watch the race. Jimmy rested his arm casually across Jessica's shoulders. She quite enjoyed the feeling of being taken under someone's wing.

The horses rounded the bend and everyone cheered as they came into the home straight, all flying hooves and gleaming horseflesh.

'Here, I got this for you,' Jimmy said and handed a ticket to Jess. It was for a horse named Gorgeous Girl. She looked up at him with a half smile to acknowledge the compliment and he winked. Suddenly a horse from the back came hurtling down the outside. The race caller picked up the momentum: 'Gorgeous Girl drops back to second, here's a surprise from dead last, coming down the outside, overtaking the field, it's the outsider Scorpio! Scorpio is first by a length, Scorpio, followed by Gorgeous Girl, then Mighty Mart . . .'

Richard looked over at Taylor, who was hanging upside down from a tree branch, and scratched his ear thoughtfully. 'A wet star . . .' he muttered to himself. 'Scorpio – an astrological water sign, of course. A long way away – well the bloody horse did come from well back to win. I wonder what that kid's doing next Cup Carnival.'

The afternoon meandered along gently – probably because Nick stayed clear of her, Jessica thought with more than a little guilt as she passed around her mini quiches. Genevieve's chicken sandwiches were well received and Tori offered her famous homemade sausage rolls (homemade by the local bakery).

Rainbow and Songbird had, of course, brought brownies for dessert but it took some time to convince everyone of their innocence.

'So, got a place to live, darl?' Songbird asked Jessica after the fifth race. 'In town?'

Caro leaned towards them eagerly. 'Yes, she's staying with me. I absolutely insist on it.'

'Well, that'll be handy,' Songbird replied, 'until you get your own joint of course.'

'No, utterly not necessary, she can stay with us forever if she likes,' Caro waved a hand in the air. 'We've got a perfectly suitable guest suite. And besides, we'll be spending so much more time down at Springforth now, she'll have the place to herself. Hopefully Angus will start to take long weekends so we can spend more time together, won't you, darling?' Caro flicked her husband on the knee.

Angus, with his face buried in a racing form, looked up distractedly. 'What's that, darling? Yes, absolutely, as soon as this next case is over.'

'So my darling sister-in-law will have that lovely Malvern home to herself all weekend, which surely beats some cramped little South Yarra rented apartment.'

Jessica wondered if it even mattered what she might want. But, she reasoned, Caro was just trying to be helpful, and besides, living with family did make sense – although she certainly intended to get her own place by the end of the year.

'You won't want to be mollycoddled for too long in the big smoke, Jessica,' Jimmy interrupted. 'You'll get yourself a trendy warehouse space in Richmond before too long and throw fabulous cocktail parties. You'll have a blast.'

Nick, after a couple of hours' absence, had returned from the tote and overheard Jimmy's comment. He glowered. 'Jessica's not really the "trendy warehouse" type, Jimmy.' He practically spat the man's name out.

'Course she is. Well maybe not today, but the city will weave its magic. You guys won't recognise her before long.' Jimmy ruffled Jess's hair playfully. 'We'll get her all citified and she'll never want to come back. In fact –' he grinned at her – 'she'll be far too good for all of you.'

'Check out the next race, Shutyeruglymug is running,' Songbird said, looking at the racebook.

Jimmy was oblivious to the dig that had Nick and Rainbow in giggles.

Jessica stood to top up the drinks. 'Well, let's just see how it goes, shall we? I'm sure I'll be comfortable wherever I am. In fact there's always Dad's place, isn't there Dad?'

'Absolutely, Princess, whenever you like,' Richard said, smiling, holding out his glass for a refill.

'You're always welcome for a visit,' Genevieve said.

'I'm off,' Jimmy suddenly said, leaping to his feet. He picked up his shades, keys and hat and bid his goodbyes to the group. 'Walk me to the car, Jess?' he said.

When they reached his convertible, Jimmy leaned inside and plucked out a bag with Kinky Gerlinki's unmistakable logo emblazoned on the side. 'This is for you,' he said with a smile.

'Oh wow! I love that shop,' Jess gasped.

'I knew you would,' he said.

Jessica removed the enormous chartreuse bow and opened the bag to find a portfolio satchel covered in a vintage fabric of 1940s Parisian women. It looked like an oversized lunch box with a chunky Bessemer handle.

'It's vintage,' he said.

'Oh, Jimmy, I can see that. It's gorgeous, I love it.' She gave him a peck on the cheek. 'It's wonderful. Just perfect.'

'I take pride in knowing exactly what a lady likes. I know

how much you love Chanel, but I thought I'd go for something different this time. It's a "welcome to the team" gift.' He leant in for another kiss, but she turned her head at the last second to ensure it remained on a professional level.

She waved the convertible off and returned to the party. She smiled fondly when she saw that Richard's hat was tipped over his face, his lean body stretched out in the captain's chair and gentle snores filling the air. Genevieve was at the car park two spaces over, chatting to some friends.

Caro stood and dragged Angus to his feet. 'Your two hippie friends are floating over there somewhere near that ragbag of people,' she told Jess, flittering her manicure towards the rear of the racecourse. 'I'm off to see if I can't get a decent decaf cap. Come, Angus, let's bond.'

Nick looked over at Jessica and smiled shyly. 'Well, this is as good a time as any, I guess,' he said and rummaged under the checkered tablecloth.

He dragged out a large timber box and, rubbing his large, labour-roughened hands over it, he collected his thoughts. 'Good luck, Jess,' he said. 'I know I haven't been your most enthusiastic backer, but I really wish you well and all the best.' He handed the gift to her with an uncertain smile. 'It's from your beach – just a memory,' he said.

She opened the lid and lifted the pink tissue that lay beneath. A collection of her favourite beach pieces lay inside: a piece of driftwood, a sea urchin – purple, the most rare – and a piece of sea glass – again in a rare purple.

'I couldn't let you go without a goodbye present,' he said looking at the ground.

'It's wonderful,' Jessica whispered. 'Thank you, Nick.' She took his hand and gripped it tightly.

'So I guess you'll be home most weekends?' he asked.

'Well,' Jessica started awkwardly. 'I don't think I'll be giving the move my best shot if I keep racing home every minute.' She saw hurt register on Nick's face. 'But you could always come and visit?' she continued hurriedly.

'Yeah, I guess.' Nick said unconvincingly. 'What about this Jimmy character, will he be a part of your new life?'

'Are you kidding?' Jess laughed a little too loudly. 'Why would you even say that?'

'Oh come on, Jess, you'd have to be thick not to see the bloke's keen on you,' Nick said roughly.

'Okay, well, you're wrong.' Jessica stood to leave. 'I have to go if I want to make the city before nightfall.'

'I'll walk you to your car,' Nick offered.

En route, Songbird and Rainbow swept her up in a monstrous group hug and made her swear to keep in touch. 'Keep it real,' Songbird said, holding Jessica's face in her two hands. 'And pretty!' Rainbow said with a pirouette.

Tori threw herself into Jess's arms. 'What will I do without you and your advice?'

'Here's a tip,' Jessica said. 'eBay: designer stuff at a fraction of the price.'

'You rock, Jessica Wainwright,' she said and gave Jess another hug, 'I can't wait to get a new computer so I can start saving!'

Jess shook her head and laughed with Nick. They continued on to the car and too quickly had reached the old Patrol. 'Well, this is it!' Nick declared and opened his arms for a bear hug. She stepped hesitantly into his embrace, then awkwardly banged her head on his chin, and pulling back, stood on his foot.

'Sorry,' she said.

'No, my fault,' Nick answered, stepping forward to open the car door for her. He noticed the other gift sitting on the passenger seat. 'What's this?'

Before she could object he was reading the gift tag. '"Can't wait to work with you every single day. Jimmy."'

Nick exploded with anger. 'This . . . this satchel is perfect for you. He knows you so well. I can't believe I thought you'd like this crappy thing . . . this box of beach junk. Shit, I'm a moron.' He walked away without looking back.

'Nick, don't go, please,' she called after him. But he kept

walking. Fine, let him act like a fool. I'm going to the city, she thought defiantly, kicking her car tyre.

She watched the angry set of his shoulders as he disappeared into the distance.

~ 28 ~

It was too good to be true. Once this council nuffer got back on the line and confirmed the final information, they were in. It would be a goer. Fantastic! On paper it looked as if it the land was Rural Farming Zone or Rural Conservation Zone, given the annoying large wetlands bordering the property, but it turned out it wasn't protected at all. The property's rear border butted against land that had recently been rezoned as residential, and now this property was included in the new zoning – albeit as a Rural Living Zone, but that would be easy to circumvent. Excellent!

Of course it would cause controversy among the neighbours, but they'd get over it eventually.

~29~

Jess checked her reflection in Caro's guest suite mirror one more time. Her new Trelise Cooper dress was an ultra-feminine, mid-calf taupe chiffon frock with black-tipped ruffles around the bust and collar. She knew the French Provincial look of the dress suited the curls that escaped her loose ponytail to frame her face. She did a spin, admiring the way the lightweight fabric floated out around her knees. Black leather cage lace-up stilettos gave a chunky anchor to the look but were a shock after several years in Blundstones and riding boots.

'Okay, world,' she said, turning away from the mirror, 'here I come.'

A wall of hot January air hit her as she stepped onto the street. A zephyr whipped leaves and litter into tiny cyclones, stinging her bare legs as she walked to the tram stop.

She planned to buy her ticket on board and had crammed her purse with gold coins to make sure she had the right change. She had checked the tram timetable and knew she had to catch the eight a.m. to Church Street, which conveniently stopped at the bottom of Caro and Angus's street.

Swinging her new portfolio with pride, she felt buoyant as she walked past groups of schoolkids with overloaded backpacks and corporate workers in their tailored urban uniforms. It felt good to be on her way to the office on a Monday morning; part of the city's busy landscape. There was something exciting about the early morning buzz of traffic and the clang of trams, the office workers gulping from cups of take-away coffee or shouting into their mobiles as they dashed along the street.

The tram arrived just as she reached the stop. Jess picked her way carefully up the wooden steps in her unfamiliar shoes. She spotted the ticket machine and stood with her finger hovering over it as she calculated the zones and times, then rummaged in her purse for the correct coins. Her ticket shot out at her and she smiled happily at her city sophistication. Then the tram jolted forward and she almost sprawled into the lap of a harried businessman, who ignored her profuse apologies, but soon she was safely seated and enjoying the view of the city from her window.

Melbourne was gorgeous, she thought as the tram trundled towards the city. She smoothly changed from the number 5 to the number 78 tram at Windsor, again congratulating herself silently.

The tram lumbered to her stop in Church Street ten minutes later and Jess climbed down the steps confidently. Woo hoo, she thought, she was early; it was only 8.30. She had plenty of time to sit and gather her thoughts, deal with her nervous bladder and grab a coffee before she was expected at Still Life.

She stepped out from the tram stop, but immediately found that her first step couldn't be followed by a second. Panic filled her. She tried to lift her left foot and realised her heel was stuck in the tram line.

Cars whipped past her on one side and another tram was just a few stops off in the distance. She wriggled her foot desperately. It was stuck fast. Jess pulled her foot out of the shoe and bent down to pull it out of its tight spot between the asphalt and metal with her hands, but it wouldn't budge. The tram was rumbling close behind her and the hot wind pulled at her curls. She grabbed the shoe again and there was a sharp snap as the heel ripped off. She stood upright, staring incredulously at the broken shoe in her hand. 'You cannot be serious,' she shouted, drawing a faint flicker of interest from two skinny men in ill-fitting polyester suits who were comparing iPhone apps as they waited for the tram.

Jess stared around her blankly, cradling the useless shoe in her hands. Her mind slowly ticked into action. A plan, she needed a plan. Her city girl smugness had evaporated in a fog of confusion.

'Okay, okay, move forward, just walk,' she said out loud, but the skinny men had lost interest; after all, there were wacky people all over the city.

She pulled off her other shoe and walked barefoot from the tram stop to the footpath. Good start, she nodded to herself. Now what? She checked her watch; it was almost 8.45. She had fifteen minutes to find a shoe shop and get to work. Easy. Surely?

The concrete was warm beneath her bare feet as she rushed down the street passing coffee shops, florists and bakeries, but not a single shoe shop. She willed the hands on her watch to slow down as they crept towards nine a.m. Damn it, she thought, stopping in a doorway, she would have to ring Still Life and apologise for her lateness. She pressed her hand over her eyes as she dialled the number.

'Still Life,' was the abrupt answer.

'Oh good morning, this is Jessica Wainwright, I'm starting a new job there this morning . . .' Silence echoed down the phone line, so Jess hurried on. 'I have a small issue, so I will be about ten minutes late. Could you please pass a message on to Mimsy Baxter for me?'

'Whatever,' a bored voice answered. The phone went dead. Jess briefly wondered if maybe a work experience student was manning the phones. Maybe she should call back and speak to Jimmy. She stood tapping her phone with her nails for a second. No, she decided, she'd sort out her footwear issue and just hope the Still Life office was flexible about start times.

She looked at her phone again, flicked to her address book and stood staring at Nick's number. He'd let her vent the morning's frustration and offer some words of support. Her finger traced his name on the screen. No. She flipped her phone closed, shoved it in her bag and stuck her chin in the air. She rushed back to the street, carefully weaving around a smashed bottle on the footpath. Suddenly she saw a Salvation Army op shop ahead, and decided to try her luck there.

The tiled floor of the shop was cool and smooth after the roughness of the concrete footpath. The clothes smelt slightly stale and musty. She hurried to the racks of shoes at the back of the store. There were tired sneakers, a pair of cracked red vinyl zip-up boots, several pairs of chunky black school shoes, strappy stilettos in a range of colours and then finally, right in the far corner of the rack, was a gift from the vintage shoe gods.

Jessica gasped with relief as she fell upon a pair of Salvatore Ferragamo sixties red suede slingbacks with pointed toes. The shoes had a large rosette and tiny kitten heels and looked as if they'd hardly been worn. 'Please, please fit,' she whispered under her breath as she bent to slip the shoes on her feet.

'Yes, oh no, yes . . . oh, well, sort of,' Jess muttered, squeezing her foot into the shoes. They were a tight fit. Her foot was too wide for the shoes' pointy toes and the slingback cut viciously into her heels, but they looked fabulous, and they weren't broken, she thought grimly, walking gingerly to the counter to pay.

The large clock on the wall behind the counter loudly ticked off the seconds, reminding Jess that she was almost fifteen minutes late.

'Hello dear, found a little bargain, have you?' the Salvation Army volunteer asked as she peered over the counter to admire Jess's shoes.

'Ah yes,' Jess tried not to stare at the clock as she handed over her money.

'I had lots of shoes like that in my day,' the lady reminisced, oblivious to Jess's impatience. 'Crippled me for life, dear. I can hardly walk for the bunions.'

'Ah . . .' was all Jess could manage. She tried to nod in sympathy, or say something relevant, but inside her head she was screaming with frustration. She finally grabbed her change and hobbled out. She made her way painfully down the street, tempted to take the cruel shoes off until she reached Still Life, but she didn't want to waste the extra seconds that would take. The straps rubbed skin from her heels, and her toes began to go numb. But then she was there.

She took a breath to ease the block of tension in her chest and calm her frantic breathing. Her feet throbbed with heat and sweat shone on her forehead. This was not how she had planned to start her first day, Jess sighed, but now she could only make the best of it.

Still Life was situated in a heritage building with huge Gothic plate-glass display windows. Jess grasped one of the large brass doorknobs and pushed her way into her new life.

The reception area was cool and hushed, the gentle trickle of an unseen water feature mingled with classical music playing softly in the background. The walls were covered in metallic, glossy silver. Beaten metal panels provided a backing for glass shelving that showcased artworks.

'Please tell me you're Jessica Wainwright,' drawled the receptionist installed behind a stainless steel desk in the centre of the room, gazing at Jess beneath hooded lids so heavily made up she could hardly lift them. 'Late on your first day. Way to make a good impression.' She stared at Jess impassively.

Jess felt sick. 'Oh, the trams . . .' she stammered, 'and then my shoe broke . . .'

'Oh, I'm sorry,' the receptionist said. 'Did I do something to indicate I actually care?' She glared at Jessica. Her heavy black fringe skimmed her eyes. She wore a sleeveless black jacket nipped in at the waist, a miniskirt, also in black, and black ankle boots.

'Er, no.'

'You're from the country, aren't you?' the girl said. 'No, wait, don't answer that, I don't care about that either.'

Jessica decided to try a fresh approach. 'Hi,' she said brightly, 'I'm Jessica.' She put out her hand.

'We've established that.' The girl ignored Jess's hand and picked up her phone. 'The new girl is here,' she droned. 'They'll see you in a minute.' She turned her attention back to her Twitter account.

Jess nodded. She wondered what she'd done to make this girl so angry. Maybe she was just having a bad day, she mused, wandering over to get a better look at the artworks displayed in the enormous picture windows. There was no denying the grace of each piece. There were works in sticks, twigs and dried flora, and more industrial pieces in barbed wire with slender copper pipe and silver galvanised wire twisted elegantly around it. The work was elegant, structural and artistically very exciting. Jess felt the adrenalin of the morning surging back. This job was going to be amazing.

She tilted her head back to stare up at an enormous chandelier that hung from ceiling. The piece was immense – six feet across at least – and seemed to be made of granite or marble; thousands of tiny pieces joined together with silver links resulting in an elegant drapery of illumination. Jess had first admired it when she'd come in for her interview.

'That is a truly amazing piece,' Jess said to the receptionist. 'Is it marble? Or white glass?'

'Styrofoam,' the girl said in a bored voice.

'No, sorry, the chandelier, I mean,' Jess said, pointing up.

'Sty-ro-foam,' the girl repeated with exaggerated enunciation. She turned her pale face towards the piece and blew. The sculpture fluttered like cherry blossom in a spring breeze. 'It's Mimsy's pride and joy,' the girl said, coming dangerously close to being civil.

'Awesome.' Jess was impressed.

A phone buzzed and the receptionist favoured her with a blank stare and flicked a finger lazily towards the stairs. 'You're on,' she drawled.

'Oh okay, thanks.'

Jessica skittered up the long thin stairwell at the rear of the foyer. She peeped into the open plan area at the top. Huge tubs of materials dotted the large space. Trestles stretched the length of the room and a team of designers was engrossed in discussing the merits of marble versus stone for a sculpture's base.

Jimmy was in a glass-walled office on the other side of the

enormous studio, leaning back in his chair as he talked on the phone. He looked over at her and smiled slowly. Jessica took the chance to drink in her surroundings.

Eventually Jimmy hung up the phone and ambled over to her. His pushed his rectangular tortoiseshell glasses onto the top of his head where they acted like a headband restraining his wayward locks. His skinny jeans clung to his muscular legs, a charcoal T-shirt from New York Design Week 2008 was worn over a white polo shirt – the sleeves of both were rolled together. A cherry bandana encircled his wrist. He squeezed her arm. 'Hi,' he said.

'Hello, Jimmy, how are you? Sorry I'm late, great place,' Jessica stammered anxiously.

'Shhh, shhh, shhh.' He raised a long finger to his pouting lips. 'It's okay. We don't want your creative energy to short circuit with angst.'

It was just what Jessica needed to hear. She took a deep breath in, let it out, then smiled back at him.

'That's better. Come and meet the team. This is La-Shea, Pandora, Jacques, Bruno, Shania, Petrice and Apsara.'

The five young women and two men flicked up their hands in a cursory greeting. They'd each coveted the position of head designer and were miffed that this inexperienced and unheard-of woman had waltzed in and stolen the job.

'They'll love you,' Jimmy whispered as they turned away. 'Now, Mimsy really wants to welcome you,' Jimmy said, steering her down the hall to Mimsy's large office.

'Mimsy, our new design head is here,' he said as he waltzed into the enormous space with Jessica in tow.

Mimsy glared over the magazine she was reading. 'Punctuality, Jessica: we thrive on it here,' Mimsy said.

'I am so sorry,' Jess began, but Mimsy silenced her with a regal wave of her unusually small hand.

'Art doesn't happen on a whim you know, my dear. It's a discipline; it's form, it's exact placement, one millimetre to the left, my darling, and the perspective is all wrong. You know this, don't you?'

'Well I guess you're right, but I'm afraid I'm not as precise as that. I go more by instinct,' Jess said, twisting her hands behind her back.

'Here you will learn to be precise and regimented in your work if you hope to succeed,' Mimsy said, waggling a stubby finger in the air. 'As you know the design team will replicate the pieces you create; their productivity relies on your inspiration; that's not something we just cross our fingers and hope will appear out of thin air. We are a well-oiled machine here: we work to a schedule and there is no place for whimsy or sloppiness.'

Jessica furrowed her brow in surprise. In her mind creativity and rigidity didn't sit well together. There was nothing in her contract for this position that suggested time-keeping was to be valued ahead of creativity. She opened her mouth to reply, but Mimsy gave her an imperious wave and she realised her time was up.

Jimmy showed her to her office, a large sparse room with blank walls. She stowed her new portfolio under the industrial steel desk, checked out the view of the city from her window and was delighted to discover there was a Saeco coffee machine installed in the corner of the room.

'How about some caffeine to get your brain firing?' Jimmy suggested, grabbing some tiny espresso cups off a shelf above the machine.

'Do I look that desperate?' Jess laughed and took a seat at her desk, relieved to surreptitiously slip her feet out of her crippling shoes.

'Not at all,' Jimmy said, as the rich aroma of coffee beans filled the room, 'But hey, you're only human, babe, and this is a sleek operation you've stepped into.'

He handed Jess a steaming short black in a dolls'-house-sized stainless-steel cup. Lattes were her coffee of choice, but what the heck, she thought, sipping the hot, bitter brew; maybe it was time to toughen up a bit.

'Right then, you're all set,' Jimmy announced, gulping down

the last of his coffee. 'I gotta get on with my day. How about you whip up a fabulous new piece by lunch, and then I'll take you somewhere awesome to eat, okay?' He gave her a mock salute as he strode out of her office.

Alone in her cavernous office Jess braved another sip of her tiny coffee and wondered how she was going to achieve 'fabulous' in the next two hours. She crammed her feet back into her painful shoes, and went back out to the design room to explore the hundreds of materials at her disposal.

She approached a waif-like girl with a pixie haircut who stood at one of the long workbenches twisting barbed wire around a reclaimed fence paling. 'Hi, it's Pandora isn't it?' Jess asked, leaning over to get a closer look at her work.

'Got it in one,' the girl responded without looking up.

'What are you working on?'

The girl put down her pliers, folded her arms and fixed Jess with a direct stare.

'Hal – that's whose job you've got –' Pandora said, 'he designed this piece for the foyer at Government House. He won an international design award for it. So now we're recreating several dozen for the sales team to pitch elsewhere.'

Jess nodded slowly.

'Hal was poached by a design company in Paris,' added Bruno, a hairy, bulky man. 'You must feel terrified to fill such big shoes.'

'Hopefully I'll bring my own touch to the company,' Jess said, fiddling with her silver bracelets.

'We'll see,' Pandora muttered.

Jess grabbed some iron pieces, copper wire and steel columns and headed for the safety of her office. This place was tough.

At one o'clock Jimmy knocked on her door. 'Let's do lunch, new girl.'

Jess gratefully put down the copper pipe she'd been wresting with and grabbed her bag. He took her to a nearby restaurant where he explained his job to her in more detail; basically he caught the big clients, schmoozed them and convinced them they couldn't live without the stunning artworks from Still Life.

'So do you consult with me to ensure the team can meet your quantity before promising the client fifty-seven lava rock candle sculptures for Cup Carnival? Jessica asked.

'Of course I do, Jess: it's a team effort. You see, I'm the key enabler yet you're on the fast-track to a super-incent, you know? As long as you keep a handle on the deliverables and recognise greater results from collaboration, then streamline efficiencies in the supply chain and reduce costs, we're all headed for a real viable growth industry.'

Jessica's fork halted halfway to her mouth as Jimmy's words tumbled forth. Dr Suess made more sense.

'Jess, your mouth is open,' he said, then grabbed a passing staff member by the arm.

'This soup is unacceptably cold,' he said and softened the complaint with a sweet smile. 'Could I possibly trouble you for another serve?' He turned his attention back to Jess. 'I think once we get your scheduling under control, you'll have no problem. You're very talented. We'll have you as Melbourne's sweetheart in no time. The world won't remember Poppy King and her lipsticks, it will be all about Jessica Wainwright.'

'Really?' Jessica said, quite seduced by the idea. She took a sip of her iced water.

It would be a battle to begin with, though. Just getting the trust and support of the design team would be hard enough, and learning to create to a schedule was going to be a real struggle. She was already behind on her first piece. It needed a good couple of hours of love before she got it right, and she knew she wasn't going to do it with the sales team breathing down her neck.

It was all giving her a thumping headache and she was only halfway into her first day.

'Hey, what's the story with the girl at the front desk?' she asked Jimmy as she nibbled the edge of her rice paper roll.

'Sventana?' He grinned. 'Just ignore her; she's been doing the ice-queen thing since she read about it in Moscow *Vogue*. It's like the heroin chic look of the nineties but with attitude instead of make-up. Great with clients though.'

Jess spent her afternoon grappling with the materials she'd chosen to make her first Still Life piece and praying for some creative magic. She tried arranging the metal pieces on top of each other, then rummaged in the materials bin for a shorter piece of copper pipe. But somehow the whole thing looked messy and unbalanced. She went back to the design room, hoping for inspiration from the materials, but no matter how many different elements she tried the piece still looked amateurish and awkward at five p.m.

Mimsy stuck her head in Jess's office door as she left for the day, took a look at the piece, sniffed and walked away.

Jess hung her head in frustration just as Jimmy came up behind her, whispered in her ear, 'I think it's wonderful sweetheart. It's only your first day: hang in there.' His warm breath on her neck sent a delicious tremor through her body. He offered to walk her to the tram stop: 'Don't want you getting lost,' he teased.

It was such a relief to finally be in the privacy of her own room that night – and doubly exciting to pull the crippling shoes off her swollen and blistered feet. But she'd made it through her first day.

~30~

. . . and furthermore, the town has the greatest potential as a newly developed retirement and tourist site, thanks to my own approved plans of an eco-village of multiple residences, which is now under threat thanks to this awful smell that now permeates the immediate vicinity.

The village can no longer tolerate the stench that is being created by this ridiculous hippie enterprise.

I urge you, Shire Council, to immediately close down this operation. The property is only zoned residential, not rural, so the residents, Songbird Patterson and Rainbow McIntosh of 38 Stumpy Gully Road, aren't supposed to be operating anything more agricultural than a vegetable patch.

I need not remind you of the loss of rates revenue should my project not proceed due to this abhorrent landfill site that is being allowed to continue to operate.

I thank you for your time and look forward to hearing from you.

Yours sincerely . . . etc, etc.

Tori had enjoyed buying the books, uniforms and shoes for the children's new school. She'd had fun choosing Tupperware lunch boxes in the new Berrylicious colour range, then selecting smart Sigg drink bottles in designer patterns, splurging on Quik-silver backpacks and finally buying each child a full selection of the bright new range of Bonds underwear. Now that they lived on the coast it was clearly de rigueur for the children to have thick, bright bands of Bonds underwear showing above their boardies during beach swimming lessons. No one could accuse her of not being a cool mum, Tori had thought smugly.

Now, sitting on her porch swing, she couldn't think of one more thing to buy them. She felt flat and bored. The children had gone off to Rainbow and Songbird's to play for the afternoon and she was alone. Tori sighed and threw down the Country Road catalogue that she'd already read comprehensively several times. She gazed over at Jess's paddock. Stupid, boring cows. They were only good for turning into shoes.

Tori checked her mobile. Still no texts. She'd sent messages off to half a dozen girlfriends, hoping for a natter with someone, but it seemed everyone was busy now that they'd all gone back to the city, leaving her behind.

She stared over at Jess's house again and wished her friend were there to share a coffee and chat. Jessica had been gone for a month and Tori missed her terribly. They'd managed a quick catch-up in the city last week during Jess's lunch break, but Tori didn't want to dampen the occasion by whining about how lonely she felt, stuck in the country on her own.

She glanced at her watch and did some quick calculations; if she jumped in the car now, she could get to the shops in Frankston in under an hour, spend an hour there and be back in time to pick up the children. There was a cute little Smiggle shop in Frankston she remembered with a happy start. The children loved Smiggle, and it was important to start the new school year with lots of bright, fun stationery items. She felt immediately revived and rushed into the house to grab her bag and keys. It was fun to have a mission.

She jumped in her car, revved the engine happily, and steered out of the driveway. Thank goodness for reasonable shops at Frankston, she thought, speeding along the local roads. It was hardly Southland, but it was certainly better than the local shopping options. Apart from the occasional little boutique dotted around the peninsula (which she'd exhausted in her first few weeks in town), there was not much shopping joy to be had.

How do people survive down here? Tori wondered once again. They must do their shopping online, she mused. How dull. She much preferred the sight of excellent store merchandising, the tangible thrill of touching, smelling and just getting the vibe of an item. It was an art form, she thought happily, plugging her iPod into the car stereo and smiling as Michael Bublé's seductive voice filled the car.

She'd always loved shopping. Her parents were just the same, she thought with an indulgent smile. They'd spoilt her rotten, and hadn't it been fun? And what an education too; she'd learned how to behave in the best restaurants, the value of natural fibres over nasty synthetics and the importance of keeping up with the latest trends and fashions.

She flicked on the air-con as she turned onto Moorooduc Highway. If only her parents had stayed together. It had all got a bit ugly after she'd turned twelve. Suddenly the arguments that had formed a backdrop to their everyday lives had reached crisis point and they'd split up. It was only the shiny new trinkets each parent bought her that made that awful time bearable.

She pushed her sunglasses on to her head and rubbed her forehead. She turned off the music and, in the quiet that followed, thoughts of her difficult adolescence flooded her mind. Her mother and father had competed to give her the biggest gifts and most exciting treats. There'd been two weeks in Paris with her mum, a trip to Disneyland with her dad and an endless stream of toys and clothes, but actually none of it really seemed to help all that much. She had just wanted to be a family again.

Now her children would have a similar life. The thought brought a wave of nausea as she remembered finding Priscilla face down on her bed that morning, shuddering as deep-throated sobs tore from her.

Tori had sighed and sat down beside her little girl and placed a soothing hand on her back. She loved this room. She had redecorated it last year to help Priscilla get over the disappoint-ment of not being selected for the aerobics team. They'd replaced the childish pink-and-white checks, white cane rocking chair and ruffled bed skirts with a Hawaiian theme. They'd draped frangi-pani lights from the window frame, found hula dolls at the huge antique barn, and had the room repainted in tropical aqua and cerise, with a mural of hibiscus down one wall. Tori was especially fond of the tropical island bed linen she'd found in the US.

'There there, darling.' She'd patted the little girl, remember-ing her as an infant and how difficult it had been to get her to sleep. 'What's the matter?'

'I . . . I . . . I . . . miss . . . Daaaaaad,' Priscilla had sobbed.

'But darling, you saw him yesterday: he came down and spent the whole day with you. You had a great time.'

Priscilla had sat up then, eyes blotchy and wet curls plastered to her flushed cheeks. 'Yes, but I want to see him all the time, not just sometimes.'

'Priscilla,' Tori had tried to reason with her, 'when he lived with us he used to work all the time during the week and play golf all weekend and you hardly ever saw him anyway. You're actually seeing him more now.'

'You don't understand!' Priscilla had screeched. 'You just don't get it!' She'd thrown herself back down onto the bed and launched into another volley of sobs.

Tori had sighed. Her back was hunched. She'd caught a glimpse of herself in the mirror and shaken her head in sad resignation. She had aged so much. Her posture was shot, her jowls sagged, her eyes were blue-bagged and her cheeks were flat and droopy.

Priscilla was wrong. Tori did understand. It wasn't about missing her dad: it was about feeling abandoned, unloved. Tori had looked at the small shoulders shaking in misery and been unable to bear the sight of her child in so much pain.

'Hey Priscilla,' she'd said gently.

'What?'

'How about you and I have a cheer-up day tomorrow, while Dustin's still on school camp? That'll fix us up.'

Priscilla had slowly sat up, wiping her face with the back of her hand. She knew all about cheer-up days. They were fantastic. She and her mother would start with a mini-makeover at a salon, then shop for new outfits. Then, looking beautiful, they would go out to lunch and finish the day by buying each other a present from their favourite gift shop, D'enfouissement. 'Okay,' she said in a little voice.

When Tori had left the room she'd felt triumphant and in control, but right now all she could think was how much her daughter's life was turning out like her own childhood.

Tori gripped the steering wheel harder and smacked her lips together and ran her tongue over them. She did it again, and again. Suddenly she realised what she was doing. It was a childhood tic, and not one she wanted to revive. She'd spent a hideous summer with a circle of dry, chapped skin around her lips when she was thirteen. She pressed her lips firmly together and clenched her teeth, making a mental note to pick up some Aveda lip gloss at the shops.

Smiggle, she thought. Smiggle was bright and fun, and the kids would be delighted with their treats when they got home. She turned her iPod on again and let Michael Bublé sweep her away.

~ 32 ~

In her first weeks at Still Life Jimmy treated Jess like a princess.

He took her out for intimate dinners, stopped by her office with coffee, sent her flirty texts after hours, praised every new creation and walked her to the tram each night.

Jess was flustered by the attention at first, but after a week or two she decided she was flattered and excited to be pursued by such a stylish guy. She started to look forward to seeing him each day and found herself dressing with him in mind; anticipating his compliments and approval.

Jess sighed as she sat behind her desk at Still Life, peeking surreptitiously at him as he chatted with the other designers.

His outfit was classic Jimmy. He wore a baggy pin-striped, gangster-style suit with a vest, mauve shirt and purple tie and black fedora. His shoes were chunky burgundy platforms. She shook her head in admiration. On any other man the clothes would look ridiculous, but on Jimmy the outfit made for sophisticated chic.

Jess turned her attention to the materials on her desk: smooth river pebbles, lengths of bamboo and bundles of wire. She tapped the bamboo against her hand. The trouble was that Jimmy seemed to have lost interest in her. All the flirting and compliments had suddenly stopped in the past week, and she wasn't sure why. Not that it mattered, she thought, putting the bamboo down and assembling the river pebbles into a pattern; she didn't know if she was interested anyway, although the flirting had been fun. He no longer accidentally brushed his hand against her when they were talking, they rarely went out to lunch or dinner on their own anymore, and he had stopped favouring her with his soulful, long-lashed stares.

It was all very confusing, she decided, gluing the pebbles into place. But right now she had other things to think about. She was worried about Tori. They'd spoken this morning on the phone and her friend had sounded tired and lonely, but Jess only had a few minutes to chat on her way to the tram so she hadn't been able to get many details. She must organise for them to have lunch again soon.

With a start, she realised Jimmy was standing in her doorway. She fumbled and dropped the rock she'd been trying to place. From the corner of her eye she could see he'd taken off his jacket and was wearing shirt-sleeve garters like a 1920s card sharp.

'Hey, babe,' he said, leaning on her door frame languidly. 'Need to remind you about the staff meeting tomorrow morning, okay?'

'No worries, all under control here. Everything's good.' She put a hand to her mouth to stop her babbling.

'Cool.' He nodded, smiled and looked at his watch, then pushed himself off the door frame and walked down the hall.

He ignored her for the rest of the day. When in the past he would have come out and listened in on her afternoon meeting with the design team, he now just continued working.

Jessica's relationship with the staff had improved dramatically. After a very productive meeting where everyone agreed, for once, Jessica farewelled the team and stayed late to finish off a piece.

She was in the tearoom when Jimmy walked in. He leaned in front of her to pick up the coffee pot. Saying nothing, he stood very close, making his coffee as if she were invisible. She held her breath. He was so damn sexy with that little tuft of beard under his bottom lip. She stood stirring her tea, willing him to stay in her space just a bit longer.

He turned around to face her. 'Is it stirred enough yet?' he asked, and he put his hand on hers to still the relentless spoon circles.

That small intimate connection reverberated like a ripple of energy that spread out through her body. She could feel every biological symptom surge spontaneously: her lips swelling, her cheeks flushing, her pupils dilating, not to mention what was happening underneath her clothing.

Jimmy took her chin between his thumb and forefinger and kissed her so softly she suddenly knew the exact meaning of the word swoon. The kiss lingered until her lips parted. When his tongue met hers blood thudded in her ears and throbbed almost painfully through her body.

Then, as abruptly as he had kissed her, he stopped and wandered off with his coffee as if nothing had happened. It took Jess a few minutes to recover the ability to walk and as she took her tea back to her office, she shook her head in confusion. What the hell was he doing?

You don't just come up to a person and sweep them off their feet then go and check your email, she thought. She should say something. No, she should give him the silent treatment back. No, she should go and confront him. No, she should . . . oh hell, who knew?

For an hour Jessica's thoughts whirled around her head; her body was on alert, charged with frustration. She'd had enough of his stupid game playing, she decided, savagely snapping wire with her pliers. There was no way she was going to sleep with a colleague anyway. She took a deep breath, pleased with her resolve, just as Jimmy reappeared at her door.

'Coming?' he asked, slipping his fedora on to his head, and looking deep into her eyes for the first time in a week.

'Yes,' she said.

Jessica leaned on her elbow and watched Jimmy fasten his baggy canvas trousers and pull a T-shirt over his head.

'Why do you always leave straightaway?' she asked. 'It's not even eleven yet.' They'd been sleeping together for a month now, but he never stayed overnight.

He shoved his hair back with one hand and flopped down on the bed next to her. 'We chat, we cuddle,' he said and looked at her closely. 'Oh, you poor sweet thing,' he said, as if he'd suddenly had an epiphany. 'Are you feeling a bit needy? Oh, that's so selfish of me.' He threw himself back on the pillow and reached an arm around her neck to draw her close. 'Let's talk.'

Trapped against his chest Jess didn't know whether to tell him to bugger off for being such a condescending bastard, or to enjoy the extra cuddle. In the end she decided to ignore the annoyance that surged inside her and just keep the peace. 'What shall we talk about?' she asked finally.

'Tell me what you're working on.'

For the past week or so she'd been thinking of using recycled tins as the base for a more-affordable art range with a high-turnover that could take Still Life's work to a broader demographic. She explained the plan to Jimmy.

'Wow, that's fabulous.' He seemed genuinely impressed.

'Really?' she said.

'Yeah, it's great, but . . .'

'What?' She was instantly disappointed.

'I don't think Mimsy's going to be too rapt, *mon petit chou*. You know how much she loves that Still Life is so exclusive. I'm worried she'll say that by introducing a lower price point with a mass appeal we'd be committing market status suicide and our top-shelf customers would ditch us. See what happened to Stella McCartney when her label went to Target?'

'Of course, you're right,' Jess said, embarrassed to have even mentioned the idea. 'I feel silly,' she said.

'Never mind,' he said squeezing her closer to him. 'Rookie mistake, could happen to anyone. Maybe you should just stick to the art, darling.'

Jess liked having the chance to share work ideas with Jimmy. The week before they'd talked for ages about a concept she'd had for an Australia-wide design contest, tapping into junior talent while simultaneously getting Mimsy into a much larger market. He was so encouraging, listening to her, prodding her to come up with the tin-tacks of each idea. It was really encouraging to brainstorm with him.

He was still aloof in the office, but Jess was accustomed to it now. She figured it was his way of avoiding gossip.

The next morning when she walked into the team meeting, she was struck once again by just how damn cool he was. He had a cotton scarf draped around his neck teamed with cargo pants and a leather bomber jacket. His black fedora worked perfectly, goodness knows how.

'Children, sit.' Mimsy stomped in, her barrel-like body launching into the high-back swivel chair at the top of the boardroom table. 'Ideas? Suggestions? Epiphanies?' she demanded.

Sventana put up her hand. 'The store needs a seat. If the husband can sit, the wife will shop longer.'

'Excellent. Go to Space; show me four photos. You know the colourway. Next?'

Sventana smiled smugly.

Jess thought it might be time to share one of her ideas and moved to raise her hand, but Jimmy cleared his throat to get her attention and frowned, so she changed her mind. She gave him a quick smile; thank goodness she had him to prevent her from making an idiot of herself.

'No?' said Mimsy. 'Good. Next: we're running an Australia-wide contest. The Still Life brand is going national, people. We're getting fresh ideas from young creative geniuses from all over the country. First prize is a job here. What do you think?'

Everyone thought they'd like to keep their own jobs, so the applause was snappy and enthusiastic.

Jessica was stunned. She looked back at Jimmy who gave her a thumbs-up signal.

After the meeting she stormed into his office. Before she had a chance to speak he put a finger to his lips and closed his door.

'You absolute legend,' he said.

'Sorry?' She was taken aback.

'I thought some more about your idea and it did have legs after all. Isn't that great? Mimsy loved it, you've done well.' He kissed her forehead.

Jess was confused. 'But does she know it was my idea?' she asked.

He arched one eyebrow at her. 'Jess, it's not about pats on the back you know, it's about the team,' he scolded.

'Yes, I know.' She felt a blush flood her face.

'Right. Off you go then and work on some more magic. Have you got anything else?'

'Yes, a few ideas,' she murmured. 'I'm working with an Aboriginal art theme at the moment.'

'Gorgeous, whip up a report and a pricing structure and email it to me, will you?'

'Shall I cc Mimsy?'

'Oh, no, that's not necessary.' Jimmy unwound his scarf and tossed it on his desk. 'She'll see it. She just loves your work, *babette*.'

Jess folded her arms and took a step back from him. 'Jimmy, I don't know. This is a bit odd. If you've presented these ideas on my behalf, I need to be involved in development and I need to get the credit.'

Jimmy smiled his best smile. 'You dear sweet thing, come here.' He stretched out his arms. She hesitated, so he moved to embrace her. 'I am so sorry if I've stuffed it up. I didn't mean to present it without you, it's just that Mimsy and I were en route to a conference and it came up. I would never steal your glory, sweetness. I am your champion.' He let his lips wander down her neck and she felt her anger dissipate. 'Tell you what, next time I'll organise a meeting and you can present, how about that? Are we still on for tonight? I want to take you somewhere fabulous.'

She nodded. He took her face in his hands, brushed the hair from her forehead and kissed her deeply. She wandered back to her office, her lips stinging with the force of the kiss.

That evening Jessica felt the heat of Sventana's customary evil stare as she left the building, but simply ignored it; she was sick of trying to make friends with the girl, whom she suspected had a crush on Jimmy. It was exhausting enough just trying to fit in with her team, trying to make the new dynamic work and hoping they weren't all bitching behind her back.

Outside, she was pleased to see that the heavy late summer rain that had drummed against the building all day had finally stopped, leaving the footpaths slick and steaming and creating psychedelic patterns of oil and water on the road. Apart from Sventana, she thought as wandered towards her tram stop, things did seem to be going well with her staff: they were polite, efficient and respectful – to her face anyway.

The job was so much more full-on than she had expected. For one thing, there was so much work – and expense – in coming up with fabulous outfits to wear every day. And Mimsy's lack of feedback about her designs was frustrating too. Sometimes she wondered whether she was doing a good job or not, but Jimmy kept assuring her that Mimsy loved her, so she just kept creating and hoped for the best.

Stepping quickly away from the edge of the footpath to avoid being sprayed with water by the passing cars, she sighed and thought of her Stumpy Gully friends. She missed the simplicity of her country life; everything just seemed so much easier there. Then she thought of Nick and the confusion between them, and of Graham and her boys, and the emptiness of the house when they'd left. Maybe life hadn't been perfect there either. She wove around the footpath to avoid puddles of water and a busker who filled the air with the mellow sounds from his saxophone. She scrabbled in the bottom of her bag for some gold coins and tossed them onto a piece of cardboard in front of him, stopping for a minute to listen to his music.

The city did have lots going for it. She loved the drama and adventure of Melbourne. From the tiny back alleys with their graffiti and late-night jazz bands, to the broad crowded thoroughfares of the Bourke Street Mall and Spencer Street, Jess enjoyed exploring the city landscapes. In her first few months she had set herself the challenge of eating somewhere new every week. She tried the Hare Krishna vegetarian food at Gopals, sat in the crowded communal dining room eating Japanese delicacies at the Chocolate Buddha in Federation Square, and travelled out to the Abbotsford Convent to be served by volunteers at Lentil as Anything.

But tonight, she decided as she breathed in the steaming air, lulled by the busker's cool notes, tonight she needed some comfort. She turned in the opposite direction and hailed a cab. She smiled as she slid into the back of the taxi. Her dad would be surprised to see her, and he'd help her sort out the confusion of the day. Her face clouded as she remembered Mimsy calling Jimmy into a last-minute meeting, which meant he'd had to cancel their date. As Mimsy was closing the door, Jess had heard her say, 'Let's talk about this Aboriginal art idea, young man.'

She didn't know what to do. Her body was leading her in one direction and her mind in another. Was she being paranoid? One thing was certain, she thought, relaxing back into the vinyl seat: her dad would help her sort things out.

~34~

Jess let herself into the penthouse. 'Hello?' she called. Genevieve walked out of the kitchen, wearing an apron and smiling broadly. A spicy aroma accompanied her.

'Hello, darling, do come in. What a lovely surprise.'

Jessica took off her damp jacket, fluffed out her hair and followed Genevieve back into the kitchen. 'Dad here?'

'No – late meeting. Sorry.'

'Never mind,' Jess said, but her throat felt tight with tears. She really needed a hug from her dad tonight, and it seemed a bit strange that Genevieve was here alone.

'I've made a green chicken curry. Would you like a bowl?' Genevieve asked, flicking off the gas and bringing a saucepan to the bench.

'Oh, yes please,' Jessica said, shaking off her sadness. 'I could do with some home cooking.'

'How is it going at work?' Genevieve asked as she served up the curry with basmati rice and roti.

Jess couldn't help herself: she blurted out a tangle of thoughts and emotions about her work and her new life.

'That's all very tricky,' Genevieve said, nodding, as they sat to eat. 'But what about Jimmy? Surely you can talk to him about it?'

'I'm worried he's stealing my ideas,' Jess murmured into her curry.

'Oh, Jess, darling, don't go all paranoid on me,' Genevieve said. 'It's a bit too spicy, isn't it?' She pointed to the meal. 'Would you like some yoghurt?'

Jess nodded as Genevieve continued.

'Look, Jess,' she said. 'I've worked with Jimmy, and he's an absolute professional. He would never do that sort of thing.' She passed the yoghurt to Jess.

'There are a few things that are hard to overlook, though,' Jessica said, staring into her glass mournfully. She related the events of the past few weeks.

'If I may say so, Jess, you are very new to the corporate world. I wouldn't go wrecking your reputation over something so small,' Genevieve warned gently. 'It's quite normal for the head of the team to present ideas on behalf of the group,' she continued.

'So you think it's all okay?' Jess asked, starting to feel embarrassed about her reaction.

'It's fair enough to be a bit sensitive, but everyone's on the same side.' Genevieve came to pat her on the arm.

Jessica traced her finger over the whorls of marble in the bench. Genevieve was right; she had overreacted.

Jessica crept into Caro and Angus's house just before ten p.m. Her sister-in-law was in the kitchen pouring a glass of wine. 'There you are. I was worried, you've never worked this late before.'

'I had dinner with Genevieve at Dad's.'

'Where was your father? Meeting, no doubt? He's as bad as his son. Well, she's making herself at home, isn't she? I bet she loves swanning around the penthouse, eating his food and drinking his wine.'

'For God's sake, Caro,' Jessica snapped. She was tired, she could feel a headache coming on and she was sick of Caro sniping at Genevieve. 'She's a nice person, and she really helped me. She listened, she didn't judge and she gave me supportive advice. That's not a crime is it? Why are you so suspicious?'

'I have every right to be suspicious. She's after more than company, mark my words. That enormous Bulgari diamond and ruby ring she's wearing would have cost more than a car. And I bet she's trying to get it on her left finger, if you know what I mean.'

During her tirade Caro poured Jessica a generous glass of merlot and made up a plate of blue cheese and crackers. She tipped a handful of red grapes onto the edge of the platter as she continued. 'It's just worrying, that's all.'

'Caro, you're being ridiculous.' Jessica stood up to take the glass. 'Genevieve was so kind to me. I've had a rotten day.'

'What happened?' Caro asked, looking up sharply. 'It's that Jimmy, isn't it? He makes my skin crawl.'

The women moved into the living room and sat facing each other on the suede couches.

'Caro, how can you say that? He is gorgeous, and so sweet. Everyone loves him; he's just unbelievable. He's creative and very interesting, and have you seen the outfits? I have honestly never seen anybody so hip, so chic – especially not a guy.'

Caro looked at Jessica and a smile crept over her face. She put her hands on her hips. 'Oh. My. God. You're doinking him.'

Jessica rolled her eyes and looked away. 'That's beside the point.'

'Yeah, right. Okay, what made your day so rotten?'

Jessica related the story for the second time that night, but remembering Genevieve's words she couldn't help but feel a little silly. 'It's probably nothing,' she finished. 'It's absolutely okay that Jimmy presented the idea on behalf of the team. Anyway, he apologised and said it wouldn't happen again.'

'What?' Caro exploded. 'But that's not fair. That's ridiculous: he's taking the credit for your work. You have to stand up for yourself.'

'Hang on, Caro, don't overreact. Genevieve reckons I should just let it go.'

'I'll bet she does. She's so manipulative. Don't forget she's mates with that Jimmy twit. Darling, you have no chance of career advancement if you let other people take credit for your work. You need to march into Mimsy's office and talk to her about it. She needs to know what a sly devil her 2IC is, and once she does she'll be grateful to you, trust me.' She leaned over and cut a chunk of cheese and wedged it between two crackers. 'He's using you. Both in the bedroom and in the office. Don't let him.'

'I don't know if I want that sort of confrontation, Caro,' Jessica replied. 'Anyway, Genevieve says it's more professional to let it go.'

Caro looked at Jessica with such silent fury Jess was worried her sister-in-law's eyes might explode. Instead of the screeched lecture Jess expected, the retort was delivered in a scary hiss.

'What is wrong with you?' Caro ran her hands through her hair. 'You are a grown woman, you ran your own business, you have always been successful, independent and fabulous. You would never have let anyone walk all over you like this in the past. Be so careful, Jessica.'

Jess kicked off her heels and swung her legs over the arm of the couch. 'You're right, I feel like a fish out of water. Completely at sea, all at sixes and sevens.'

'Come on, Jess,' Caro said and smiled as she topped up their glasses. 'You must be able to think of more clichés than that.'

Their laughter eased the tension.

'How did you get so bolshie and tough, Caro?' Jess asked. 'Nothing fazes you.'

'I got independence the hard way,' Caro explained, settling into an armchair and tucking her feet beneath her. 'It was my dream to float down an aisle in a white dress with my future family life spread out before me; I had visions of cherubic babies, picnics and roast dinners. But the reality, as you know, is shocking.'

'What do you mean?' Jess asked, but she had a fair idea what Caro meant.

'It's just so lonely, Jess, even with girlfriends, or other families to hang out with. When you have a husband as hard-working as mine you soon learn that you're on your own. That all the jobs are on your own shoulders. That you can't rely on anyone else. It would almost be easier if I were a single mother; then I wouldn't have the expectation each night that Angus might actually turn up for dinner, only to be disappointed every single evening when that phone rings at 6.30 p.m. with last-minute excuses.' She sighed and took a big gulp of wine.

'Well,' Jess said, trying to be tactful. 'It does give you all this.' Her arm swept around, indicating the high ceilings of the lofty Malvern mansion.

'Yes, it does,' Caro nodded. 'But often it's not worth it.'

'But why do you care, Caro?' Jess was confused. 'Why don't you just enjoy life as it is and have fun regardless, whether he's home or not?'

Caro turned her glass around and around while she thought about her answer. Finally she looked straight into Jess's eyes. 'Because I love him. And I miss him.' The hum of the outside traffic was the only sound that cut through the silence as each woman stared into her own wine glass. 'In fact, I've planned a little surprise for him in a few weeks' time.' Caro smiled as she thought about it, then looked up.

'But enough about me, Jess. I worry about you. You've moved to the city but you've left your fortitude back in the country. You're being pushed around in the office, blinded by Genevieve and seduced by that awful weedy Jimmy.'

Jessica sighed and looked at her sister-in-law. What she was saying was completely the opposite of Genevieve's advice. Who was right? Who should she listen to?

~35~

Jessica couldn't sleep. Her stomach churned with wine and curry and her mind flickered with questions and worries.

She wished she could talk to Nick; he'd help her sort it out. But she could hardly talk to him about her and Jimmy. Bloody Jimmy. She punched her pillow into a more comfortable shape. Why did he have to be so irresistible? Damn him.

She'd been so proud of herself for setting up this new life in the city, and making a go of it at her new job. And it was going well, it was. But she still felt like the same person inside. Still as confused and lost as she'd felt for the past year. That hadn't changed.

Kicking off the doona, she flipped over on to her back to stare at the ceiling. Somehow she'd thought she'd feel different in the city; better. But here she was, plain old Jess, with a new job, a new address and a new boyfriend, but still the same woman. What was she doing wrong, she wondered? What the hell was it that she wanted? In frustration she got up and padded into the dark ensuite to pour herself a glass of water.

She'd hoped that living closer to her boys would mean that she could see them more often, but despite dozens of calls and emails to Graham she'd only once managed to see them for half an hour, one afternoon when Samantha had called to say she was at the park with them. Jess had raced out of the office and into a taxi but the visit felt stilted and uncomfortable. The boys were distant and grumpy. 'They had a really late night,' Samantha had explained, but Jess had gone away feeling empty and hurt.

She sipped her water slowly and stared out at the sliver of

moon outside her window. She loved her job, but she didn't enjoy feeling she was being cheated by Jimmy, and no matter how much she tried to rationalise his actions she still felt used.

She flung herself back onto the bed and flicked on the television where a self-help guru was banging on about how YOU have the power to change and only YOU can find direction and steer your life. She was about to switch it off, but the hypnotic nature of the ad kept her transfixed, and instead she lay there half-listening, half-thinking. She was so convinced by the guy's message in the end that she almost bought the bloody DVD set for four easy payments of $49.95. But the message was clear enough without it: she had to stop floating aimlessly. She needed to listen to her own instincts; a skill her father had that she'd always admired.

It was time to take action, to make a plan. She drifted off into a troubled half-sleep narrated by the television voice-over, which wove into her unconscious. She dreamt she was the captain of a ship, guiding it towards an idyllic island, where her boys frolicked happily.

When she awoke, sunlight was streaming in through the window. She turned off the television and lay staring at the blank screen. She felt clear and light. She knew what she wanted.

That weekend was a flurry of activity for Jess. Her sense of purpose held strong and she viewed apartments all Saturday morning until she found one she liked. She delivered her application for a small flat in Prahran by hand to the real estate agent that afternoon, and was rewarded for her efforts by Sunday morning, when a call informed her that her application had been successful.

With a plan in place to move in during the week, she rang Graham's new wife, Karen. Graham was interstate and the boys' stepmother was such a mousy little pushover that Jess soon had an afternoon with her children organised. Things were looking up.

36

'Cheers!' Three glasses clinked. 'Here's to us,' Songbird said and raised her glass to the back paddock and to the future of the planet.

'Cheers,' Rainbow said, and Nick joined in. The night was still. Nick looked up at the treetops where not a breath of wind shifted the tallest leaves. The three of them were wrapped warmly in coats and hats in anticipation of a frosty night.

'I can't believe we might actually have an investor,' Songbird said. 'We're going to be able to expand, bring in loads of compost and manure and really go to town on this thing.'

'Aren't you going to tell me who it is?' Nick asked.

'Nah, sorry, Nick. It's all hush-hush. This company wants complete confidentiality: they're terrified that word will get out before the deal is done.'

'They probably think that another company will come and pay you double,' Nick said.

'No, the coin this investor's spending is phenomenal. And they're supplying land, too, so we can do it on an enormous scale. We'll be able to power the whole village in a couple of years.'

'I can't believe it,' said Nick. 'It actually works; it actually makes power?'

'You'd better believe it, buddy boy,' Songbird said.

'How? It still doesn't make sense to me.'

'Well we've developed further from that pit in the ground you saw last time.' Songbird leaned forward and rubbed the chill from her fingers, then glanced up as a nearby wombat shuffled into his hole.

'We now make the terra preta in that construction that we were looking at earlier.'

'Your bio-char lab?' Nick asked indicating the fridge-sized metal container sitting atop the terra preta pit. 'I remember you telling me all about it in great detail last month but I hadn't imagined it would look quite like that. So it all breaks down in there, does it?'

'Yep, and as the manure, the mould and the carcasses do their decomposing work and the timber turns into charcoal, the gas that is released is collected and fed into the fuel cell, which produces electricity.'

Rainbow pointed overhead to a paper Chinese lantern holding a single light globe. 'Isn't it gorgeous? It's our own homemade electricity. It's so exciting. I feel a bit like God, you know. I reckon She'd be proud of us.'

'How do you keep the power coming as a constant, you know, so it doesn't drop out?'

'We're working on that now, actually,' Songbird explained to Nick. 'We've devised a series of six pits. They work in annual cycles, with the seasons. Our first pit is at power-making stage. It will run out of the vapour that is the by-product of the process after two to three months. We have a second pit all ready to go, full of seaweed, manure, cuttings, clippings and compost, and we fired it yesterday. It has a week before it settles into a lovely, organic, living, breathing beast. Then we shift the lab onto that second pit. But our fuel cells will be fully charged at that point so there is no interruption to the power supply. And then the first pit will be ready for seedlings. It is the most outstanding soil you could ever imagine. Black as tar, soft and rich. Seeds grow into plants overnight. The fruit will grow to enormous proportions.'

'You'll do well at this year's agricultural show,' Nick said as he stamped his feet to stop his toes going numb.

'Yeah, I'll say – we'll be accused of giving them steroids,' Songbird laughed and went on. 'Basically each pit will be at a different stage of development. One: freshly filled with rubbish, poo, and seafood and about to fire; two: producing power; then three: seedlings; and four: growing; five and six: mature plants and harvest. It all depends on the season. The four green pits will be growing each season's plants. The summer pit, for example, will be fruiting strawberries, tomatoes, beans and whatever else fruits in summer, and then in winter it will become the pit making the power as that pit doesn't grow winter fruit and veg.'

'It really is a remarkable system,' Nick said, and took a sip of his elderberry wine. 'And it's wonderful that it's finally up and running after all our hard work over the last few months.'

'It's amazing how little space it takes up, too,' Rainbow said. 'You can do it on less than a quarter acre, really. Obviously the larger the pits and the bio-char lab the greater the power, but we're already running one light globe and our fridge off the small test operation.'

'It's so incredible,' Nick said. 'I'm honoured to have been along for the ride.'

'It is pretty amazing. But the thing is, Nick, there's still a lot of construction involved if we want to seal the deal with this investor and we're going to need your help.'

'I'm here for you right now, girls: you can count on me at the moment. But I am thinking of going walkabout for a while. I'm just feeling a little bit . . . I don't know.'

Rainbow's blue eyes melted in concern. 'Awww, Nick, you miss her. You're such a sweet thing.' She patted him on the back of the hand.

Songbird leaned back in her chair with her workboot-clad feet stretched out and her arms folded. 'He is a stupid, dozy bugger. That's what he is.'

Both Rainbow and Nick looked up at her. 'Excuse me?' Nick said.

'What did you bloody let her go for? Rainbow misses her, Tori mopes around here like a misery-guts, the girls in the store miss her. You could have stopped her and you didn't.'

'I get to speak to her a couple of times a week when she rings,' Rainbow protested. 'We have a good old natter.'

'You miss her!' her mate said forcefully. 'I can tell: you're all mushy. It shits me.'

'You miss her too,' Rainbow accused.

'Yeah, yeah, all right. I miss the stupid cow too.'

Nick sat listening to the exchange before he stood up for himself. 'Songbird, it's not as easy as that. I couldn't have stopped her. First of all, she had to go and do this, she had to prove that she was good enough with her art to earn a real living out of it. I think it's very important to her professionally. She needed it. And if I had stood in her way, she would always have resented me. She would forever have wondered what might have been. And I don't want to be that guy.' He swirled his wine around his glass, then looked up at the women. 'And anyway, Songbird, what makes you so sure she would have said yes? She's not interested in me; she's interested in that dickhead in town.'

Songbird snorted with derision.

Taylor appeared before them in his pyjamas, shivering in the cold night air. 'She'll be back by the end of the month,' he said, then shook himself off after relieving himself on the lemon tree, and went back inside.

37

'Home again, home again, jig-a-jig jig,' Jess sang loudly to herself as she drove into Stumpy Gully. It was a song she and the boys had sung whenever they came home, and tonight that's just what she was doing. She felt light and giddy with excitement to be coming back after five long months. There was the old church with the op shop attached, and the playground where she used to take the boys. There was the town hall, which looked as if it had had a facelift.

The weatherboard houses shaded by rows of eucalypts seemed to beam their welcome to Jess as she drove past on her way to the pub to see one of her favourite bands.

Linda, Jessica's maître d' from the General Store, had called her that afternoon in a frenzy.

'Cousin Leonard's back from their European tour!' she'd squealed down the phone. 'And guess what? Songbird was in this afternoon and she heard from Les the hairdresser who cut Wayne the publican's hair this morning, that they're making a surprise guest appearance at the Stumpy Gully Hotel tonight!'

Jessica had spent her teen years dancing to Cousin Leonard in the town hall. But now that the band was constantly touring and enjoying international success, it was rare for them to come home and there was no way Jess was going to miss out on seeing them.

The pub was rocking when she walked in. Obviously the secret was out. Three-quarters of the town's population was there. As she squeezed through the crowd, the band's first song came to an end, and suddenly Jess found a spotlight shone on her. She blinked in the bright light.

'The prodigal daughter returns! Welcome home, Jessica. You back for good, darlin' girl?' the band's front man Marty asked as the crowd cheered.

Jessica, both chuffed and a bit shy to be singled out, called back good-naturedly, 'No, just visiting, Marty.'

Marty led the chorus of a disappointed 'Awwwww!' from the room.

Jess laughed and made her way to a group of townies in the corner.

'Here she is,' Fi called out. 'Our city girl, down for a weekend.'

'Just like us,' Cat said. Jessica shuddered. She looked at the group in their well-fitting denims and padded pastel quilted jackets, designer sunnies perched on their head. Each one looked like a clone of the next. God she hoped she wasn't just like them.

Tori smiled and gave her friend a hug. 'How is it going? You'll excuse me for saying, darling, but you look absolutely shattered. I hope you're not overdoing it.'

'Oh, it has been a busy week.' Jess accepted the hug gratefully. 'Quite a bit on. More importantly, how are you?'

'Not bad, honestly. Just trying to keep it all together.'

'Good on you, Tori, I'm proud of you,' Jessica said seriously.

She briefly considered asking Tori's advice about Jimmy, but decided she couldn't stand one more opinion on the matter. Besides, it was her ship, after all.

Jessica sat down and smiled her thanks as Tori poured her a glass of sauvignon blanc. She looked around fondly at the beautiful Stumpy Gully Hotel with its Victorian terrace lacework, heritage colours and etched windowpanes. This had been Jess's favourite pub ever since she and Nick had tried to sneak in under-age.

The band took a break just as Jess noticed Nick walk in. The flood of sheer pleasure washing through her body startled her. She wanted to run across the room and throw herself into his arms, but instead she took the conservative approach and stood as he made his way through the throng of rowdy locals to her table.

She was about to put out her arms to embrace him when he gave her a thin smile and said flatly, 'Hello, stranger.'

'Hello yourself,' she replied, relieved she'd opted for the more sedate greeting.

Nick looked around the crowded pub, searching for a spare table.

'Let's go outside, down to the lawn,' Jessica pointed and followed him after excusing herself from her friends.

It was freezing. She was glad she'd brought her puffy coat. Their breath billowed like clouds of steam as they walked onto the grass to sit at the old timber table. Jessica was suddenly struck by the sea and sky before them.

'Wow,' she said. 'I've been coming to this pub for nearly twenty years and I've never seen it like this. It's remarkable.' The stars were so plentiful it was as if the sky had been sprinkled with glitter, the air was crisp and clean and the salt tanged in the back of her throat. 'It's so beautiful here,' Jessica said under her breath. 'I'd forgotten.'

Nick sat down at the table. 'Yeah, it's amazing how you don't know what you've got until it's gone.'

She looked at him. 'You're right.' She looked back to the view, aware his eyes were still on her.

He raised one eyebrow and looked at her. 'So, Red, how have you been?' he asked eventually, just as she was starting to squirm under his frank gaze. 'I haven't heard from you.'

'I've been good, Nick. I've seen the boys a couple of times: they're getting so big. How are you?'

'Busy,' Nick said. 'Your dad's really cracking the whip. And Caro's been down heaps lately; she says she wants to give you your own space.'

'Yeah, well, she needn't bother, I moved out of her place last week.'

'On your own? How does that feel?' Nick asked, gouging his nail into the tired timber.

'It's good,' Jess told him.

'Are you safe though?' he asked.

Jess laughed and punched his arm. 'A – I'm not a teenager, B – this isn't Victorian times, and C – what's it to you anyway?'

'I just care about you,' Nick said.

The flutter in Jessica's stomach was undeniable. She looked up at him, feeling a slight flush in her cheeks. 'Do you?' she asked.

'Yeah,' Nick said and sipped his beer. 'Like a big brother, you know.'

'Of course,' Jessica said, embarrassed.

They sat in silence, nursing their drinks and watching the seagulls torment a young couple eating fish and chips at a fore-shore picnic table.

'Nick?' Jessica asked, folding her arms protectively around herself.

'Hmmmm?' Nick said absently, his eyes on the band inside as they picked up their instruments to start the next set.

'Tell me about Imogen,' Jessica said. Even though Nick's eyes were fixed on the lead singer tuning his guitar, and his face remained impassive, Jessica could tell she'd struck a raw nerve.

'Why?' Nick asked.

'What happened? I'm just curious.'

'You know the story,' Nick said, turning his steady gaze onto her face.

'Nick, there's more than just a story,' Jess said, leaning towards him. 'Of course I've heard the local gossip but I wanted to hear it from you. We've never actually talked about it.'

Nick stopped tapping his foot distractedly and sighed. Jessica knew she'd won.

'Look, you remember what a difficult time that was for us.'

'How could I know that, Nick? I never saw you. If you remember, Imogen wasn't my biggest fan. And she couldn't stand my boyfriend either.'

'No, you're right about that. God, you and Pete went out for years,' Nick said.

'And now he's happily working in the mines in Port Hedland, but that's not what I want to talk about.' Jess finished her last mouthful of wine and put the glass firmly on the table.

He sighed again, dragged a beanie out of his pocket and pulled it over his head. 'Well, she didn't really hang around with everyone here at the pub,' he said, rubbing his hands together in the cold air. 'And I admired that in her, in the beginning. Coming from Melbourne to go to high school in this hick down; she always acted a little superior. I guess that's what I fell for: her city sophistication, or some crap.' Nick downed his beer and stared out to the black waters beyond the ti-tree foreshore.

'We got married too quickly, straight out of school, but I wanted to do the right thing; she was pregnant, and well, I was pretty obsessed with her anyway. And when she said yes, I can't tell you how that made me feel. To be accepted by the beautiful ice queen? I felt like a superhero.' He pushed his hands into his pockets.

'And then after the wedding?' Jessica asked.

'That's when things went bad. She blamed me for every thing – being pregnant, stuck in a tiny fibro shack in a two-horse town. Her family told her she'd made her bed, so she could lie in it – that sort of thing. I was working my guts out, but nothing made her happy. Then little Matilda came along . . . Oh, Jess, I loved her so much.' His voice cracked. He reached to the napkin holder and pulled out a wad of paper.

Jessica took his hand in hers. 'It's okay Nick, take your time,' she said quietly.

He cleared his voice roughly and continued. 'That's when things got seriously out of control. She was such a bitch during the pregnancy and after the baby came she got post-natal depression but neither of us knew it then. It was bloody awful. She actively hated me and barely tolerated Matilda. I overheard her on the phone one day saying she'd never wanted to be a mother anyway.' He wiped his eyes. 'Obviously she was sick, but I didn't have a clue. And she treated me like shit, though that was pretty normal for her.'

Jess squeezed his hand. 'Did you try talking to her? Or counselling?'

'Of course I did,' he said. 'She'd just scream at me that she deserved better than this "shithole". She was chain-smoking by then. She always had a fag in her hand. I am sure she smoked in the house when I was out – the place reeked.'

'It must have been a nightmare.' Jess shifted closer to him.

'I didn't know what to do, Jess.' He looked her straight in the eye, the pain still raw in his face. 'Imogen refused to breastfeed so although most days were hell, I had these incredible moments with Matilda, holding her tiny body and feeding her. I was totally in love.' His eyes shone with the memory.

'I'd sit there in the early hours of the morning and just gaze at her little face. It was magic, Jess.' He sat up straighter, charged with emotion. 'It was the most magnificent time of my life. Sure, I was dog-tired, my wife hated me and I was working constantly to support us all, but I feel so lucky I had those moments.'

For the first time it occurred to Jess that she and Nick had experienced a similar loss. She hadn't thought of it that way before, but she now understood why Nick had been so empathetic when she lost her boys.

His voice dropped. 'It wasn't like that for long. Matilda only lived four weeks, Jess. I remember waking with a fright because it was seven a.m. and she hadn't woken up for her four a.m. feed.' He took a slow breath and blew it out like white fog in the cold air. 'I ran to her room and Imogen was standing there like a ghost. Her skin was practically transparent. White, with blue veins in her forehead and temple; I'll never forget it. Her eyes just stared at me. They looked like glass. Grey glass. Tears were running down her face and dripping onto the baby.' His voice faltered, and Jess put an arm around his back.

'Matilda looked like she was asleep, but –' His voice caught and he swallowed hard before continuing. 'But I could tell right away that she wasn't, you know, *there* any more.' He hung his head and his shoulders heaved with pain.

'Oh, Nick,' Jess whispered, grabbing a napkin to mop up her own tears.

He looked up into the trees as an owl hooted softly, then he continued with his story. 'Imogen didn't speak, she just lay Matilda on the mattress, and walked out. She didn't come back the whole day. I was in shock; I didn't know what to do.' The owl hooted again and Nick turned to watch it launch off a nearby branch and beat silently through the still air.

He turned back to her and went on. 'Eventually I rang the doctor, and he came and sorted everything out. By the time Imogen returned it was all over.' He wiped the back of his hand over his face. 'I found out later she'd been seen in the town fifteen kilometres away. She was still in her nightie with bare feet. She must have just snapped, Jess, to walk all that way and back.'

'I had no idea,' Jessica said quietly.

'I barely remember the funeral. I do remember Imogen was whacked out on sedatives. We drifted through the next few months in a daze.' Nick screwed the napkins in a tight ball in his hand.

'It must have been dreadful,' Jessica said. 'And then you finally broke up?'

Nick stared at Jess as if he was deciding something. He pursed his lips and ran his fingers through his scruffy hair. 'One night I came home late. Imogen was obviously drunk. She had out a box of my stuff that I kept locked in a trunk under the bed. She had broken the lock and had all my things spread out all over the kitchen table. She went absolutely nuts, Jess. She swore at me, screamed at me, tore strips off me. At least she was communicating for once.' He gave a bitter laugh. 'Then she called me a fucking bastard, stormed out of the house and that was pretty much the last I saw of her.'

Cousin Leonard struck up the crowd-pleaser 'Oh My Goodness' to a riot of applause and wolf whistles.

'Nick, I'm so, so sorry. What was it? What did she find that upset her so much?'

'You know what, Jess? I think story time is over. I have to go. I've got an early start.' He stood, picked up his jacket and turned to go.

'Nick, I have to know.' Jess stood and grabbed him by the arm. 'What did she find?'

Nick looked at Jess and shook his head. 'Okay, fine. You want to know?' he said hoarsely. 'I'll tell you. It was love letters, Jess. She'd found all the love letters I'd been writing for the previous two years. And they weren't addressed to her. So I guess I'm not the innocent victim I made myself out to be, after all.' With that, he turned and left, walking back into the pub, pushing his way forcefully through the crowd.

Jessica stared after him. Hidden love letters. Then it was true – Nick had been having an affair.

~ 38 ~

The display home was at the lower end of the range. Well, to be honest, it was at the bottom end. But that wasn't going to make a zack of difference, as it could potentially cost a further twenty per cent less: there were savings to be made everywhere. The garage could be shorter. The deck could be made of a recon timber instead of merbau. One coat of paint was more than enough to make a sale. And who needed all those power points anyway? Overkill. It did seem wasteful, too, to have insulation in the ceiling when no one would see whether it was there or not. There was a cheaper alternative to timber for the frame being manufactured in Taiwan. Costs could be cut everywhere. Suddenly the potential forty per cent profit on each residence just went up to fifty.

Jess stood back to assess her work. Mimsy had been thrilled with the idea of low-cost artworks with a high creative element that would extend her brand out into the Melbourne suburbs. The trouble was that Mimsy thought it was Jimmy, not Jess, who had come up with the concept.

Jess stabbed at the sculpture with her pliers. She was such an idiot for not speaking up, but she hadn't wanted to come across as whining and pathetic. Now, as she assembled another 'Trois Boucles' – three anodised metal rings of varying sizes, connected with a pivot ring between each, hung from a metal chain – she wanted to shout with frustration.

It was a fabulous idea, and people from Prahran, Richmond and Glen Iris were rushing in to buy them at under a hundred bucks a pop from Mimsy Baxter's Still Life, and Jimmy was enjoying all the credit. He still assured her he had presented the plan as a 'team idea' but Jess wasn't so sure. She really needed to break up with him, she thought for the twentieth time that day, as she selected three more metal rings for the next piece.

The trouble was he was quite lovely. Sometimes. And it wasn't as if there were men lining up to take her out to dinner; it was convenient to have him in her back pocket. At least he wasn't cheating on her in the bedroom, the way Nick had treated Imogen. She quickly shooed the unpleasant thoughts away.

Jessica arranged the rings in order and searched for a different type of chain to hang them on. She wanted to try a twist on the standard 'Trois Boucles' to keep the range fresh and interesting.

There was no way she'd be sharing this idea – or any others – with Jimmy, she thought. He might be great in bed, but she wouldn't be silly enough to engage in work-related pillow talk again.

She was twisting the chain in different directions, frustrated by its lack of cooperation, when Jimmy came up and slid his arm around her waist. 'Let's get it on tonight, hey?' he whispered. 'I've been thinking about you all day.'

Despite her best intentions, she smiled, but his words didn't set off their usual barrage of physical reactions in her. Instead she felt quite in control, and in the mood for a little game-playing of her own.

'Sure,' she answered, slipping out of his grasp. 'I'll see you then.'

That night Jessica sat staring out of the window of her flat into the darkness, her mind calm and decided. She stood as his knock echoed on the door.

'Hello, my lovely angel,' Jimmy said as he came in. He placed one arm around the small of her back and the other around her head as he expertly dipped her and gave her a gentle nibble on the neck. He pulled her up again and went to the fridge, where he knew his favourite Asahi beer was waiting.

They sat on the couch together and she found herself feeling mischievously excited.

'I've got exciting news,' he said, rubbing her upper thigh. 'Mimsy's going with your Aboriginal art idea. She loves it. We're flying guest artists in to start creating next week. She's so impressed with you.'

'That's funny, she hasn't said anything to me.'

'Oh you know what she's like, she's so hopeless at compliments. But take it from me, she thinks you're a legend.' He took a long swig of his beer.

'That's good,' she said, picking at a stray thread in her top.

'Here, let me rub your neck, sweetheart. Turn around.' He

massaged her neck for a minute, then stopped and tugged her shoulder so she would turn back to him. 'So, anything exciting happening at work?'

'Well,' she said, pretending to be thoughtful. 'I've had a tremendous idea to elaborate on an existing piece, to give Still Life a fresh new face for the public.'

'Really, angel? You are so clever, my darling.' He leaned in and gave her a light kiss on the lips. For once it didn't turn her on. Well, not very much, anyway. She got up and stuck her iPod in the dock on random selection. The upbeat sounds of 'Beautiful Place' by Good Charlotte filled the room. She inwardly grinned: it made her think of Stumpy Gully. God she missed home.

'Go on, go on, what is this brilliant idea of yours?' He reached forward to get his beer.

'Okay, it's pretty out there, pretty wild, but it would be so amazing, a real artistic statement.' She widened her eyes and watched him sit up straighter with interest. 'You know how the white chandelier in the foyer is the Still Life signature piece? It dominates the entire area above the shop floor.'

'Yes, it's wonderful, it catches everyone's eye. It's Mimsy's favourite thing, next to her red sculpture, of course.'

Jess nodded. 'Well, it's been there for fifteen years, so, although it's still beautiful, it's no longer fresh. And we can't get rid of it because it's the Still Life icon, but it needs a makeover: something to give it a lift, a new life.'

'I'm listening,' he said, tapping his hands against his knees in anticipation.

'I propose that we spray the entire piece with a commercial spray adhesive. The glue will make it heavy and weigh the foam down. Then we turn on a dozen small household fans and blow large petals of fluoro-coloured silk at the piece. The chandelier will double in volume and the silk will quiver in the breeze and look amazing; like some kind of eighties Cyndi Lauper disco. Most importantly, it will bring the look of the shop into this decade, which it desperately needs. The recession is over, the future is bright and so is the next colourway. Neutrals are finished.'

She sat back to see if he'd taken the bait. He was looking at her, mulling the idea over, nodding gently. The nodding increased, then a smile reached his lips. 'Angel, you're an absolute genius. I love it.'

He picked up her hand and started nibbling her wrist, then her forearm, and then he moved up to her shoulder while gazing into her eyes. It did feel very nice, but she knew that this was his prelude to foreplay and ultimately sex and she had to stop now.

'Jimmy . . .' she started.

'Shh, you know I can't talk when I'm lovemaking,' he murmured as his nibbles reached her ear. She put her hand up to his mouth and forced him to sit back and look at her.

'Jimmy, we need to talk.'

'What about, darling?' He cocked his head on the side and assumed his patient listening face.

'I don't think this is working out. I think we should stop seeing each other.' She watched him carefully.

'Really?' he said, wrinkling his brow briefly. 'That's a shame. Well, if that's what you want. As long as we're still friends at work, and can enjoy our little chats, then that's the most important thing. Right then.' He swallowed the last of his beer. 'I guess I'll be off.' He chucked her on the chin and rose to retrieve his boots.

That was easy, Jess thought with surprise.

Just then the phone rang. She glanced in the bedroom. Jimmy was doing up the buckles on his boots and would be gone in a few seconds. She'd better answer.

'Hello?' She glanced at the kitchen clock. Midnight. Who was calling at midnight?

'Jess, it's me,' the voice said thickly.

'Hello, you.' She smiled. Nick had obviously been at the Stumpy Gully Hotel.

'I need to tell you something, Jess. It's really important. I need to talk to you.'

Jessica didn't want to have this kind of conversation while Jimmy was in her flat.

'Can it wait, Nick? Just give me fifteen seconds and I can call you back.'

'No, Jessica, it can't wait another second. It's already been too long. It's already eighteen years overdue. I'll be really quick.'

Before Jessica had a chance to put him off he started spilling his feelings down the phone line. 'Jessica, I wasn't entirely honest with you the other day –'

'Nick, wait –'

'Can't wait, Jess. Just let me finish . . . please . . . it's important. You asked me to tell you the story, which I did, but I didn't tell you the entire story. You know those love letters I told you about? Well there were hundreds of them, all of them from me pouring my heart out about how I felt. About my love, my passion, my fantasies, Jess. But Jess, why did I still have them in my trunk? Did you think about that, Jess? Why did I still have them? Why hadn't I sent them?'

As Jimmy entered the living area, she urgently put her finger up to her lips. Jimmy smiled at her and made a big pantomime of tiptoeing to the front door.

Meanwhile, Nick's drunken ramblings were continuing on the other end of the phone. 'You know why? Jess? Do you know why? Obviously because I never sent them, Jess? And why Jess? Why didn't I send them?'

Jessica held tight to the mouthpiece. 'Why?' she whispered.

'Because the person I was having the affair with, the person I was so in love with, never knew. She never got the letters so she never knew. I wasn't having a physical affair, Jess. I'd never betray my baby and my wife, but I had to talk to someone. And that was the someone I had always been in love with. You know who, don't you, Jess? It's you, Red. You're the one I wrote the letters to, you're the one I was having the affair with . . . and you never even knew.'

At that moment Jimmy called out from the open front door in an intentionally loud voice. 'Bye, Jessica! Thanks so much, darling, you were great!' He slammed the door behind him.

There was about twenty seconds silence. Jessica finally whimpered. 'Nick?'

His icy voice returned. 'Was that . . . Jimmy?'

'Please Nick, it's not what you think. It's not what it seems.'

The burr of the disconnected line was the only response.

~ 40 ~

Well, it was official: today was her worst city day ever, Jess decided as she watched a deep pool of soy sauce soak into the fabric of her brand-new shift dress.

It wasn't even that she liked the dress, she thought, throwing down her sushi lunch and rushing to mop up the stain in the office kitchen, but there were clients coming in that afternoon. She sighed and tied on her work apron to hide the disaster.

The whole day had been a mess. This was the second spill she'd had; this morning she'd sent her coffee cup flying at their team meeting, soaking her notes and earning her scowls of disdain from the designers.

And just to clearly illustrate the sort of day she was in for, the evil Sventana had stuck out one anorexic ankle as Jess had passed her desk earlier and tripped her up. Was the woman insane?

Then Mimsy had been brutal about her work. 'It's completely unbalanced,' she'd drawled. 'What are you thinking, Jessica?'

It annoyed Jess the way Mimsy, with her slightly Japanese accent, pronounced her name 'Jess-eee-ca'. In fact, the more she worked with Mimsy the more her affectations got up her nose. It was one thing to be a successful businesswoman, but would it kill her to say hello in the morning?

It was all too much, and beyond her care anyway. Her mind was consumed with thoughts of Nick.

She was relieved when it was finally time to go home. She arrived at her new Prahran flat with her arms laden with goodies. Tori was coming to stay the night and she wanted to spoil them both with a fancy home-cooked dinner.

She whizzed around the room clearing magazines, picking up towels and making the place respectable. She'd fallen in love with the funky 1970s look of the building. Random glossy brightly coloured bricks dotted the exterior wall, a large screen of hollow cinder blocks flanked the front entrance and the letterboxes were in seventies turquoise with angular white lids.

She'd carried the look into the interior, using acid orange as her base and adding a modular couch, tie-dyed cushions and a chocolate-brown shag pile rug that brought the whole look together. She had enjoyed collecting the bits and pieces to furnish her flat, wandering happily down the backstreets of inner-city Melbourne, stumbling across eclectic vintage stores.

The doorbell rang, Jessica opened it and gave Tori a warm hug. 'Come in and sit down, love,' she said.

Tori threw her Chanel bag onto the couch and sat down on the mission-brown cushions. Jess passed her a gin and tonic and placed a platter of club sandwiches on the tinted glass coffee table in front of them.

'So, how's life?' Jess asked.

'Oh, it's pretty bad, Jess. I've been going over and over things all the way here.'

Jess patted Tori's hand. 'The divorce?' she asked.

'Well, it's more than that, actually,' Tori admitted. 'It's money too. I just want to buy more and more things all the time, and well . . . I think it might be a bit of a problem.' Her eyes filled with tears. 'I used to buy stuff when I felt flat or down – I mean we all do, don't we? Indulge in a little retail pick-me-up?' She twisted her hands together and turned her head away from Jess.

In a whisper, she said, 'But I think it might be getting just a tad out of hand.' Her fingers flew to her throat. 'Promise me you won't ever breathe a word of this to anyone,' she implored, her eyes dark with fear.

Jess moved to sit beside her friend on the couch. 'It's okay, Tori, you know you can trust me.'

Tori nodded and closed her eyes as she continued. 'I bought a two-thousand-dollar pair of shoes the day before Joseph and I split up. That's what finished us: a stupid pair of shoes.'

'But why, Tori? Why do it when it's destroying your life?'

'It's difficult to explain. I just don't feel any joy anymore. Christmas is hard work, my birthday is tedious and unwanted, going out is dreary, scenic walks are boring. And that's not like me. I used to have such passion for life, but ever since I became a parent, everything's become so grey, so dull, so lacking in joy. Where's the joy gone, Jess?' She looked sadly at her friend, twisting her scarf in her hands.

'I think I know what you mean,' Jessica murmured. 'Go on.'

'But when I shop, it's just so fun, Jess. More than fun for me, though, it's like . . . a drug, like a high. And it can be anything, really it's ridiculous. I could be at the doctor's office for a Pap smear and if they're selling something at the counter for charity – a red nose, a pink ribbon, a daffodil – I'll buy one of each. And love it. I love getting stuff.' Her voice was high and brittle.

Tori took a deep swallow of her drink and continued. 'When the kids came along there were so many things to buy: I was on a high with cots and mobiles. And when they grew up it was so much fun to take them out for a day's spoiling and let them have whatever they wanted. I have given away so many six-month-old puppies.'

'Oh, Tori,' Jessica said in shock.

'I know, it's sick. But I just love it. Look.' She turned out the pocket of her blazer, revealing a mini tape measure. 'What do I need this for? But the petrol station had them on special tonight and they looked so cute. I think I'm going insane, Jess.' She threw her head into her hands and started sobbing.

'No you're not, you're not,' Jessica soothed her, rubbing her back. 'You've done a really brave thing tonight and I'm so proud of you.'

'What?' Tori looked up through wet lashes. 'Buying the tape measure was a good thing?'

'No, you goose,' Jess laughed, 'but recognising that you have a problem is awesome, and you've done that tonight.'

'I guess so,' Tori sniffed. 'But what am I going to do?'

'What about therapy. Could you try that?'

'Maybe,' Tori said softly.

Jessica got up to make more drinks and grabbed a box of tissues, which she handed to Tori. 'Let's think about some options,' she said, draping her arm around her friend.

~ 41 ~

The relaxed tones of Chris de Burgh's 'Lady in Red' flooded the Mercedes. Richard sang along joyfully. He looked at the duck-egg blue ring box sitting on the passenger seat. He couldn't wait to slip the one-point-five-carat solitaire diamond ring onto Genevieve's finger.

Christ, he was lucky, he thought, swinging onto Punt Road. He had it all. He had his Peninsula estate, his family and now Genevieve would be his wife. He adored her and was pleased at how well she was fitting into his family and even acting as surrogate mother to Jessica.

He knew his girlfriend wasn't perfect. He knew she had her little secrets and schemes, but it made the relationship all the more invigorating. He laughed to himself. Genevieve thought she could keep things from him, but he was way ahead of her. She'd even hinted about ideas for the Springforth property and he'd let her have her fun; she'd soon be surprised to find out just what he had planned for the estate, and he looked forward to her being a part of that.

The trip down Punt Road was surprisingly clear tonight, and the Yarra River twinkled as reflected lights from the nearby buildings danced on the water.

He pulled up at the Domain Road intersection lights, indicating left. Suddenly his body was forced to the right of the car. He thought he must have been hit by another vehicle, but he was on the inside lane, it was impossible. When he tried to look to the left to see what was there, he couldn't move his head. His right arm was paralysed, his head leaned against the window. What's happening to me? he thought in terror. Am I having a heart attack?

The driver behind gave up his impatient tooting and came to tap on his window. Richard struggled to move his head slightly but couldn't look right either. He started to panic. This couldn't be real.

The other driver rushed around to the passenger door. He pulled it open. 'You'll be right, mate,' he said reassuringly, and quickly dialled triple zero while Richard remained frozen, staring terrified out through the windscreen.

Jessica wasn't thinking; she was just moving. She needed to see her dad, to see that he was okay, that her life hadn't just come crashing down around her. She rushed down Epworth Hospital's busy halls, her coat flying as she searched frantically for the Casualty waiting room. In her haste she ran right past and had to double back, breathless with anxiety. Then she had to wait, stamping her feet impatiently, while the triage nurse dealt with a severed digit. Finally it was her turn.

'Richard Wainwright, he's my father, I'm Jessica Wainwright, I'm his daughter,' she stammered, and the nurse pushed a button to admit her into the Casualty ward.

It was controlled chaos: a maze of the sick, injured and frail, with a soundtrack of moans of pain and the wails of frightened children. Jess looked from face to face, searching for her father.

She peered around a curtained-off cubicle at the end of the room. The breath was stolen from her lungs and she felt as if she had been slammed bodily against one of the nondescript walls.

Her dynamic, athletic dad appeared to have aged twenty years. His skin hung from his face, yellow and lifeless beneath the ruthless fluorescents. His lines and wrinkles were deepened and doubled. His usually busy, muscular arms seemed frail, flaccid and elderly.

Genevieve stood to hug Jess. Although she seemed calm and serene, Jess could see the concern etched onto her face.

'How is he?' Jessica said. 'Is he unconscious?'

'No, he's just sleeping, it's okay,' Genevieve reassured her.

'Oh, thank God. Caro rang me about twenty minutes ago with the news. She's such a drama queen that I didn't know what to expect.'

'The doctor thinks he's had a stroke. They've just done an MRI and we will know more when the doctor has looked at the results.'

'Oh, Genevieve,' Jessica burst into tears. Genevieve's arms went around her as she sobbed into the older woman's cashmere-clad shoulder.

'There, there,' Genevieve said calmly. 'It'll be okay.'

'How do you know?' Jessica asked, looking up.

'The doctor is fairly confident. Given the symptoms Richard displayed and the excellent results from the initial examination, the doctor said that it looks like a stroke with a good chance of recovery. However . . .'

'What, Genevieve, what is it?' Jessica felt like an elastic band stretched to snapping point.

'It's likely he will need an operation. They have a surgeon and an anesthetist on stand-by. Although there is definitely hope, you need to know it's quite serious, Jessica.'

Hearing Genevieve's words, Jessica's terror and panic dissipated like sugar in water. That was it. She needed to be strong. There was no time to be flapping about panic-stricken. Jessica put her chin up high. 'Tell me absolutely everything you know, Genevieve.'

~42~

The pyrolysis process – and its resultant energy creation – continued to be a success on the hippies' farmlet. Songbird and Rainbow were in the full swing of energy production. Their potential investor had been down and seen their plant in operation and was duly impressed – especially with the octagonal metal container the women had fashioned from scrap. He had told them that barring any unforeseen circumstances, the deal would go ahead and his solicitor would contact them the following week.

Their spring onions, spinach and broad beans in the first pit were lush and tall – way beyond their usual growth.

Songbird was at the kitchen sink washing the dirt from under her nails. Rainbow was making chamomile tea. They were thawing out from early morning weeding in the harsh June chill.

The children also understood the importance of the vegetable pits and were fantastic little gardeners; identifying and removing weeds and keeping the precious plants watered. 'The ground is so black, Mum,' Taylor had said with wide eyes. 'It must be really, really good for the plants.' Songbird had smiled and tousled his dreads with pride at his understanding of the process. 'It does stink, but,' he added, and scampered off with the other children.

She had to admit, the compost storage did get a bit on the nose. They needed a lot of organic material to make each terra preta pit and as they collected it in an old mini-skip, it went quite putrid, especially in the sun. It wasn't anywhere near as bad now that the weather was a lot colder. For a while there, though, their backyard made everyone's eyes water.

The children were off in the yard playing Pin the Tail on Eugene, and the two mums sat down to discuss the energy plant. 'Beetroot loaf?' Rainbow offered her partner.

'Mmmm, yes please. Imagine how good it will taste with our first terra preta vegies.'

'Exactly,' Rainbow nodded, her dreads bouncing up and down.

The women were discussing the move to the one hundred hectares the investor was giving them rent-free, when the phone rang.

'Hello?' Songbird said.

Rainbow watched her, concerned about the look on her face.

'What do you mean?' Songbird said, then listened. 'But you can't be serious. It's my land.' She looked at Rainbow aghast. 'But it's zoned semi-rural, which means we're allowed to produce anything of a rural nature.' She listened to the voice on the other end of the phone.

Rainbow could see she was distressed and stood up to hold her partner's arm in support.

'Yes, we are producing electricity . . . What do you mean a semi-rural farmlet isn't allowed to produce electricity? I know we're not a power plant. It's not like we're mining uranium, we're just making compost basically . . . Well it doesn't smell today, not that badly . . . What if we start a different system to store the compost? Surely there's some-thing . . . Okay . . . Yes . . . Goodbye.' She hung up the phone.

'What is it?' Rainbow asked, panic-stricken.

'We've been shut down, babe, as of now. No more power plant. No more bio-char, no more pyrolysis.'

'What? But they can't do that,' Rainbow screeched in outrage.

'They can. There's been a complaint from someone in town, which is what brought it to the council's attention.'

'Well stuff them. Let's just ignore them.'

'We can't, babe, the fine's enormous. Which, by the way, he said we're lucky that he's going to waive.'

'Oh my God, Songbird.' Rainbow slumped heavily into her chair.

'I know, it's all over. We're going to lose our investor. He won't want to invest in a business that isn't allowed to operate.'

Rainbow looked up. 'Who complained? Who's whingeing? Maybe we can just get them to change their mind.'

Songbird looked, with pursed lips, at her partner. 'Yeah, you might be right. And you know who'd know?'

'Who?'

'Who knows absolutely everybody in this entire town, both tourists and locals.'

'Jessica.'

~ 43 ~

The next morning the atmosphere in Richard's private hospital room was much more optimistic. A burst of sunshine streamed in through his window.

'How are you?' Caro asked in a hushed voice, dropping a ludicrously large chocolate bouquet on the end of the bed.

Richard smiled wanly and patted her hand in response. Angus did his best to wrap his frail father in a bear hug.

Jess and Genevieve moved over to make room for the new arrivals.

Richard gave them all a lopsided grin. He had those he cared for most around him, and it helped him face the cold knot of fear that had enveloped him.

Jess grimaced. She was shocked by the force of terror and horror she felt at seeing her father this way; so reduced and feeble. But she forced a smile back onto her face and looked at him encouragingly. After all, there was good news: a CT scan had shown a bleed but its origin hadn't been identified so Richard didn't have to face brain surgery.

And his recovery was promising to be swift. The medical staff was encouraged by his early progress. There were still a few small residual effects – the left side of his face was a bit slack, which slurred his speech, and his right arm simply refused to cooperate – but his neurologist had told them that this was all normal, and in many similar cases a full recovery could be expected.

Caro, who hadn't left Richard's side, was squeezing his hand. 'Oh Richard, I just can't believe it.'

Richard smiled at his daughter-in-law.

'These things happen,' Genevieve said, briskly plumping his pillow. 'No use whining over spilt milk.'

'I was hardly whining, Genevieve,' Caro snapped, dropping her hospital voice for a minute.

Angus grabbed Caro's hand. 'Darling,' he said, barely disguising the threat in his voice. Caro turned her face into her husband's shoulder as he pulled her out of Richard's earshot.

'I hardly think it's accurate to compare a brain haemorrhage with spilt milk,' Jess heard Caro whisper angrily.

'She's being efficient, don't be narky,' Angus hissed back. 'Behave.'

'All right,' she snarled and turned back to Richard with a smile. 'Richard,' she said. 'I'm just curious, have you got your affairs in order?'

Jess, Angus and Genevieve gasped as one.

'Caro!' Angus said.

'Oh, so *she* can be efficient and I can't?' Caro asked.

'I give up,' Angus said and crossed his arms in resignation.

Caro smiled sweetly and topped up her father-in-law's water. 'It's just that there's no time like the present and I was offering to help, that's all. I'd hate to see you inundated with paperwork during your convalescence.'

'You're unbelievable,' Jess hissed at her sister-in-law across the bed. There had been a time Jess would have never spoken up. She would have kept quiet to keep the peace. Perhaps her city experience had toughened her up, she thought.

'Oh stop it, someone has to be practical here,' Caro returned with equal venom.

Richard held up his good hand. 'Caro is right. I do need to be sure everything is in order. Especially now there has been a development.' He struggled to push himself into a more upright sitting position. 'Gen and I are getting married.'

There was a moment of silent shock.

'Oh Dad, Genevieve, that's so wonderful. I'm delighted for you.' Jess felt all sense of doom evaporate from the room and instead it was filled with possibility and thoughts of the future.

'Well done, Dad. Welcome to the family, Genevieve,' Angus said, smiling broadly.

The siblings looked pointedly at Caro, whose face had turned an interesting shade of puce.

'Ah, yes, good . . .' was all she could manage.

'The will,' Richard went on, 'is about to be changed to reflect my wife's entitlements. There are other business developments, so the will has to be updated anyway.'

Jess looked across the room and giggled inwardly at Caro's obvious fury. Angus had a firm grip on his wife's white-knuckled hand.

'But Richard, this is all a bit sudden. Surely you need to think about this massive decision,' Caro said.

'For God's sake, woman, he knows what he's doing!'

Genevieve looked up from tucking in Richard's sheets and was surprised to discover the brusque voice had come from Jess.

Richard interrupted. 'Caro, darling, you don't need to worry. You'll be well looked after.'

'Richard, it's not me I'm worried about – it's the children. I just hope your grandchildren will be looked after.'

'They will be; have no fear.' He patted the back of her hand.

Jessica had had enough emotional stress for one day. She kissed Richard goodbye, hugged Genevieve, slipped out of the room and got into the closest lift.

'Hold it,' an unseen voice called.

Jess instinctively thrust her arm into the red eye's sensor. Caro got in and punched B2. Jess stared at the overhead LED display, praying Caro would just stay quiet.

'Look, I know that sounded bad,' Caro tried to explain, 'and I know I come off as hard as nails sometimes. But I love this family so much, I really do. It's the only family I have, and I hate to see it threatened by an upstart like Genevieve.'

'What is with you?' Jess turned to face Caro, her hands on her hips. 'You're so jealous and so bloody greedy. I wish you'd back off.'

'Jessica, I am so sorry you feel that way, I really am.' Caro turned away. The lift arrived at the basement level.

Jess stepped out. She turned back to face Caro, who said, 'Just be very careful, Jess, I don't trust her.'

~44~

Jess balanced her Nokia against the steering wheel, hardly seeing the roads and traffic around her.

'Tori,' she told the speaker-phone, 'it's been horrendous. I just can't believe that Dad could look so old and so weak. I was so scared.'

'Oh, Jessica, darling. You poor thing. Do you want me to come to town? I can be there in an hour.'

'No, no, I'll be fine. Thanks anyway.' She dropped the phone into her lap. 'Can you still hear me Tori? My loudspeaker isn't very good.' She grabbed a styrofoam cup from the cup holder and gulped down some bitter, lukewarm coffee.

'Yes, I can hear you fine, sweetie. What does the doctor say?'

Jessica filled her in and vented some steam about Caro's insane behaviour at the hospital.

'That woman is so full-on,' Tori said. 'When will you know more about your dad?'

'In the morning, I guess. I hope so. I have no idea how to keep myself busy until then.' Jess came to a stop at the busy Toorak Road intersection, and looked incredulously at the usual Saturday crowds who sat sipping lattes at sidewalk cafes and casually browsed the stylish shops. Life seemed so normal. It didn't seem right when her dad was lying in a hospital bed.

'What can I do to help, Jess?' Tori asked, pulling Jess from her reverie.

'Could you ring Nick and Rainbow and Songbird and let them know what's happening?'

'Of course,' Tori assured her.

The traffic finally started to move. 'Now tell me,' said Jess. 'How are you doing? How's it going with your therapist?'

'It's going well,' Tori said cautiously. 'I'm scared most of the time and still just want to go shopping and forget everything, but I'm getting there. I've learned that I've been using shopping as a coping strategy and it's actually quite destructive.'

'That sounds like positive progress.' Jessica pulled up to the lights next to a pimped-up Monaro and tapped her speaker volume up to hear over the roaring engine. 'So what's the next step?' she asked.

'I have to cut up all my credit cards.' Tori's voice dropped to a whisper. 'I'm not sure I'm ready for that yet, but I'm working on trying to find more effective ways to get through when I feel bad; it's just at the moment I can't think of any . . .'

'Maybe you could give me a call and we could talk things through?' Jess suggested.

'Thanks love, you're a good friend. I promise to try that next time,' Tori said, and Jess could hear the smile in her voice. 'Anyway enough about all that, you have plenty of your own worries,' Tori said. 'Will you tell the boys what's happened?'

Jess slammed her foot on the brake as the car in front of her stopped suddenly. 'You moron, bloody moron,' she shouted. 'Sorry, Tori, just a crazy driver. I'm not going to say anything to the boys yet. I'll wait till things are a bit more stable, then I'll sneak them away from Graham so they can visit their pop.'

Jess pulled into her apartment building's car park and turned off the engine.

'How has that been going?' Tori asked.

'Not bad since I got all bolshie, actually,' Jess laughed. 'The new wife Karen's okay. I feel quite sorry for her. She's doing her best to let me sneak the occasional quick hello when they go to the park, so I feel much more connected to them.'

'That's fabulous, darling,' Tori said. 'Why don't I come up next week and we'll have lunch and big talks, okay?'

'Thanks, Tori, that'd be great.' Jess picked up the phone and her bag and climbed out of the car.

'Love to Richard and the family. Tell him to get well really soon.'

'Shall do. Bye, Tori.'

The heavy front door of her father's apartment closed behind Jessica with a resounding click that echoed through the marble foyer. She couldn't face sleeping alone at her flat tonight. She'd spent the day there catching up with Still Life paperwork, but as darkness fell she wanted the comfort of her dad's things around her.

She had dropped in to the hospital on the way to his apartment. There was no more news, but it was good to see her dad sitting up and looking a tiny bit better than he had that morning.

She switched on the lamp at the entrance to the opulent living room, the soft greys and silvers providing the perfect foil for the jet black Eames day lounge framed against the French windows, which were draped in metallic platinum sheers.

Jessica stopped in front of what her father lovingly named the Hall of Fame. But unlike his contemporaries, who proudly displayed images of themselves rubbing shoulders with power brokers and dignitaries of the globe, Richard's shots were framed prints of family and friends.

She wandered down the wall of memories, giggling at Richard with sideburns holding a six-year-old Angus, and laughing out loud at a photo of her parents dressed for a dinner dance: her dad in white shoes and a grey suit with lapels so wide he could potentially fly, and her mum, with long straight hair and lurid green eyeshadow, in a caftan. Jessica felt the stress of the last twenty-four hours slipping away.

She smiled at a photo of Eva Wainwright pulling a silly face. It was such a relief to be able to think of her mother with love and happiness instead of only the pain of loss. Jessica was relieved she'd made the decision to stay here tonight. She felt practically joyous. Everything was going to be all right.

Just then her mobile rang. A nugget of panic suddenly lodged in the back of her throat. She inwardly cursed herself for her premature optimism.

'Hello, Jessica Wainwright?'

It was the doctor. 'I have good news,' he said, immediately allaying her fears.

Jessica's throat cleared; her heart surged.

'Your father's latest scans are back and it's looking very positive,' he said. 'It would have been much worse had your father not been so fit,' he said. 'But barring another stroke, we anticipate he will make a complete recovery. As we were unable to locate the source of the bleed, however, it is crucial that Richard rests while his body heals.'

'Thank you so much,' Jess breathed, hanging up.

Her world suddenly made sense again; her thoughts were clear and ordered. Her dad was going to be okay, and she couldn't imagine better news than that right now.

She burst into hot tears of relief and folded herself into her father's favourite chair, delighting in his smell that lingered in the fabric.

Jessica was cooking dinner for herself in Richard's granite and stainless steel kitchen an hour later when her mobile rang again.

'Hello?' she said and, flicking the little Nokia onto speaker-phone, rested it on the bench so she could continue to stir her pasta sauce.

'Hi, Jess, it's us.'

'Hey, Rainbow. Hiya, Songbird.' Jessica was thrilled to hear their friendly voices.

'How's your dad? ' Songbird's voice was strained through the little speaker.

'So great, guys. I can't tell you how relieved I am. He's expected to make a full recovery.'

'That's brilliant news, doll. We're rapt, aren't we, Rainbow?'

'Yaaaayyyyy,' Rainbow's voice was faint in the background.

'Rainbow can't come to the phone right now: she's skipping,' Songbird said.

'So what's up with you? Any news on the terra preta plant?' Jess asked.

'Yeah, I'm afraid it's all bad. We're being shut down,' Songbird said woefully.

'Shut down? By whom?' Jessica said, staring at the phone.

'The council. Someone's dobbed us in. The council reckons we're breaking zoning laws. Apparently we're not allowed to make electricity in a suburban backyard.'

'Bloody cheek!' Rainbow called in over Songbird.

'They're probably right, but there's got to be a way around it. What does your mystery investor say?' Jess asked, serving her pasta onto a plate.

'We haven't told him yet, but the problem is he'll just pull out: there's no sense in investing in a business that's not allowed to operate.'

'Oh no, what a shame. He will too. So how did the council find out about you?'

'We thought you might be able to help us with that one. You know everybody in town. Somebody complained to the council about the smell and, when I rang up to look into it, apparently that same somebody has been asking a lot of questions around the council and is planning to take a huge chunk of land down here and turn it into a housing estate. Of course, there are no plans submitted yet and we could be panicking over nothing, but my source at the council is the same bloke that told me about the new marina in Harbourtown that ended up ripping out all those mangroves, and he was right about that, so why wouldn't he be right about this? I asked who it was that had been enquiring and he said there was no name given. We're freaking out down here, Jess.'

'Jesus, Songbird,' Jess flicked her phone off speaker and picked it up so she could hear more clearly, 'that's outrageous. We can't have a housing estate in Stumpy Gully! It will destroy the town. What next? Formula One?' Jessica was appalled. How could this be possible? She felt almost personally responsible. As if by leaving her village unsupervised, everything had spun out of control.

'I'll come down as soon as Dad's out of hospital,' she said, pacing up and down the kitchen in anger. 'But I'll also do what I can from here, okay? I'll look into it. Off the top of my head though, girls, I can't think who would do such a thing. Where is this subdivision meant to be taking place? It's all zoned regional down there, except for our property, of course. Perhaps it's that farm behind the supermarket? That's due for a restructure. I bet that's it. Leave it with me: I'll get right onto it in the morning and phone you back.'

'Thanks, Jess, we just knew you'd know what to do. Oh, and by the way, Taylor has a message for Richard. He woke up in the middle of the night desperate that we pass the message on.'

'What is it?' Jessica stopped pacing.

'The union wants to build,' Songbird said.

'What the hell does that mean? Like a trade union?'

'I don't know,' admitted Songbird. 'His messages only ever make sense after the fact, which kind of defeats the purpose of premonitions. Anyway, just pass it on, will you? I told him I would.'

Jessica hung up. It was a disaster. Songbird and Rainbow's terra preta operation had failed before it had even started. She wished she were there to help.

From the foyer came the sound of the front door opening. Jess gave a start as footsteps approached the kitchen.

'Oh, Genevieve, it's you!' she said as the older woman appeared. 'How lovely, I could use some company. Would you like to stay for dinner?'

'Er, why yes, thank you,' Genevieve said, seeming a little startled to see Jessica at the apartment.

Cate Kendall

'The doctor rang, the test results were all good and they expect Dad to make a full recovery,' Jessica explained, taking another plate from the cupboard.

'Yes, I know. I was there when he came in with the news,' Genevieve replied.

Jessica considered discussing Stumpy Gully's latest dramas but something stopped her. She didn't think that Genevieve would truly understand the seriousness of the situation.

She served up a second plate of pasta while Genevieve whipped up a salad and opened a bottle of wine. They were soon sitting across from each other at the bench discussing physiotherapy and Richard's recovery plan.

After a while silence fell over them. Jessica couldn't help notice the ring on Genevieve's right hand. The ring that had Caro in such a flap. She considered Genevieve's response to the news of Richard's recovery. She hadn't seemed terribly excited. But then again, she'd had an hour to absorb the information and she was no doubt exhausted.

'What a beautiful ring, Genevieve,' Jess said finally, embarrassed that she had obviously been staring at it.

'Thank you,' Genevieve said, glancing at the ruby-and-diamond piece. 'It's Bulgari.'

'Where did you get it?' Jessica asked, hoping she sounded innocently curious.

'Just up here at the Collins Street store,' she replied.

'For a special occasion?' Jess asked.

'Yes, actually, I bought it for myself to celebrate a work promotion earlier this year.'

'Oh, congratulations! I didn't know you'd been promoted,' Jess said. 'That's great news.' She cleared their plates and wiped the marble bench down with a flourish. Ha! Wait till she told Caro that her fears for the family fortune were completely unfounded after all. Genevieve was no gold digger.

~ 46 ~

Jessica slept deeply, safe in the knowledge that her dad was going to be okay. She woke in his guestroom feeling lighter and more optimistic. Outside the weather was bleak and grey, but nothing could dampen her bright mood. It was three days since Richard's stroke and his doctors were becoming increasingly confident about his recovery. The next step was rehab, and eventually he would be back to normal. The world was good and beautiful, Jess thought, staring out the window where the wind was whipping the city into a frenzy of dancing litter and fallen leaves.

Her father and Genevieve had a planned a meeting for that morning so Jess decided to leave her visit for the afternoon. She had taken some time off work and felt at a loose end on a Monday morning when she would normally be briefing her team and starting a new week at the office.

She dressed quickly in a thick jumper and jeans, made herself some tea and toast and decided to spend the morning sorting out Richard's study.

The pile of paperwork was simple to work through. After all, she had set up his filing system ten years ago, and it seemed she was the only one who kept it up. She gave a rueful smile as she went through the trays. Telstra bills: all but one were marked paid. Old board papers she shredded in case they held sensitive information.

As the pile got smaller – receipts filed, junk mail turfed, bills paid – Jessica came across a receipt from Bulgari, dated December twenty-second. The description was clearly outlined.

A two-carat ruby, flanked by two half-carat diamonds. Jessica gasped out loud at the price. You could buy a house and land package in the outer suburbs for that. Then she saw the payment advice. Paid, by *Richard Wainwright's Amex card*. She sat on Richard's office floor holding the paper in her hand as the realisation sunk in.

Genevieve had lied to her. An outright, bare-faced lie. Jessica was furious. She grabbed the phone and dialled Genevieve's advertising agency.

'Kendall, Keyes and Morton,' a chirpy voice answered. 'How may I help you?'

'Hello, my name is Mary. I work for ER PR,' Jess said. 'We need to send a sample to your Head of Creative. Who is that, please?'

'That's Mike Mulligan,' the girl replied.

Jess asked a second question: 'And what about Genevieve Walters, what's her position?'

'Oh, she's been one of our creative directors here for ten years.'

'So she still holds the same position she's always held?'

'Oh, yes, same position as always.'

Jessica said goodbye and slammed the phone back into its cradle. There was no promotion.

'That bitch,' she spat, and then her mouth dropped open as another thought filled her mind.

She raced down to the master bedroom and pulled open doors until she found Genevieve's slick patent leather briefcase. Jessica rifled through the papers it contained and found what she was looking for. She slid the elastic from the cylinder of paper and opened it onto the bed. Just what she thought: first draft rough drawings for the subdivision of the farm.

It was Genevieve who had shut Rainbow and Songbird down and was planning to turn Stumpy Gully into a concrete jungle. But worse than that, she wanted to subdivide the Wainwright property. How could she?

Jess carefully replaced the plans and returned the case to the cupboard, trembling with anger and shock. It took all her self-control to stop herself from shredding the plans then and there. She suddenly felt so stupid for trusting Genevieve; even looking to her as some sort of mother-substitute. Genevieve had fooled everyone – except for Caro, who had tried to warn them all along.

She would have to tell her dad straightaway. He deserved to know the truth about this woman he wanted to marry.

~ 47 ~

'Richard's dead.'

'Excuse me?' Jess looked up from where she sat cross-legged on the floor of the study. Her world tilted. Had Genevieve just said that the lift was broken? That they had run out of milk for coffee? Surely that must have been it. There wasn't enough emotion in her voice for it to be anything else.

'Your dad died this morning,' Genevieve repeated. 'I'm so sorry, Jess.'

'Don't be ridiculous,' Jess scoffed at the woman. 'Last night the doctor said he was doing really well. He's going to be fine. I'm just sorting out his desk for him. He'll be so pleased when he comes home: he likes everything neat and tidy . . .' Her voice was high and wavering; her heart a thumping boulder in her chest. He had been in hospital for three days; he was doing well. The doctor had said. Genevieve was just making a bad joke.

Jessica needed time to stop; for the room to stop spinning so she could take a breath, just get her thoughts in order, because something bad had just happened and she couldn't quite work out what it was. She looked down at the papers in her hands, at the solid reliability of her father's desk. He loved that desk: it was strong, dependable, the kind of desk that would be in a family for generations, he had told her when he'd bought it.

What was I doing? Jess thought. She shook her head uselessly. There was a very bad noise humming inside it and a terrible pain somewhere in her body. She looked up. Genevieve was staring at her blankly. It was something that woman had just said, wasn't it? She really had to talk to her dad, she had important things to tell him . . . Something broke deep within her and realisation floated to the surface of her mind.

'Dad,' she croaked.

~ 48 ~

'Yes, hello, it's me again. Sorry I had to get off the phone before. Look, it's all go, thank you, that's the plan I'd like to go with. Please draw it up as a final draft. I'll send a cheque this week. There has been a rather tragic development, but never mind, at least we won't have any more hold-ups. I'll call you later today to arrange a meeting. I might be in a position to lodge plans with council in a couple of months so I need the plans ASAP. Goodbye.'

~ 49 ~

Jessica mashed her lips together to stop herself from crying and picked up the phone. She dialled and waited.

'Graham here,' came the voice on the other end.

'Hello Graham, it's Jessica.' She stared across the paddocks at the cows trying to huddle under gum trees to escape the driving rain. Their faces were forlorn and their ears drooped as if they were aware of the sadness enveloping the property.

'I know it's you, I have caller display,' Graham said.

Jess sighed. 'I'm ringing to tell you that my dad, that Richard, passed away on Monday.' One cow raised its head and let out a deep, mournful bellow.

'Oh, I already knew: I saw it in the paper,' Graham said.

'Right, okay then.' She steeled herself and continued, 'I am ringing, Graham, to ask you to please bring the boys to the funeral on Thursday.'

She needed her boys with her; she needed to feel the energy from their vital little bodies and to remind herself of the good, positive things in life. And besides, Richard had been their grandfather, he had loved them and they had adored him and they had the right to farewell him with the rest of his family.

'Thursday! Jessica, that's tomorrow. It's a bit inconvenient, honestly,' Graham said. 'I've got a conference all day. And all the way down there . . . You can't do it in town, I suppose? I could escape for an hour, maybe. No, I guess not. Look it's just not doable. Sorry.'

Once, Jessica would have conceded and hung up. But, no, fuck him, she thought. 'No,' Jess said. 'No, that's not good enough, Graham.' Her voice was thick with tiredness and grief, but for once her thoughts were clear and she felt her resolve strengthen; she'd had enough of this bullshit. 'You listen to me, you nasty, nasty little man. Those are my boys too. I have contributed to most of their lives, I love them and I need them here tomorrow. You will get them here or I will make your life so ugly, so bloody messy with court orders and custody hearings that you'll wonder what's hit you. You got it?'

'Right . . . okay . . . I'll see what I can do,' he answered, too shocked to fight back.

The morning of the funeral crawled around. The sense of deja vu for Jessica was stifling: it was the same house, the same mourners, even the same kind of miserable, drizzly weather, as when her mother died. Jessica floated through the homestead, distant from the action, unable to anchor herself to any reality.

Caro had bustled in with her usual efficiency and had taken over – which was a relief. This was so much worse than when her mother had died. Jess hadn't known then how terrible the pain was going to be. Now she could see the long road of sadness and grief that stretched out before her, and she couldn't shake the dreadful, painful thought that she was an orphan. The natural order of things seemed out of balance: there was no one behind her, supporting her. She was grief-stricken, mad with sadness and furious at Genevieve.

The house was packed with family members busy finding rooms, changing into funeral-appropriate clothes and setting up for the wake that would take place on the property afterwards. There had been no sign of the boys yet.

Nick came into her bedroom carrying a steaming mug of chamomile tea. She smiled at him warmly. 'That's exactly what I needed, thank you.'

He looked down at her fondly. 'Why are you sitting in here by yourself? Don't you want company?' he asked as he perched on the corner of her bed. From her seat in the large floral wing-backed armchair, she stared out over the fields. She envisaged Richard striding up the hill in his gumboots. Her eyes started to water again.

'Not really,' she whispered. 'How am I going to get through this, Nick?'

'You're a very brave, strong woman, and we will all be here with you,' he said, squeezing her shoulder.

The family rallied around the cars in the driveway and the somber convoy to the church drifted down the hill. Although there was a seat in Angus's family car, Jessica decided to travel with Nick.

The family was ushered to the side door of the church to be seated before the congregation was admitted. Caro linked her arm into Jessica's as they stepped through the side door. They gasped: front and centre, as proud as the Queen Mary, sat Genevieve in the family's front pew. Jessica grabbed Caro's hand.

After she'd heard the news of her father's death, Jess had taken a taxi straight to Caro and Angus's house, where the family had held each other and grieved. Jessica had told them at once what she'd found out about Genevieve. The women had looked immediately to Angus: as a solicitor surely he could make it all okay.

'This is undeniably a nasty situation,' he'd said, pacing the room, frowning. 'I am sure it will be okay, but I need to get on to Dad's solicitor immediately.'

'This is ridiculous,' Jessica had wailed. 'The day Dad's gone, we're already bickering over the will.'

'Don't say that,' her brother had responded gently. 'It's not like that at all. We don't know anything for sure. Let's wait until we have the facts.'

But walking into the church to see Genevieve acting like a mourning widow was almost more than Jess and Caro could deal with. Angus made a diplomatic move and sat next to Genevieve to separate her from the others.

As the church began to fill, Nick went quietly up to Genevieve and whispered in her ear. She looked horrified and rushed out of the church. Angus, Caro, Jessica and the rest of the row slid up. When Genevieve returned a few minutes later, her seat was gone and she was forced to sit a few rows back.

'What did you say?' Jessica whispered to Nick as he sat next to her.

'That her car had been broken into,' he replied.

'Oh, no, really?' Jessica asked.

'No, not really,' Nick replied and looked to the front as the service began. Jessica marvelled at how even today Nick could make her smile.

Just as the minister began, Jessica heard feet clattering down the aisle of the church. She gasped and her eyes filled with tears. It was Callum and Liam, all dressed up in neat little suits. The family shuffled left and right and the boys wedged themselves on either side of her. Her arms went around each slender set of shoulders and squeezed. She kissed each little head, then turned back to acknowledge Graham. But it wasn't Graham at the back of the room, it was Karen.

The funeral service was less painful than Jess had feared. It celebrated the life of a great man – a family man – and Jess felt privileged to have been his daughter.

The eulogy, delivered by Richard's best friend, Uncle Al, was magnificent and even evoked a few laughs as the congregation remembered some of Richard Wainwright's finest moments.

Jessica travelled back to the house with Callum and Liam in Karen's car. She couldn't keep her hands off them. She stroked Callum's plump little cheeks; slicked Liam's hair out of the way. Instead of squirming away, both boys revelled in the ministrations, chattering and snuggling up to her in the back seat. As soon as they got to the house they ran inside to check out their old rooms and Jessica was relieved she had left them as they were.

The wake was an awkward affair, with everyone trying to outdo each other with service, catering and cleaning – anything to distract from the real reason for the day. Even Tori, Pip, Fi and Cat were working their designer-clad butts off.

Jessica was in the living room, holding the boys' hands while they talked to Angus, when Karen sidled up to her. She was such an awkward woman, Jessica thought. 'Hi, Karen,' she said.

'I'm sorry, Jessica, but I have to get the boys back.'

'No! No, wait a bit longer. I know, let's all go for a walk.'

'I really shouldn't – I'll be in trouble. I wasn't even supposed to come, Jessica.' She hopped from foot to foot, pulling at her cardigan sleeve.

'Oh, come on, the fresh air will do us all good.'

Jess led them all down the back stairs, through the garden and out the back gate. The winter westerly whipped their hair into disarray. Much to their delight, the boys' jackets blew into instant superhero capes, and they whooped off into a caped crusader game.

'How's it going, Karen?' Jessica asked as they walked together, arms folded against the cutting wind.

'Oh, you know, it's okay.' Karen flicked a nervous glance up at Jessica.

'It's hard to keep up with his demands, isn't it?'

'Oh, yes,' Karen said. 'He expects me to be a mind reader. And he's not particularly tolerant.'

'I know all about that,' Jessica said.

Jessica watched the boys play chasey. It hurt that they called her Jessica now instead of Mumma. But Callum explained that their dad had insisted. But at least she could see that they were happy and healthy and well-loved. That was all she ever wanted for them. To insist on making them come to her every week would just be unnecessary and cruel, but she was damned if she was going to be completely cut out of their life.

The two women stood side-by-side and watched the boys hollering into the wind.

'I'd really like to see the boys more regularly, Karen,' Jessica said. 'Just once a month or something. I could pop in. It wouldn't hurt anybody. I would just have a play and a chat. You or Graham could be there if that's what you're worried about.'

'Oh dear, oh dear,' Karen twisted her hands together. She was so brow-beaten, Jessica thought. She recognised something of her old self in Karen. 'Graham warned me you were going to say this. I'm sorry but he says no. He says that they're doing fine and we need to just leave it as it is. I wasn't supposed to even be here. We were meant to leave straight after the church.'

Jessica felt sorry for her, caught in the middle. 'Never mind, Karen, I shouldn't be bringing this up with you anyway. I'll talk to Graham. Thank you so much for bringing the boys down.'

As she stood on the step waving goodbye, Jessica didn't even notice the tears begin to run down her face. She felt like she'd been crying for years. The boys leaned into the back window of the little BMW and waved until they were out of sight.

She turned and went inside the house. Rainbow and Songbird were putting on their coats.

'Oh, girls,' Jessica said. 'I am so sorry that I haven't done anything to help you yet. I will get onto it next week, I promise.'

'Don't be daft, you stupid cow,' Songbird said. 'You have a lot on your plate at the moment. We'll be apples. Anyway, we're chucking it in.'

'Why?' Jessica asked.

'The universe isn't with us on this one,' Rainbow explained. 'Once you have to fight cosmic forces you may as well just stop. We're waiting though: something will come up – it'll happen. But we can't keep battling to make this work.'

'It's too late to save the planet anyway,' Songbird said gloomily.

'What about your investor? They didn't really drop out, did they?' Jessica asked from the door as the girls walked towards their Smart Car.

'The investor was –' Rainbow started.

'Not interested, never mind,' Songbird finished for her mate. 'Cheers, see you on the flipside.'

'Jessica,' Caro called from the doorway, 'this arrived for you earlier.'

Jessica turned to look. It was a potted lavender plant, from Jimmy. 'How, um, thoughtful,' she said. He wasn't to know she hated lavender with a passion.

~ 50 ~

It was the creepy little lavender plant that spurred Jessica into action. Her family was surprised when she announced she was leaving early to get back to the city just a few days after the funeral. But she couldn't sit around feeling miserable for one more minute.

Richard's death prompted an urgency in her to get on with life; to grasp it with both hands. She felt a sense of clarity that seemed to have been missing for the past two years, and she didn't want to waste a moment before getting things sorted out. She knew from experience that grief was unpredictable and vicious: although today she felt seized with strength and resolve, tomorrow she could be dashed by despair once more.

Her mind was filled with pictures of her dad as she sped down the freeway towards the city, and hot, fat tears plopped onto her lap as she drove. She'd loved him so much; he'd been a rock, and she wasn't sure how life could continue without him. Sobs hiccupped from her belly and she had to pull over to wipe her eyes and wait for the storm of grief to pass.

She took a few deep, shuddering breaths and for a moment considered turning back to the farm and her family. But she wanted to get things moving; she'd have time with her family soon. She swung the car back onto the road and tried to distract herself by thinking about her job.

It was a fantastic opportunity; she knew that. The work suited her and the money was great. But it was the designing and creating she enjoyed most, not her workplace and certainly not her colleagues. She missed the warmth and inclusiveness of

Stumpy Gully; she missed her store and her friends. She knew now she could have the best of both worlds: an art career and an idyllic lifestyle.

She pulled her Patrol into a car space in front of her flat. There was no way she'd dare go to her dad's place; she was nervous she might find Genevieve there. Angus said he was having the locks changed first thing in the morning, when the evil witch would be at work.

The next morning Jess awoke from a night of troubled dreams and lay in the cold dawn as the sense of loss and grief washed over her once more. But her sense of purpose was still strong, so she dragged herself out of bed and splashed water on her face, avoiding the dark-rimmed eyes that stared back at her from the mirror.

She quickly drank a chamomile tea, grabbed her favourite denim jacket and charged down the flight of stairs, arriving at the stop just as her tram did.

She walked into Still Life as the clock ticked over to nine a.m. Sventana kept her nose in a magazine, ignoring her as always.

'Morning Sventana,' Jess waved breezily as she passed. Then she stopped and turned back. 'Oh, and by the way, Sventana dear, you can have Jimmy back,' she said nonchalantly. 'I've finished with him.'

She felt outstandingly bitchy as she swung up the stairs, but it was quite a pleasant feeling, she decided.

She entered the workshop and greeted her team. 'Love your skirt,' one of the girls said. 'It looks like a tablecloth.'

Jessica smiled and thanked her for the compliment. The project she'd briefed them on last week was coming along perfectly. And she knew Mimsy loved it; she was able to read the woman now. When Mimsy took off her red specs and looked Jess straight in the eyes, it was her way of saying 'Sensational'.

Not that it really mattered much anymore. Jessica knew her work was good. She was proud of it and no longer needed the approval of others. She finally knew she was ready – ready for success, ready for the big time. And there was only one place in the world where that was going to happen.

Jimmy came in to her office to offer his condolences and express shock that she was back at work so soon. He tried his best puppy-dog look on her. 'You must need some comforting, sweet pea,' he soothed.

'I do,' Jess answered, amused to see his eyes light up. 'It's lucky I have such a wonderful family and close friends in Stumpy Gully.'

'Well, I'm here for you too,' he said, putting his hand on her shoulder and giving her one of his trademark deep-and-meaningful looks.

Jess laughed and Jimmy walked away, unsure how to deal with her. She turned to her desk and started clearing out her drawers. As she gazed at the display of artworks on her shelf, she felt a jolt of pride. She had done well here, she was a success, but it wasn't what she wanted.

She loved creating, but she missed working on her own stuff. This work was manufactured, uninspired, and to a formula. She needed the creative surge of the Peninsula, of Stumpy Gully. She missed her community. She missed being home, where everybody knew her name (and her business). Jess threw old papers in the bin, washed out her coffee mug for the last time and threw it in her briefcase.

She needed to be home to defend her township. She and her brother had to fight off Genevieve. Rainbow and Songbird needed her help to win their battle to save the planet. And Nick . . . well, that was more than she could think about at the moment, she decided, giving her pot plants a last watering. She was pretty sure any chance of them working out as a couple had been ruined, but if she could keep him as a friend that would be enough.

When her office was packed up she went to see Mimsy.

'Sit,' Mimsy commanded when she saw Jessica standing in her open doorway. Jessica chose to stand.

'Mimsy,' she said, 'I'm resigning. I need to go home and take care of things, since my Dad . . .' She couldn't say the word out loud.

'Hmm.' Mimsy looked up. 'In that case you will have to leave today. Our policy is same-day departure as we have a lot of confidential work we would hate to see fall into the wrong hands, thanks to a disgruntled former employee.'

'Yes, Mimsy.' Jess turned to go.

'It's a shame you're leaving, I quite liked your work.'

'Did you? You never said.'

'Didn't I? I thought I had. Still, it's not the end of the world. Funnily enough, I was probably going to have to let you go anyway.' She pushed her glasses on to her head.

'Really?' Jessica was unable to hide her bitter tone.

'Yes, young Jimmy's had some brilliant ideas lately.' She leaned her heavy bosom on the desk. 'In fact he's turning the styro-chandelier into an exquisite piece that will bring us to the cutting-edge of millennium design. Brilliant. We don't need a separate head of design if Jimmy can do it.'

'Well, good luck with that,' Jessica smiled.

'You can go now,' Mimsy said. She pulled her glasses down and turned back to the photographs on her desk.

Jessica took the back stairs out and walked through the rear warehouse where the larger work took place. It was all set up for the work on Mimsy's precious chandelier, which had been transported from the shop to the rear of the warehouse in a large truck as it was too big to go through the building.

The fluoro silk petals were ready in bins and a team surrounded the sculpture, ready to take part in artistic history. Large commercial spray adhesive pumps were whirring into life. Jimmy stood at the helm, directing the process.

'Bye, Jimmy,' she called and waved as she stepped out the back door.

'Goodbye, angel, happy travels,' he replied with a wave and a wink. Sventana scowled at him and stomped off back to reception.

And so Jessica left Still Life for the last time. As her car crawled through the stop-and-start city traffic she reflected on her knowledge of chemical reactions. It really was a fascinating field. For instance, she mused, when styrofoam was sprayed with adhesive it instantly shrivelled up into tiny lumps. A shame, that.

~51~

It had been a week since the funeral. Carrying a cup of tea, Jessica walked out to the deck to watch the sun's pale rays flood the valley. This had been Richard's favourite time of the morning. She was choked with sadness. 'I can't believe he's gone,' she whispered for the thousandth time. She had spent the weekend locked up in the house with the blinds down, caught in a fog of introspection and old photos.

It was frightening how permanent the pain felt. Logic and experience told her it would wane. But at that moment it felt as if it would have her in its tight grip forever. The only small consolation was the clear sense of purpose she felt about her own life, and her drive to put things in order since his death.

She'd spent a day packing up her Prahran flat, leaving it furnished for the tenants she hoped to attract, but now she sat in quiet contemplation for a couple of hours, unable to summon the motivation to move.

When she heard a car driving down the driveway, she stood up to see who it was. She opened the front door and looked out. It couldn't be. Genevieve's Mercedes? Surely not. That woman had more balls than a bull run. What on earth could she want?

Then a ute pulled up in the driveway behind the Mercedes. Eugene's haughty face looked over the cab at Jessica. Songbird and Rainbow got out.

'Hello, Genevieve,' Jessica said.

'Hello, Jessica darling. How are you?'

'What do you want?' Jessica said coldly, with her arms folded. Rainbow and Songbird hung back and watched.

'Now, Jess, dear, why are you being like that? What's wrong? I thought we were friends.'

'We were friends, until I found out you were a cheat and a liar.'

'What on earth are you talking about?' Genevieve laughed as if it were all a silly misunderstanding.

'The ring, Genevieve.'

'Oh, for heaven's sake. That ring has caused nothing but scandal and gossip. Yes, your dad bought it for me, okay? Happy?'

'Why lie about it?' Jessica asked.

'You saw how ridiculous Caro was getting with the whole thing. I couldn't eat a bloody Tim Tam without her screeching "Gold-digger". I had to lie to stop her from ripping the thing straight off my finger. Besides, Jess, it's really nobody's business where I get my jewellery. If Caro thinks that's bad, she'd be thrilled to find out where my diamond bellybutton ring came from.' She put her hands on her hips defiantly.

'But the development, the subdivision, the plans.' Jess waved her hands angrily in the air. 'You'd been in touch with council, you had the entire property drawn up as an estate, and all behind my dad's back. That's pretty deceitful, Genevieve.'

'Jessica, you don't understand at all. Your dad knew all about the plans.'

'What?' Jessica scoffed, stamping her foot angrily. 'That's a lie.'

'Okay, he didn't know the exact plans.' Genevieve leaned against her Mercedes. 'We spoke about it in broad brush-strokes. I didn't want to frighten him off the idea until I was sure that it would work.' She held her hand up to admire the glint of her ruby in the weak sunlight. 'The plans were actually going to be a surprise for his birthday. He'd been talking for months about developing the property, about going into partnership with someone, about a whole new frontier for land down here. I knew he meant real estate. There is absolutely nothing else more profitable. You'll all be multimillionaires when I've finished. You'll be thanking me by this time next year, trust me.' She wiped a tiny smudge off the car's spotless paintwork.

'When Richard spoke to me about his dreams for redeveloping the property I just knew I could help him out – and considering I am now the owner of it . . .' She let her voice trail off as Jess swapped angry looks with Rainbow and Songbird. 'That was the meeting Richard and I had just before he died. He wanted to be sure that I got my fair share so we met with his lawyer in the hospital room and he bequeathed the land to me.'

Jess couldn't speak. Her face was hot with rage.

'You're getting the penthouse,' Genevieve continued, ignoring Jess's reaction. 'Your dad was so relieved you were happy being a city girl, and Angus is getting the homestead. And I'm getting –' she turned with arms outstretched to indicate the two hundred hectares that fell below them – 'the rest.'

'Don't ever talk to me about how my father felt,' Jess said in a low, threatening voice. 'How dare you come here and tell such outrageous lies, you complete and utter bitch?'

Songbird and Rainbow came over to stand beside Jess, their arms around her as she trembled with rage. 'Dad would never, ever have agreed to split up this land.'

Genevieve looked smug and relaxed as she flicked her hand in the air. 'I may not have mentioned my exact plans to him, but he knew I always wanted rural acreage, and there's something you need to know about me, my dear: I always get what I want.' She smiled slyly, then held out her right hand to admire the Bulgari piece once again. 'Oh, look, a matching one.' She fluttered her left hand and a solitaire diamond engagement ring glinted in the morning sun.

'We were engaged to be married, dear, so the will was altered. It recognises me as his betrothed.'

'But you didn't actually get married,' Rainbow said.

'It doesn't matter: it's whatever the will says,' said Genevieve. 'Anyway, you grotty little hippie, what business is it of yours?'

Songbird couldn't stay silent anymore. 'It's our business because Richard gave the land to us.'

'What?' Genevieve and Jessica both turned to look at Rainbow and Songbird.

'Sorry, Jess, he swore us to secrecy until it was finalised,' Rainbow said.

'He was our investor the entire time,' Songbird explained. 'And rather than investing one hundred per cent capital, he's actually given us a fifty-year lease on the property so we can make our terra preta on a grand scale.'

'You're kidding! Girls, that's wonderful, I'm so happy for you,' Jessica clapped her hands and laughed. 'I can't believe it. He said he wanted to develop the land and had launched into a new agricultural scheme, but I had no idea it was you.'

Genevieve scoffed. 'There's no way Richard would turn his precious Springforth into a compost-producing tip.'

'That just shows how little you knew him, Genevieve,' Jessica said, shaking a finger at the woman. 'This is exactly the kind of thing he would have done.

'But I was there in the meeting.' Genevieve's voice was starting to sound panicky. 'I signed the document; the solicitor was instructed to draw up the will to leave the land to me. Richard would have signed on Friday but . . . well, he wasn't around anymore. Nonetheless, it's still legally binding.' She ran her hands through her hair.

'You have to understand, I loved him, Jess, and he loved me too. We were going to be unstoppable together. Property moguls.'

'Oh, thank God, here's Angus,' Jess said as her brother's car came up the driveway.

'Hello all,' Angus said, leaping out of his car to join the impromptu meeting. 'I'm the executor of Dad's will and I've just had a phone conference with the solicitor who drew up the will. Look, Genevieve, I'm sorry but it seems you have been the target of one of Dad's pranks.'

'What? No, I think you've got that wrong.' Genevieve folded her arms. 'He wanted to develop the land.'

Angus just shook his head.

'But,' Genevieve said weakly, 'surely he wouldn't do that. It's too big a deal to just muck around with like he's playing Monopoly.'

'He did, Genevieve,' Angus said flicking through the document in his hand. 'He had his own plans for this land, but he was obviously keeping them from you for the time being. He was committed to a green energy plant and to that end he has in fact given the land to Rainbow and Songbird.' He turned to them. 'Well done,' he said, grinning. 'I guess we're business partners.' He shook their hands.

'I'd been discussing with him for over a year how I wanted to get out of the city scene; change careers and spend more time with the family. He'd intimated that he had something on the back burner I might be interested in. It was only over the weekend that I read the documents regarding his business partner-ship with you ladies. I must say I'm impressed and very excited to be involved. In fact, here –' Angus passed across an overflow-ing folder to Songbird – 'are the engineer's drawings for a large working power plant based on your design. There is a marketing and engineering plan outlining the creation and capture of energy produced by the fumes from the terra preta, which can then fuel a generator or be stored in a battery or fuel cell.'

Songbird and Rainbow grabbed the document and eagerly pored over it.

'You can't do this, Angus, you're completely wrong,' Genev-ieve said. 'You don't know about the updated will. This land is mine: as of last week darling Richard said so.' Genevieve was confused.

'This is for you, Genevieve,' Angus said, passing her a sealed envelope. 'Dad's solicitor gave it to me late last night. It's why I'm here. I was warned you might come down today.'

Genevieve ripped open the letter. Jessica could see the hand-writing on the front was Richard's. It was eerie to see his unique script on the paper, as if he were still with them.

Genevieve quickly scanned the missive. 'Oh, bugger,' she yelled. She screwed the letter into a tight ball and threw it on the ground. She looked from person to person, her face white with shock, then turned to get into her car. She spun her wheels in the dirt, creating a cloud of dust, and drove away.

Angus picked up the crumpled letter and handed it to Jessica. They read it together.

Dear Genevieve,

I'm in hospital, love. Things look good, but I figured if something happens I might owe you an explanation.

You're a silly thing, aren't you? We were having such fun. I love your spunk, your feisty manner. Everything about you. Especially your ferocious boardroom, terrier nature. You always get your own way and I really love that about you. In fact, I really do love you. But you went too far, Gen; you got too greedy. You could have had it all but you went behind my back. I don't mind a bit of initiative, but things seem to have got out of hand.

Preparing for a worst-case scenario, I arranged a little trick with Tom Brown, my solicitor, just for the fun of it, really. Just to let you know that no one really pulls the wool over Richard Wainwright's eyes.

It's a shame, Gen, we've been having such a fabulous time.
Thanks for the memories,
Richard Wainwright

PS – I found the plans you'd hidden. Recon decking never would never have worked – it would have rotted in the sea air.
PPS – Bugger! I guess this means I'm dead.

Angus and Jessica finished reading at the same time and looked at each other, their eyes wide. He'd been onto her the entire time. To think Jessica had been so sad that at the end of his life her dear Dad had been duped by a con-woman.

The siblings threw back their heads and laughed. Songbird couldn't stand it a minute longer and snatched the letter so she and Rainbow could join in the joke too. Soon all four of them were cracking up, standing halfway up the hill in a paddock in the sun.

52

Nick pulled up in front of the old homestead. He turned off the engine and looked at the house, then past it to the fields beyond. He loved working here.

He missed Richard Wainwright a lot. He had been a fantastic boss. But more than that, he'd been a good friend. He'd listened to Nick's suggestions and allowed him to be the true manager of the place. It hadn't run better in years, the old bloke had said. But that was over now. Nick had heard of the new plans for the property. He laughed as he remembered Caro relating the tale to him that afternoon in the supermarket.

What a joke. That Richard: in control to the very end.

Angus and Caro were at the helm of the property now. He knew they'd do well. They didn't need Nick. And even if they did, it wasn't his place anymore. There was nothing here for him. Jessica had obviously moved on. He couldn't believe she'd been sucked in by that loser in town.

His heart had broken that night. He'd phoned, admittedly a bit drunk after a session at The Stump, to tell her his innermost thoughts. That was stupid of him, really, to try to have such a deep conversation over the phone, but he'd missed her so much. He'd needed to tell her the truth behind the love letters.

He'd been in love with her ever since they met at school. But she'd always had somebody else, or he had, and then when they were both single, a best friend pall had shadowed the relationship. It would have been possible to spark it up by showing romantic interest in her, by pursuing her as a suitor, but he'd been terrified of destroying the beauty of what they had. He'd been so close to doing it, to sweeping her off her feet, when Jimmy came to town. His chance had passed. All he had left was the role of friend, but he lost that too by being overly open, baring his heart on the phone that night. How stupid of him. Of course there was another bloke in her flat. Why wouldn't there be? She was gorgeous.

So here he was once more at her house, as a friend; a companion. Tonight, though, he'd come to say goodbye. It was Nick's turn for a change: he was well overdue for his own adventures. He was off to visit Pete in Port Hedland, where he would be a miner for a while. There was some good money to be made up there and his old mate Pete was happy to have the company.

He walked around to the back door. Jess was on the deck. Her wild, crazy curls fluffed about her head. She must have just washed her hair. Nick could imagine how she'd smell, just like freshly picked strawberries. Maybe she'd like one of his neck rubs. She'd always said they were the best. She was sitting on Richard's favourite Adirondack chair, staring up at the stars. She hadn't seen him yet and he took the moment to look at her.

Her knees were drawn up under her Dad's old jumper. She didn't look sad, though. She looked peaceful. She leaned down to scratch her ankle. There was something so fragile in that action that made Nick's heart ache: it was a movement so real and touching.

'Hello there,' he said.

She turned and saw him. 'Hi, Nick,' she said brightly and stood to greet him. He kissed her – just a soft, gentle kiss on the mouth. A kiss that meant nothing more than 'hello, dear friend'.

She leaned forward and poured them both a glass of Montalto Pinot Noir. A cheese platter sat untouched, awaiting his arrival.

'Nice tucker,' he said, helping himself to a slab of blue.

'It's chilly out, but so lovely,' she said looking at the view. 'Caro tells me she filled you in on this week's antics.'

'Yes, she did,' Nick laughed. 'What a great bloke that Richard is . . . sorry, was.'

'That's okay. It'll be months before we get the right tense, I expect.'

They both sipped their drinks and chatted about the property's future. Jess seemed sure there would be a job for him. 'You'll be invaluable, Nick,' she told him. 'I'm sure Angus will have you working your arse off here.'

'I don't know, maybe,' he said. 'He hasn't mentioned it.'

'I'll tell him,' she said.

'Don't – just leave it. I've got some stuff on anyway.' He looked at his hands.

'Like what?' she asked, reaching for a handful of biscuits.

'Just stuff. Look, thanks for the drink, I should go.'

'Nick, wait, we haven't talked about the other night.' She brushed her hand over his knee.

'Oh, Jessica, must we? I am so embarrassed about that. I was a bit under the weather, I shouldn't have called. It's none of my business who you're seeing. I have to go.'

He stood to leave when she called after him, 'It's over with Jimmy, Nick.'

He turned back and looked at her. 'Really?' he asked.

'Yes, really.' She stood to take his hand. 'It was a mistake getting involved with him and it didn't take long for me to see through his bullshit and realise what a tosser he was. I am the one who should be embarrassed: I can't believe I fell for it for as long as I did.'

Nick reverted to his gruff blokey manner. 'Doesn't matter, Jess, it's your life. You don't have to explain anything to me. We've always just been about bad timing. Anyway I'm off, stuff to do.'

She pulled him into a hug. 'See you soon,' she said.

'See you round,' he replied and walked down the steps until his workboots crunched on the gravel.

'Nick,' she called.

'Yeah?' he said and looked up. She was washed in moonlight, her face pale in its glow.

'Did you keep the letters?'

'Yeah,' he said and looked at the ground.

'Can I see them one day?'

'Maybe,' he said looking up at her, 'if you're very good.'

She grinned.

He left. That night he got as far as Bordertown, South Australia, before he was able to pull over and sleep.

53

That night Jess lay in bed thinking back on the joyful, busy week she'd spent at the General Store, enjoying the bittersweet happiness at being back where she belonged, tempered with the constant weight of sadness that shadowed her.

Her grief had been soothed and she'd been distracted by the pleasure of returning to her store and throwing herself into styling and merchandising the displays. She'd spent hours trawling the local second-hand shops, picking up bits and pieces to enhance her beautiful space.

She had decided on a display of old apothecary bottles and had just today sourced a beautiful set in shades of purple and blue. They would be perfect along the top shelf above the display of tins.

Being back in the General Store had meant she'd been able to meet Tori for lunch, and was relieved to hear her friend was sticking with her therapy and continuing to deal with her shopping addiction. But there seemed to be no hope for reconciling her marriage.

'That ship has sailed,' Tori had told her sadly, her eyes bright with tears. 'I thought that now I am addressing the issue Joseph might be interested in trying again, but he doesn't want to even discuss it.'

Jess had squeezed her hand in sympathy. 'All you can do is face one day at a time, Tori,' she'd said, knowing how trite her advice sounded but unable to think of anything else to suggest. Sometimes life just didn't turn out the way you wanted.

Now she sighed and turned over, her mind racing with

everything that had happened in the past year. It'd been a difficult, challenging year, but she'd got through it.

She was so proud of how the General Store was looking, and
she knew her dad would have been proud too. She would invite
Nick to come in for lunch tomorrow, he'd love it.

Suddenly the Country Fire Authority siren wailed into life.
The eerie call sent a chill through her bones – it was always
an ominous noise in the country, and unusual this early in the
spring. She rolled over again and pulled her doona up over her
shoulders. She hoped it wasn't anyone she knew.

Then her phone rang. Oh God, no.

It was Merle from the supermarket. 'Jess, it's the shop,
love,' she said in a shaky voice. 'You'd better get down here,
quickly.'

Jessica stood and watched in disbelief as flames licked from the
front windows, up to the facade and pulled at the letters spelling
out the store's name. The stench threatened to overpower her.
She was aware of arms around her pulling her back. Explosions
came from the rear of the building. The noise of crashing tin;
the rabble of onlookers. She was confused, she didn't understand: how could this be happening when she'd just started to
get her life back on track? It didn't make any sense.

The firefighters had assured her no one was inside, so where
was Nick? She shook her way out of Rainbow's embrace and
shouted to Merle, 'Where's Nick? Why isn't he here?'

'Didn't you know, love?' Merle seemed confused by Jess's
question. 'He's moved to Western Australia. He left earlier
tonight.'

Jessica's knees gave out. She wobbled to the ground. Merle
supported her head. 'But why?' Jess asked, the fire momentarily
pushed to one side.

'Oh, Jess, you don't need this right now. Let's just get this
sorted out,' Merle said.

'Why, Merle? What did he say?' Jess's face was terror-
stricken.

The old woman stroked the hair from Jess's forehead and said quietly, 'He said that there was nothing left here for him anymore.'

~ 5 4 ~

Late the next day, Jessica sifted through the rubble at the site. The Fire Chief had declared the blaze an accident. One of the gas burners might have been left on, a tea towel must have caught and the tinder-dry remainder of the building had just gone up. It was completely and utterly gone. Not a thing remained.

Jess felt as if she was going mad, wading through charcoal, metal and rubbish. What could she possibly find in this mess, except for miserable reminders? A little gingham foot poked out from a burnt metal box: one of her Christmas decorations. They were all charred and ruined, but still merrily smiling with soot-blackened faces.

A wave of desolation swept over her. How could she get through this with no Dad and no Nick? She had no idea what to do, or how to even fit this disaster into her mind. She stood on the street at the front of the building, still clasping one of the little gingham people by the hand. Looking at where the store had once stood, she tried to make her addled brain understand what had happened. There was nowhere to go from here. There was nothing to be done. It was over, all over.

A car toot behind her caused her to turn. She vaguely recognised the little BMW, but her brain was in too much shock to place it.

The back door flung open. 'Jessie! Jessie!' It was Liam, swiftly followed by Callum. As they darted across the road, Jessica looked quickly left and right, relieved to see there were no cars. 'Boys! Callum, Liam, darling boys, come here this instant.'

They were already in her arms, squealing with happiness. 'What a mess, Jessie,' Callum said, pointing at the fire site.

'Yes, it is rather.' She turned to follow his gaze and had to admit that it was just a mess. Not a disaster. And messes could be cleaned up.

'Wasn't that your shop?' Liam said. 'Was there a fire?'

'There was a fire last night.'

'Oh, no,' Liam said. 'That's terrible. I loved your shop. What are you going to do?'

'That's an excellent question, Liam, and I'm very glad you're here so I can ask you both your advice. What do *you* think I should do?' She glanced over their heads and waved at Karen, who was waiting at the car.

Looking back down at the boys, who were now standing side-by-side surveying the damage in exactly the same way she'd been doing when they arrived, she marvelled at their growth in the last couple of years. She also marvelled at how her love for them had only strengthened in that time.

'So? Do you have an answer for me?'

'Build it again?' Liam said and looked up at Jessica, seeking her approval.

'Yeah, we can fix it!' Callum said quoting his favourite TV program, *Bob the Builder*.

'What a brilliant idea! Should we do that? Should we build it again?' She felt a seed of optimism deep within start to bloom.

'Yeah!' both boys yelled, jumping up and down at the prospect.

Karen came over as the boys skirted the cordoned-off site, poking at its perimeter, fascinated by the destruction.

'Was this your shop?' Karen asked.

'Yep, 'fraid so,' Jessica replied.

'What are you going to do?'

Funny how everybody kept asking that question when the answer was so clear.

'Rebuild it. I've just had some excellent advice.'

'Wow, you're brave,' Karen said. 'I could never do anything like that.'

'Why are you guys in town?' Jessica asked, turning to look at Karen. 'It was perfect timing, by the way – I really needed the boys at that exact moment. Thank you.'

'Well, it's about the boys really. Graham and I are getting divorced.'

'What? Oh, Karen I'm so sorry.'

Karen's mouth twisted with sadness. 'He's leaving me for someone else.'

'You can't be serious?' Jessica was aghast. She knew he was bad news, but this was too much, even for him.

'Never mind, that's life.' Karen wiped her eyes, sighed and continued, straightening her posture. 'But the good news is, as Graham's wife and stepmother to the boys, I'm getting joint custody. It was a battle, let me tell you, but I told the judge about you and the death of their biological mother so the court felt the boys needed a stable maternal figure, and that's me!' She said it with such pride and love that Jessica was suddenly choked up by how much she obviously adored her stepchildren. 'And I was thinking that maybe we could share my half of the custody.'

Jessica was stunned with happiness. 'I would love that, Karen,' she beamed.

Karen nodded happily and rushed on with her story. 'The boys have missed you terribly, Jessica. Callum still cries every other night. Graham hasn't been at all honest when he's told you that they've moved on.' She wrapped her cardigan around herself.

'Graham not honest? What a surprise.' Jess rolled her eyes.

During their conversation both women kept a close eye on the boys. Liam started to tug at a lethal-looking piece of timber.

'Liam, put that down,' they called in unison and laughed at their joint-mothering.

The four went down to the beach for a quick walk to discuss future plans and let the boys stretch their eager young legs. The seagulls were at their mercy and flew away squawking at each ambush. When the group climbed the beach steps and returned to the car, they all stood once more and faced the wreckage of the old shop. Callum looked up at Jessica.

'So, can we fix it?' he asked.

'Yes, we can!' Jessica replied.

~ 55 ~

Front Cover, *BRW* December 2010: Photograph of Rainbow
and Songbird
Cover headline: Eco-Warriors Billion Dollar Deal with
Peninsula Energy
Story, page twenty-two:

*In an unprecedented Australian energy deal, Rainbow McIntosh and
Songbird Patterson, of Stumpy Gully, Victoria, have just signed a
$1.1 billion dollar deal with power company Peninsula Energy, while
saving the planet at the same time.*

Report: Simon Jarvis

*McIntosh and Patterson, Greenpeace members and self-proclaimed
hippies, are unlikely tycoons, yet have taken on the energy market with
a unique invention based on the rich agricultural fields of the ancient
Amazon.*

*Partnering with solicitor and entrepreneur Angus Wainwright, son of
the recently deceased business tycoon Richard Wainwright, the women
formed BlackGold, a company whose name describes its product to
a tee.*

*'Black gold is what we call the bio-char that is created during the
pyrolysis process,' Songbird Patterson, Electrical Engineer and one of the
inventors, explains. 'The earth is so dark, rich and fertile that plants grow
three times more quickly, fruit is larger and more plentiful.'*

*The two women began the business a mere two years ago. It started
as an idea based on their research into the Amazon and the unique fertil-
ity of certain areas within the region. Horticulturist Rainbow McIntosh
explains, 'These agricultural fields were initially developed by the Incas*

*five hundred to two thousand years ago and to this day they are still
fertile and rich. They are essentially self-producing.'*

The bio-mass begins the process. A conglomeration of compost,
organic cuttings, animal waste and carcasses are collected and then burnt
underground. The resulting slow burn, deprived of oxygen, is a process
known as pyrolysis and the result is bio-char, a charcoal that literally
sucks carbon out of the atmosphere and into the earth. The by-product
of this process is a vapour or gas that when contained can power a fuel
cell, a generator or even be converted to petrol.

'It was a very exciting day for us when our own home-grown terra
preta plot actually produced enough energy to power a fuel cell and then
illuminated a sixty watt light globe for thirty minutes,' McIntosh says.
'When we approached our dear friend Richard Wainwright, he immediately offered his two-hundred hectare property and a large amount of
working capital for us to expand our operation.'

Angus Wainwright, Wainwright Snr's son, took over the operation
shortly after BlackGold moved to the large Peninsula property, where the
team wasted no time in starting the energy creation process.

'It's fairly straightforward really,' Wainwright says, 'in fact I don't
know why everybody doesn't do it. Even if the agriculture industry
doesn't harvest the energy, it makes so much more sense for it to slash-
and-char instead of the current method of slash-and-burn, which sends
damaging carbon into the environment. And the output using the resulting earth is phenomenal. My wife, Caroline, is running the agriculture
by-product side of the operation and has won every category at every
agricultural show she's entered in the last few weeks.'

One of the most phenomenal attributes of the BlackGold operation is
that it's only in its infancy and yet Peninsula Energy saw the potential
and rushed in with the offer before the company even began producing
its own energy.

'When Angus Wainwright approached us, we were ripe for a green,
locally produced energy,' Frederick Nordstrom, CEO, Peninsula Energy
explains. 'In fact, we were desperate. A recent survey of our customers
showed us that 87% preferred a green method of receiving their power.'
Nordstrom continues to explain why the marriage between the companies
was mutually beneficial. 'It's a perfect product for us. The Peninsula has

the land availability, small townships, and infrastructure already in place for energy distribution. It's an ideal test market for what will surely be the energy of the future.'

The small town of Stumpy Gully, population 2500, will be Black-Gold's first test site at the end of 2011. 'We are going to light up that little town,' McIntosh says. 'Everybody in this place helped us get started and offered their support. And on the night the lights go on, we're hosting an enormous vegetarian banquet with our organic by-product to thank them.'

Many universities and research centres around the world are investigating terra preta and bio-char and its essential role in arresting global warming.

Johannes Lehmann, Associate Professor at Cornell University, says bio-char is indeed the key to the future of our planet. 'I think it (pyrolysis) is a very important opportunity that we should have a very close look at. I can't see that there's another opportunity such as pyrolysis with a bio-char return to soil that offers clear carbon-negative bioenergy where for every unit of energy that you produce you're actually net-sequestering carbon in the terrestrial ecosystem, anywhere on Earth.'

Songbird Patterson and Rainbow McIntosh, two women who wanted to save the planet. It looks like they might just do it.

Caro scooped up another load of eye-tearing compost and dumped it into the skip. Springforth, the beautiful property she'd shared with her family for the past fifteen years, had become a tip. A stinky, fly-blown, tip. A compost collection dump-truck came daily and dropped yet another load of refuse onto what once had been a manicured front lawn. The stench was unbelievable. The place was an eyesore. And she'd never been happier.

She waved as Jessica pulled up in her old Patrol. 'God, it's bad on a hot, still day, isn't it?' Jessica said holding her nose as she came over.

'It certainly is,' Caro said, removing her face-mask. 'But we're only at the beginning. We have systems we're about to put into place to house the bio-mass so it doesn't smell so badly while it's waiting its turn to enter the pit. It's no wonder it creates such energy – just feel the heat coming off the decomposition.'

Caro was right, there was a definite warmth emanating from the rubbish heap.

'So how goes it at the building site?' Caro asked as they headed to the back verandah for a cold drink.

'Brilliantly,' Jessica said. 'Thanks to the plans left from the renovation fifteen years ago, we'll be able to build an exact replica of the General Store. And I just found a demolition site in Schnapper Point with hundred-year-old oak floorboards for sale.'

'Perfect. You're a marvel. And how's the mobile camp kitchen working out?' Caro asked as they sat and she poured the iced tea.

Jessica had opened a temporary cafe in an old shipping container at the edge of the site. Her staff served espresso coffees and a minimal menu in a quaint picnic-style set-up. Only Jessica could have given a slap-dash cafe an atmosphere of such quaint quirkiness that it drew tourists and locals alike. And to be close to the action she'd rented and moved into the little cottage next door, in which she baked the daily treats for the cafe.

'It's working wonderfully, people don't mind at all – as long as they can get their coffee and their paper they're happy.'

'Is breaking ground far off?' Caro asked.

'Next week! The plans zipped through council and the same builder from last time is free and knows what he's doing. We should be operational in just over nine months. How about you? How's your new career working out?'

'Oh, Jess, I'm so happy. The kids love their new school and it's just wonderful to be working side by side with Angus. I've never seen him so stress-free. He's completely embraced his new country life. I still can't get used to seeing him without a tie.'

'Yeah, he seemed pretty chipper this morning when he came in for coffee. I'm glad you're getting along so well,' Jessica said.

'Jessica, I must apologise for my behaviour over the last year. I was just sick with worry, and I came across as a bit of a cow.'

'God, no, Caro, it's me who should apologise to you. You were right the entire time. I didn't listen to you. I was seduced by Genevieve's maternal ways with me, the way she babied me and fed my shaky ego. I was so blind. I was looking for a mother figure when I had a perfectly good big sister here all along. But what was with you telling Dad about the property value and all that? You did come across as quite mercenary.'

'I was just ensuring Richard was one hundred per cent committed to retaining the property for future generations, no matter how valuable it was,' Caro explained. 'I would never sell this place,' she added with fierce determination. 'Anyway, I'm just so thrilled how it's all worked out. You know the ad agency sacked Genevieve?'

'No! Where's she working now?'

'At McDonald's head office as their advertising manager.'

'Oh, that's just perfect!' Jessica laughed. 'What a career change. Speaking of career change, look at you! Your boots are filthy and your jumper has holes in the sleeves: not at all what I'm used to seeing.'

Caro laughed and kicked a clump of mud off her gumboot. 'And fancy me being a producer of fruit and veg. I've always loved my garden, but to have it be practical instead of picturesque is so thrilling. I have to keep an eye on my greenhouse, though. I keep scolding bloody Songbird and Rainbow for trying to grow their 'special' plants in there. I have to remind them constantly we're partners with Peninsula Energy, who could pop in at any time.'

The women looked down across the property. The lush cornfield was reaching its peak and rustled in the sudden breeze. The other crops fought for space as they stretched up for the sun. The shiny canisters bordering the bottom paddock hummed as they created their organic energy. Caro and Jess laughed as Angus waved and made his way towards them, then tripped over a hillock of black soil.

Caro took a packet of tobacco from her back pocket and made herself a rollie cigarette as her husband approached.

'It's remarkable that all this has come from Dad's belief in the girls' vision. It's such a shame he's not here to see it,' Jessica said.

'Yes,' Caro mused, 'I loved that man like my own dad and I knew how important this place was for him. It made me sick to think somebody could whip it away from under his nose. But he had the last laugh, didn't he. This place is more like paradise now than it's ever been.'

Jessica was busy serving tables, taking orders up to Linda in the temporary shipping container kitchen and seating guests. Although the cafe's capacity was only a quarter of what it used to be, it was still a tricky business juggling the customers.

It did look very beautiful and was perfect for the summer season. Jess would have to organise a marquee for winter, but the market umbrellas and floral tablecloths were gorgeous and elicited many compliments from her customers. Small glass juice bottles filled with jasmine kept the place fragrant and the sea breeze was never too strong, thanks to the bulk of the foreshore acting as a windbreak.

The small menu of the old General Store's standards was a hit. One muffin flavour – different each day, the famous flourless chocolate cake and a range of toasties were all that was on offer, yet no one complained. It was a simple enough operation that one girl and Linda could manage most days, leaving Jessica free to concentrate on the building. Except on crazy days like today, where all hands were required on deck.

Jessica was so proud of herself. She couldn't believe how far she'd come. She'd developed fantastic organisational skills at her job in the city, yet managed to maintain her creative spirit. She often felt like pinching herself that she was personally in charge of building her General Store from scratch; with no help from the men in her past who'd usually stepped in and taken over. Angus gave great advice, but the majority of the project was her responsibility. She was doing it on her own and she loved it.

She walked over to clear the cups from the front table, when a shadow fell over it.

'I'll just clear this up and the table will be free,' she said without looking up.

'That's okay, Red, I'll wait.'

She squealed and spun around.

Nick wrapped his arms around Jessica and squeezed so tightly he thought he'd break her.

'Where have you been? I needed you!' she scolded.

'Do you still need me?'

'No,' she said proudly, 'I did it on my own.'

'Well, I've timed it perfectly then, haven't I?' he said. 'I should have said this long ago, Red, but will you please not go anywhere ever again? Will you please stay with me?'

She cocked her head and pretended to think. 'Okay,' she said and they grinned, holding each other's faces in their hands.

Acknowledgements

Lisa Blundell:

Thank you to Mark Smith of Sunrise Energy Management for his determination to make this a better place to live, and his knowledge of terra preta as a good basis for a big idea.

The bio-char system in this novel has been subjected to creative licence for the sake of the story. The concept, however, is real and for information on the magic of bio-char or terra preta start at Wikipedia – the links take you from there.

Cousin Leonard is an actual popular band although their number one hit success in the book is my personal future projection for them: www.cousinleonard.com

Thanks to Rie Southwell of Chook Leaf and Danni Brancatisano for their fashion knowledge.

A special thank you to my husband, Ian Blundell, for his knowledge of science and great research skills. But more importantly, for his untiring patience and support.

Finally thanks to Leisa Wharington, Steve from the coffee shop, Lisa from Hardware and all the other lovely Balnarring locals who inspired this book.

Michelle Hamer:

It takes so many people to make a book and I feel privileged to have such talented, generous people supporting Cate Kendall's endeavours.

Big thanks to our publisher Larissa Edwards, our editors Jessica Dettmann and Chris Kunz, and the Random House marketing team.

Thanks as always to my agent, Selwa Anthony, and to my co-writer, Lisa Blundell.

At home Harley, Ruby, Darcy and Ollie continue to be my own personal cheer squad.

Kell, Ads and Benji, thanks for the bed in the spare room, the dating advice (so he will call, right?), the telephone counselling and the hilarity of hard-rubbish day. You all mean so much to me.

To Tracey, who always has my back. My world makes more sense with you in it.

To John, thanks for trying to make me laugh when the editing made me grumpy. Thanks also to Kyan, Mirrami and Pier. I can't wait to see your book in print one day, Pippi!

To Jasmin and Vince, thanks for the coffee-and-crying sessions – and everything else!

Thanks to Suzy and Zak, who make family life so much fun.

And to Mum and Dad. You helped to get me through the year in so many ways. This one's for you.

You've finished the book but there's much more waiting for you at

www.randomhouse.com.au

▶ Author interviews

▶ Videos

▶ Competitions

▶ Free chapters

▶ Games

▶ Newsletters with exclusive previews, breaking news and inside author information.

▶ Reading group notes and tips.

▶ VIP event updates and much more.

ENHANCE YOUR READING EXPERIENCE

www.randomhouse.com.au